Isadora's Dance

A Literary Romance

Donna Wootton

ISBN: 978-1-927882-64-1
Cover image: iStock/Constantinis
Cover and interior design: Shane Joseph
No part of this book may be used or reproduced without prior permission
of or notification to the publisher and author.
This book is a work of fiction. Names, characters, locales, events, and
incidents either are the product of the author's imagination or are used
fictitiously or for purposes of reference in the context of the story and are
not intended to resemble actual places or persons, living or dead.

Library and Archives Canada Cataloguing in Publication

Title: Isadora's dance: a literary romance / Donna Wootton.
Other titles: Isadora & Lucia
Names: Wootton, Donna, 1947- author.
Description: Originally published under title: Isadora & Lucia.
Identifiers: Canadiana (print) 20210269480 | Canadiana (ebook)
20210269502 | ISBN 9781927882641
  (softcover) | ISBN 9781927882658 (Kindle) | ISBN 9781927882665
(EPUB)
Classification: LCC PS8645.O68 I73 2021 | DDC C813/.6—dc23

This book is dedicated to
the late Doreen (Wladyka) Gorsline
truly a writer's friend

Other Books By Donna Wootton

Leaving Paradise

Moon Remembered

What Shirley Missed

Chapter One

Before the plane came to a full stop, the pilot announced that the loading dock at Heathrow was out of order. I moaned. It had been a long overnight flight. Being told we had to wait for an alternative arrangement to disembark seemed anti-climactic.

Pieter, who sat beside me, stood in the aisle. He too was impatient to get off the plane, as he was on his way to Amsterdam to visit family. I'd learned he was a scientist who worked in Edmonton, Alberta, as a technical adviser to a water filtration company. He was interested to hear what I was on my way to Oxford to do at the Bodleian library. With his technical expertise he was employed. With my M. A. degree, I wasn't. Undaunted, I had told Pieter I was going to prepare a proposal for a thesis about Lucia Joyce, daughter of the acclaimed Irish author James Joyce. Pieter thought he'd heard of him and wondered what I would do with my doctorate. "Probably the same as my parents," I said, shrugging. "They're both professors. I have an introduction to a Dr. Antonia Galsworthy. Someone my dad knew in his undergraduate years here when he was at Oxford."

Eventually, we saw a set of stairs being wheeled out just like in the old days. Some damn cheery native Brit behind us started harking on about, "Just like the royals."

If that were the case, where were the dignitaries to greet us, I wanted to ask. How was James Joyce greeted? Better than his daughter. Poor Lucia! Treated badly by her father who had been neglected by his father. Worse, even.

"Actually, it feels more like arriving in a Caribbean island," I said. "Only it's too cool and grey for that."

I bent my head to peer through the small window and saw a dark sky threatening rain. With the waiting I began to feel cranky. When I pulled out the coloured map of Terminal 5 I had printed at home, it struck me.

Terminal 5! That meant there were four other terminals. How big was this place anyway?

Finally, we disembarked only to find the escalator inside the terminal wasn't working either. Pieter and I walked up the flight of metal grid stairs together, laughing like two drunks returning home after an all-nighter. After standing in line for a while, we both got our passports stamped. He gave me a big bear hug when we parted, before rushing off to catch his connecting flight. Lucky for me, my luggage was already rotating on the carousel. Unlucky for me, I got stuck behind two people walking slowly side by side pulling their luggage behind them like reluctant dogs. As soon as I could, I rushed past the pair and, like a lemming, followed the crowd. I followed and followed for what seemed like an eternity. Using my map, I located where I could buy a bus ticket to Reading. From that city I would catch the train to Oxford. My imagination clouded the scenery more than the weather. How eager I was to tackle the story of that dear daughter who could have been as brilliant a dancer as Isadora Duncan.

I sat on the platform waiting, listening to the announcements of delays up and down the line. A polite voice told us we could look forward to upgraded service in the future to offset any current inconvenience. "The future is now," I thought; but all the Brits around me were waiting patiently. Reluctantly, I resigned myself to more waiting. When the train finally did pull into the station, I joined all the passengers in queues. I struggled with my heavy piece of luggage. "Mind the gap," the passing porter said.

"I am minding the gap," I mumbled under my breath.

By the time I finally reached the porter's gate at Keble College where my mother had arranged accommodation for me for two nights, I was filled with relief and joyful anticipation. I had finally arrived!

A young man, about my age, greeted me. "Isadora Duncan," he said, repeating my name while looking it up in the register. Did he know my namesake? There was no hint of recognition let alone mockery in his tone, yet right then and there I felt I might be the ghost of that tragic dancer. Often people had teased me for having the same name as a historically famous woman. What could I say? My parents are idiots.

He was cute and I wanted to ask him his name, but he showed no particular interest in me besides wanting to explain why he was giving me three keys. I tried to pay attention, but how could I absorb all the detail when I was exhausted from my travels and distracted by his good looks. If I knew his name I'd know if he was of Sri Lankan, Pakistani, or Indian heritage. He definitely had an Oxford British accent. Oh well, he probably had a girlfriend.

Inside the quadrangle I marveled at the geometric patterns on the brick buildings and noted the dining hall. Then a group of students came out of the building and crossed the quad, talking and laughing. I practically squealed. They all wore short, black gowns that flowed behind them like wings which made them look like bobbing crows. Maybe they'd just finished writing an exam? The cutie in the porter's lodge had said breakfast would be early because of examinations. Only last week I had written my last exam. I wanted to cheer and celebrate with the students but thought better of it. They might think I was some gauche American. It probably wouldn't matter to them that I'm Canadian. My parents said it mattered, but what did they know?

I fumbled with the keys, trying to find the right one for the door leading to the entrance to the chapel and the residences. Behind me a woman with an Irish brogue said, "You have to push the door tight before putting the key in the keyhole. That one's for your room. Here, allow me."

Stepping aside, I let her. Not bad, I thought, when I entered my room. There was a single bed, an upholstered chair, a floor lamp, a built-in desk, and, on the desk, a kettle. Excellent! I could make a cup of tea. As I was doing so, the phone rang, startling me. It was the porter calling, but he didn't sound like the young man I had just met. Leaving the tea to brew, I hurried back to the porter's lodge to retrieve a message which had arrived earlier. There I found an elderly gentleman in a porter's jacket. Disappointed I kicked myself for not being more forward.

Walking back to my room I wondered who Clive was? I was to meet Clive somebody at eleven the next morning to tour the colleges. Squinting, I made out the last name. Galsworthy. Ah, Clive Galsworthy. Obviously related to Dr. Antonia Galsworthy. Husband? Son? I began to look forward to meeting them.

3

Chapter Two

The quadrangle at Keble College was empty. Standing outside, I realized all I had with me was the message from the porter's lodge. The big brass ring with the three numbered keys was still sitting on the desk beside the pot of brewing tea. I thought about the Irish lady I had met earlier. After she had opened the door for me, she had headed upstairs, saying how lucky I was to be on the first floor. Standing back, I raised my eyes and there she was, looking out her window. I waved. She smiled, returning my wave. I shrugged, gesturing that my hands were empty, and pantomiming that I could not get into the building. Smiling again, she retreated from the window.

"Thank you," I said, when she held the door open. "I forgot to take my keys with me when the porter phoned."

"Didn't you lock your door, dearie?"

I felt foolish. "Maybe the door locked automatically behind me?"

"No, you have to use the key."

"That's good then because now I can get back into my room. Would you like to join me for a cup of tea?"

She laughed. "Oh yes, tea would be nice. There's nothing like a cup of tea to break the ice." Inside my room, she said, "I'm Anne Stirling."

"Isadora Duncan."

"Like the dancer?"

"Yes," I said enthusiastically "My mother has a doctorate in dance theory, so she named me after her heroine."

"Do you think she married your father because of his surname?" Anne Stirling laughed at her own joke.

I joined in her laughter. Somehow, when chatting with Anne Stirling my parents didn't seem like such idiots. "My dad is a James Joyce scholar. Aren't they a pair? Do you take milk?"

"Yes, please."

"Isn't it good the dorm provides two mugs?" I said, passing her a cup.

"The facilities here are excellent," Anne Stirling said. "Are your parents at Oxford?"

"Oh no," I spluttered, spraying hot tea over my hand which hurt, but I didn't want to complain. "Mother teaches at a small university in Ontario, Brock University, and my dad teaches at the university in Toronto."

"Ontario? That would be in Canada?"

"Yes. Please do sit," I said, offering Anne Stirling the upholstered chair. Pulling the swivel chair from the desk, I sat opposite her.

"I've never been to Canada. In fact, I've never been abroad, just Britain and Europe. I have a nephew who lives in Australia. He's my sister's eldest son."

"Has your sister been to visit him?"

"No, though he's been home twice. It's a long way."

"Yes," I said, acknowledging her excuse, but finding it just that, an excuse, not a particularly good reason.

"You're a long way from home."

"I'm here to do research on Lucia Joyce," I said, launching into a full explanation about my proposed thesis. Anne questioned me to learn more details, keeping me talking for over half an hour.

"Do you have plans for this evening?"

"No, nothing planned until tomorrow morning."

"Would you like to go out to see a play?"

"Sure," I said, perking up at the prospect of an evening's entertainment.

"The Oxford Theatre Guild is performing 'Blood Wedding'."

"Is that a vampire play?"

"No, no, nothing like that. It's the title of a play by Federico Lorca."

"Oh, right," I said, pretending to be well versed in the world of prominent playwrights.

"At the Oxford Playhouse, walking distance from here, across from the Ashmolean."

"Good," I said, not wanting to further reveal my ignorance. Maybe the Ashmolean was connected in some way to the Bodleian.

"I'm peckish. Would you like to go out to a restaurant beforehand?"

"Yes," I said gratefully. "I haven't even thought about what to do for dinner. I would like a bite to eat."

"I'm glad you can join me and happy to have your company. Well," my new friend said, standing. "I'll just go back to my room and freshen up. Meet you in fifteen minutes?" Before departing, she nodded at my set of keys lying on the desk. "Don't forget to lock your room when you leave."

Left alone I thought that if Mother had reminded me (at age twenty-four) to lock up, I probably would have snarled, yet here I was being cheery. Friday night, and I didn't have a date. Instead, I was going out with a woman my mother's age and looking forward to the evening. I wondered if Anne Stirling was married? I decided she wasn't. She hadn't mentioned a husband or children, yet she did talk about her sister's family.

At the Playhouse, Anne bought a ticket at a reduced rate for people over sixty. I got the same rate on my student ticket. In a way that made us equals. People of all ages were milling about, talking and drinking in the front lobby. It was exciting to be in a crowd, feeling as if I belonged.

"Are the doors locked?" I asked. There were no ushers to take our tickets. I was eager to read about the play.

"As the play doesn't start for another fifteen minutes we have to wait here."

When we did take our seats, I opened the programme that listed the particulars for the evening's performance and turned to the article, 'Lorca's Poetic Realism'. It was subtitled, 'A Tragedy in Three Acts. First performed in 1933'. I saw there would be dancing which really appealed to me. I wondered why I didn't know about this play? My family often attended the annual Shaw Festival at Niagara-on-the-Lake, not far from where we lived. Maybe Lorca's plays didn't fit into the Shavian mould? As I read, I learned that Lorca's poetic realism included a blend of music, movement, and dialogue.

At intermission Anne and I stood along the side aisle rather than going back to the crowded lobby. "How are you enjoying it?"

"I really like the dancing, so much rhythm and movement, but the mother's obsession with death is a bit much."

"That's the part I find fascinating, especially the personification of Death as a beggar woman."

I shivered. "I think she's creepy."

During the second act I concentrated on the music, seeking out the beauty Lorca saw amid the hateful society that shortened his life. As we were leaving the theatre Anne pointed to a flyer posted on the billboard outside the building advertising a concert the next evening. "I'm going tomorrow," she said.

Anne may have expected me to join her, but I didn't commit myself. Maybe Clive Galsworthy would prove a suitable source of entertainment. Instead, I pointed to the large building across the street. "Is that the Ashmolean?" I asked.

"Yes. You must visit it," she said.

Blackhall Road was busy with passing vehicles and pedestrians. We walked along, sharing our thoughts on the music from the play, which ranged from flamenco to Spanish folk tradition. When we turned onto Keble Road, I was grateful for Anne's company. The road was just a cobblestone lane and darkly lit. Another turn brought us to Parks Road, where there was traffic, though very little at this late hour. Fumbling with the big key to the main gate left us giggling like school girls. Once inside, I couldn't help but glance through the window while passing the porter's lodge.

Despite my contentment, once inside my room, I felt with glum precocity that I was not going to remain resigned to my situation. Yes, the iconic places in Oxford were spellbinding, but why be blissful when I could be happy? The grandeur of a foreign culture like Spain tantalized me. There was heat and rhythm and colour and rebellion and much unorthodox behaviour. I would find that. Academia may require my discipline but living demands more risks.

Chapter Three

On Saturday morning Broad Street was riotous with activity. I watched Morris Dancers who were dressed in folk costumes: the men in white shirts and long pants with bells tied around their shins, the women in white blouses with colourful skirts. Clapping wooden sticks together, the men lifted their prancing legs, making their silver bells jangle. They wore felt hats; the women had hair ribbons that bounced while their skirts swayed. Further along the street, local farmers sold fresh produce. Antique furniture and book dealers hawked their wares from open-air markets which blocked traffic, forcing buses and cars to make a broad turn back to Parks Road. Adding to the mayhem were swarms of bicycles. Cautiously I crossed the broad street to get a closer look at the proceedings. I was training myself to look for oncoming traffic from the left, only now I found I also had to check traffic coming from the right, too.

Eventually I made my way to the gates in front of Trinity College where I was to meet Clive Galsworthy. In front of me, a man of about sixty or sixty-five pushed a bicycle between a double-decker bus and a throng of tourists. He leaned his two-wheeler against the gate, then turned and asked for tickets. After greeting a dozen people, he called into the crowd, "Anyone else here for the tour of the colleges?"

I hesitated, then decided to give it a shot. "Excuse me," I said. "I was asked to meet a Clive Galsworthy at this spot. Would you know him?"

"You must be Isadora? I'm so glad you've come."

"Yes," I said, wondering why I was being sent on a scheduled tour of the colleges with a tour guide.

Seeing my confusion, he pointed to his name tag. "I'm Clive Galsworthy."

"You are?" I blurted.

"Come over here please, everyone," Clive Galsworthy called loudly, "away from the crowd. We'll get started." Leaning his head close to mine, he said quietly, but clearly and crisply, "We'll speak later."

As the others gathered around the tour guide, I studied Clive. Was he Antonia's husband? He seemed to be my parents' age, or older. Yet why was a professor's husband serving as a tour guide? Why come out on a Saturday morning and lead visitors around the town? Maybe he was simply enthusiastic about the colleges of Oxford. Maybe he liked to get out of the house on the weekend. Maybe he wanted to get away from his wife and family. Not every couple was joined at the hip like my parents, who exhausted themselves trying to do everything together while managing separate, full-time careers.

"The students are writing exams, so we can't go inside Trinity today," Clive said. Then he introduced himself and part of the mystery was solved. After retiring from the registrar's office, Clive decided to keep himself busy and useful by giving tours of the place he knew and loved.

Ye gads, I thought, old enough to retire. He was older than my parents.

"We'll walk down Broad Street away from this noise, but please note Blackwell's Bookshop just a few doors along," Clive said.

In a herd we jostled through pedestrian traffic. As I was passing the noteworthy bookstore, a group of young people came out and paused on the stairs. It was him.

"Hello Isadora."

"Hi," was all I could manage, turning bright red as my heart flipped. Craning my head to look back at the young man who had often popped into my thoughts since my arrival in Oxford, I saw his mates elbowing him and asking who I was. He was laughing, which made him even more gorgeous. For a fleeting moment I considered leaving the tour group to join him, but I became caught up in the flow of the tour and found myself stopped outside some black hoarding. Besides, I was supposed to be with Clive. I ended up in front of Clive and out of sight of the young man. What a missed opportunity. What a fool I was. As if he cared anyway. If he was interested, he would have knocked on my door last night, as he knew where my room was, and found some excuse. Anne Stirling had.

Clive was explaining the black hoarding around the new library which was being refurbished. I didn't catch why a new library needed renovations, but I did hear Clive say that the personalities pictured on the temporary wall in alphabetical order represented leading figures of Oxford. We had stopped in front of Jane Austen. Beside her was Sir Thomas Bodley. Clive expanded on the written biographies, "He was the founder of the Bodleian Library. Although there had been a library at Oxford since about 1320, it was denuded by an early king, and Bodley volunteered to restore it. The Bodleian was opened in 1602, and Bodley appointed Thomas James as its first librarian. James later had to ask permission from Bodley to marry."

Imagine an era when a librarian had to have permission to marry? My mind was abuzz with other thoughts, but I pulled my attention back to Clive when he pointed out an elegant building across the street. It was the Sheldonian Theatre, designed by Christopher Wren who also designed St. Paul's Cathedral in London. We learned that Wren hadn't studied architecture formally. Clive was full of anecdotes and behind-the-scenes tidbits. He was tall, so it was easy to follow him along the crowded streets. He counted the number in our group. Apparently, we had lost one person, a young man. Someone guessed he must have decided he was on the wrong tour. I had not even noticed this young man among the group, made up mostly of elderly tourists with a smattering of middle-aged couples. That left me as the only young person. Maybe I could sneak away to the pub Clive was describing, located somewhere down the narrow lane we were passing. In Shakespeare's time, it had been a seedy place full of gamblers. Now it was a tourist attraction. In the Inspector Morse series, an episode had been filmed there. Everyone nodded their heads in recognition. Even I recognized the name from hearing my parents discuss the detective shows at home. We all had Inspector Morse in common.

Someone asked about Harry Potter. "When we get to New College, we will see the Ilex, which is the evergreen holm-oak you'll recognize from a scene in Harry Potter and the Goblet of Fire," Clive said.

When we finally did get to New College, I became fascinated with the place for other reasons. Outside its gate were remnants of the ancient city wall dating from the twelfth century. Walled cities intrigued me; in my imagination they housed fairy tales. The tall section of wall outside the college gate was blackened with soot from the nineteenth century. We were standing in an alley surrounded by stone. When the college was built in 1379, they had to reinforce the gate to keep out the riffraff who would often beat up the educated elite. Here was the dark side of fairy tales, the underside of education. Toughs beating up the upper classes. Brawn versus brains. I pictured scenes of men taunting students. They were all men. Surely nothing like that would happen nowadays with gender equality. Wasn't I fortunate to be living in the modern era?

Inside the Cloisters everyone else scrambled to take pictures of the infamous oak tree. I didn't; I never took photos as I found it distracting. Instead, I meditated. This was why cloisters were built in the first place. I thought about William of Wykeham, who had founded the college. A man of humble origins. It was ironic that, in front of his college, the humble had tried to bring down the privileged.

Clive led us into another quadrangle and pointed out the oldest dining hall in Oxford. We had to be quiet and respectful of the students who were writing exams.

"Another time I'll take you inside," Clive said for my ears alone. "I want you to see the linenfold panelling on the walls and the portraits, especially the one of the Reverend Spooner, well known for the spoonerism."

Clive was a large man, not just tall, but broad and big boned. He wasn't fat and seemed reasonably fit. Maybe cycling around Oxford helped. His hairline was receding; his forehead was wide; his eyes bulged out of their sockets, emphasizing his natural enthusiasm. I was growing to like him.

At the end of the tour Clive asked me to join him for a drink at The King's Arms, a pub, a pink stucco building frequented long ago by the likes of Shakespeare, and which now served as a favourite hangout for students.

Once there I was happy to see people my own age and younger crowded around the wooden tables outside, sipping beer and talking boisterously. This felt more like my milieu. I followed Clive indoors rather than express my preference for staying outdoors, recognizing that he might need some peace and quiet. After getting our drinks, we settled at a table along the side wall under heavy, dark beams.

"Great atmosphere," I said.

"Toni asked me to invite you to Sunday roast tomorrow. It's the one meal of the week she cooks."

"Thank you. I would love to come. What time?" I asked.

"Around eleven."

"Oh," I said, remembering my situation, "that's when I have to checkout of Keble College."

"Where are you going then?"

"I don't know yet," I answered, frowning and realizing I had given no thought to my future accommodation.

"You needn't worry. You can stay in our son's room. He's left for Italy."

I was taken aback. Being invited to a meal on a Sunday seemed appropriate, but an invitation to stay in the home of virtual strangers was another thing altogether. Would his wife approve?

"Toni would be delighted to have you," Clive added, as if reading my mind. "She's already suffering the empty-nest syndrome with Rufus gone. He's about your age—twenty six."

"I'm turning twenty-five this summer." So, an only child like me.

"Excellent. I could pick you up tomorrow morning. It isn't far. Just down the road and across the bridge. On Cowley Place."

"I only have one piece of luggage," I said, "but it's a gigantic piece, on wheels. Actually, it's easy to pull. Maybe I could walk."

"You could if you really prefer to," Clive said. "It's all downhill."

"You're sure your wife won't mind?" I asked.

"No, she's the one who suggested I invite you if you hadn't made other arrangements. She's a Fellow at Lady Hilda's College, you know? Lewis Dodgson will be joining us for dinner," Clive said. "He's the librarian at the Bodleian who will be working with you. Toni has made all the arrangements."

"Great," I said. How appropriate, and something to look forward to tomorrow: Sunday roast cooked by my thesis proposal sponsor, joined by a dinner guest who would mentor and oversee my research. It was all sounding very academic, but it would be good to get to know them so soon after my arrival.

"Jolly good, then. That's all settled. Do you have any plans for the rest of the day?" Clive asked.

"Yes, I do," I said without hesitation. Suddenly I felt overwhelmed by his enthusiasm, generous hospitality, and paternalism. I didn't expect him to start organizing my life. "I'm going to the Ashmolian this afternoon and to a concert tonight at the Sheldonian," I blurted out.

The dear man expressed genuine pleasure on hearing my plans. After thanking him for the tour, I crossed the road to the theatre. Everything was falling into place.

Chapter Four

Over breakfast with Anne Stirling on Sunday morning, I learned that the dining hall at Keble College was the longest one in Oxford. I decided to tell Clive this as, on the tour, he had said that the hall at New College was the oldest one in Oxford. Facts like these seemed to matter to people like Anne and Clive.

When I shared with Anne that I'd been invited to the Sunday Roast, she told me that it is a traditional noontime meal served at homes and in pubs. "Usually beef," Anne said, "or possibly lamb." Her comment made me think of all those baby animals I'd seen from the train in the lush green fields.

Even though I ordered only a continental breakfast, I found the staff were very attentive. Despite there being a buffet, they brought me coffee with cream and chilled juice.

"The service is good here," Anne said.

"Yes," I smiled, "I could get used to such service."

"And we don't have to do dishes."

I laughed. "At home my mother rinsed the dishes and stacked the dishwasher, while my job was to empty the machine and put everything away in the cupboards. Mother insisted on this separation of duties when it became clear my father had no regard for where anything went. The turning point came when she finally found the hand whisk she was searching for inside a large pot. She asked me what it was doing there. How was I to know?"

When it came time to say goodbye, Anne thanked me again for finding her after the concert the previous evening so we could walk home together. My cheap seat for Springtime Baroque had no back; it was a bench without a cushion, but from there I'd spotted her below. I really had enjoyed meeting her.

After packing, I handed my keys in at the Porter's Lodge, hoping I might see the young guy again, but instead there was a young woman behind the desk. Disappointed, I hauled my bag over the stoop and walked down Parks Road.. The streets were quiet compared to yesterday and I enjoyed the calm, mindful of my surroundings and the many sights now becoming familiar to me.

I turned onto the High Street and followed it over the bridge. The first street on my right was Cowley Place. Locating the Galsworthys' number, I left my bag on the sidewalk and climbed the stairs to ring the bell. Clive answered, welcomed me, and insisted on hauling my luggage up the stairs for me. He was such a sweet man, so attentive and helpful. By now I felt easy in his company. Turning around in the cramped hallway, I found myself face to face with a woman.

"Hello Isadora. I'm Antonia." Her voice had the ring of royalty to it. Extending her hand to me, her fingers loosely touched mine.

Of course, you are, I thought, and immediately wondered how she could be Clive's wife? He was so warm and enthusiastic; she seemed tense and aloof. Antonia's handshake was cold and limp. Her thick, grey hair was pulled back starkly from around a thin face, and her large, dark eyes were set deeply above protruding cheekbones. Her wide nostrils flared with each intake of breath. Antonia's lips were painted bright red.

"Clive will show you to your room," Antonia said, speaking like the owner of an inn and in no way reassuring me.

Clive, already perspiring, picked up my luggage. I feared he would have a heart attack; yet he managed, all the while talking to me between breaths.

"I emptied the closet for you, Isadora. The washroom is just down the hall. We have a two-piece ensuite so we're only sharing the tub with you. Toni likes to have a bath at night, before bedtime, whereas I start my morning with a shower. I get up early so I'm sure I won't be in your way. You just make yourself at home. Here we are."

I followed Clive into the small room at the front of the house overlooking the street. It was bright and crowded with furniture: a single bed, a tall chest of drawers, a reading chair, and a desk with a computer.

Opening the door to a large closet, I found a custom-built, stacked, wire mesh unit.

"You can use Rufus's computer. I'll show you the password."

"Thank you, but I have my laptop."

"Well then, I'll just leave you to unpack. Take your time, my dear."

I did, realizing that, despite Antonia's attitude, I would be happy to be sleeping in the room for more than two nights. After unpacking, I looked for a place to store my big piece of luggage. In the end, I simply left it on the floor of the closet, underneath my clothes. The full-length mirror hanging on the back of the closet door reminded me that I looked nothing like my namesake. In truth, I looked more like the woman I was about to study, Lucia Joyce. I even had big feet like hers. While gazing at myself, I heard voices coming from the front hallway. Concluding that the other guest must have arrived, I went downstairs.

What can I say about my first impression of Lewis Dodgson? Mostly, how he fixed his eyes on me as I descended the staircase. I felt as if he was undressing me. Somehow, he seemed to take in my entire being without moving his eyes. Later, when I learned he was a skilled photographer, as well as a librarian, I was not quite so surprised, rightly concluding he was very observant in both areas.

"I'm very much looking forward to working with you at the Bodleian, Isadora," Lewis said, after Clive had introduced us.

"Toni wants us to start with drinks in the garden," Clive said, leading the way to the back of the house. Their lovely English garden had a rose arbour where we sat overlooking the public pathway outside the gate. Beyond that was a small canal where a group of students were punting under a stand of overhanging willows. I felt as if I had arrived at the quintessential English home and decided that I would remain for the duration of my stay in Oxford.

"How is your father?" Antonia asked.

"Fine, thanks. But that reminds me, I must let my parents know where I am." I turned to Clive before he retreated into the house. My voice was clear. For some strange reason I wanted Lewis Dodgson to know I had parents who were concerned with my well-being. I guessed that, while he was not as old as my parents or our hosts, he was much older than I was, maybe in his forties. He had a small frame and elegant hands. His face was pleasant, almost boyish, while not really handsome. His thick, soft, brown hair was straight and long enough to touch his ears without covering them. I wasn't attracted to him the way I was to the young porter, but I was fascinated by this older man.

"Antonia's being very generous," I said hoping a positive comment would set a good tone. "Really, I can't quite believe I've been invited to stay."

"Whereabouts in Canada do you live?"

Knowing I had to find my tongue in front of this man if I was going to get any help with my research, I gushed, "I live with my parents in St. Catharines, a town close to Niagara Falls. My mother teaches at a small university there and Dad commutes to Toronto which is quite a long way; but he only does it for part of the year because he concentrates his classes into the fall semester. I went to high school there, and I attended the university in town, Brock."

"Is this your first time away from home?"

"No, but it is the first time I've left home to study. I don't plan on returning soon. I'm still making plans. Have you ever been to Canada?"

Lewis smiled. "No, I could ask you to take me, but I guess I can't now that you aren't returning."

I smiled.

Clive reappeared with drinks and Antonia followed with hors d'oeuvres. I hoped their arrival would divert Lewis's attention away from my red face. Was he flirting? Flustered, I proceeded to drink and eat too much.

When Clive explained that I had spent two nights at Keble College, but would now be staying with them, I dropped my little statistic about the dining room.

"Oh yes," Clive said. I should have known he'd be up on all the details about the dining rooms at the different colleges. "Keble was founded in 1870 by the friends of John Keble as a college for gentlemen."

"By then things had settled down at Oxford. In the 1850's," Lewis added, "there were immense drinking parties and wanton vandalism."

"Really?" I asked naively, studying Lewis. He seemed to stammer or lisp over his words, something I had not noticed earlier.

"There's still immense drunkenness," Antonia said dryly.

"Is that even a word?" Lewis questioned.

"It's a drunken word."

"Rather," Clive said. "Well, they've certainly curtailed the vandalism. You won't find graffiti on the walls in Oxford nowadays."

"Not on any wollege calls," Lewis said. "Sorry, college walls," he added carefully.

"Just eggs," Antonia said.

"Don't mind Lewis," Clive said quietly to me. "He's our present-day Spooner."

"Oh," I said, feeling embarrassed for the man, then speaking too loudly in an attempt to cover our private exchange, I added, "Clive told the tour group yesterday about the violent clashes outside New College in the past."

"Beastly behaviour," Antonia pronounced.

"Nothing much has changed really," Lewis said. "There's still class warfare between various colleges on the ground. Mostly at the Tuft Tuff Tavern."

"Turf Tavern, Lewis," Clive corrected. "Still, it's not like the olden days."

I was beginning to wonder if Lewis could be suffering early dementia. Wasn't disordered language a symptom? Maybe Spooner had it, too?

"Getting a degree at Oxford is an elite activity," Antonia said.

Recognizing that my hostess was something of a snob, I refrained from agreeing that Oxford was better than a whole host of other institutions. I didn't say anything as I didn't want to sound like a snob, too.

Lewis was watching me intently, not in a predatory way, but in a studious manner. "Isadora was telling me about where she lives," he said, without taking his eyes off me, but he was speaking to Clive and Antonia.

Clive laughed. "In the future it is predicted that there will be more Spanish-speaking Norteamericanos than English-speaking in the U.S. Where does that leave Canadians?"

"Learning Spanish and forgetting French?" Lewis answered.

"Learning Spanish and keeping French, too," Antonia added.

"*Par la force des choses,*" I said.

"Ah," Lewis remarked, "you speak French?"

"Only a little," I said, not about to admit I'd been a French immersion student as an adolescent.

"Rufus is trilingual," Antonia said. "He speaks Italian, too."

"Is that where he is," Lewis asked, "In Italy?"

"Yes," Clive answered.

"I've never been to Italy," I admitted.

"Then you must come and visit us there, too," Clive said.

Lewis turned to me. "I have been to their villa in Vignolo. In the Piedmont district, close to the Italian Riviera. It is wonderful."

"Maybe," I pondered, wondering about Clive's invitation and if the villa belonged to Antonia. Was I making a false presumption? "I'll see how it goes with my work."

"And what is it exactly you're working on?" Lewis asked.

"I'm looking for Lucia." I was deliberately being cryptic.

"Lucia?" Lewis asked, his eyes wide.

Antonia looked startled. "Why her?"

"Not your niece," Clive said.

"I've met Lucia, in Italy. In Vignolo. You don't know Lucia?" Lewis asked.

"Of course, she doesn't," Antonia snapped.

"No, I'm talking about Lucia Joyce," I said to clear the confusion.

"As in James Joyce?" Lewis asked.

"Yes, his daughter."

Lewis nodded and said I would find books Basil Blackwell had written about the Joyce family in the Bodleian.

Feeling a need to diffuse the atmosphere, I reminded Clive that I wanted to phone home. Antonia announced that dinner would be ready shortly. At this, everyone rose and moved indoors.

Chapter Five

The next morning, I crossed Magdalen Bridge in the rain. Despite the weather, I walked slowly and let my thoughts revisit the previous day. Mostly, I thought about Lewis. After hours of attentive engagement over dinner, he had left in a hurry with the briefest of farewells. This struck me as rather strange, but Clive explained that Lewis lived out of town and disliked travelling in the dark. Now, there was no controlling the flood of memories. I would no sooner tell myself it was no good thinking about him, than I began thinking about him again. I didn't feel physically or romantically attracted to him. It was another kind of tug, not of the heart strings, more an awakening of senses. Something more mature. Something more like an awareness. Lewis made me more aware of myself. It was unsettling and uplifting at the same time. With a new sense of purpose and direction, I picked up my pace. I was on my way to meet him in Radcliffe Square.

Now my thoughts turned to my phone call home. My mother was thrilled that I was staying with Clive and Antonia Galsworthy. However, Dad had seemed confused, wondering how I had ended up there on a permanent basis. Talking to both of them on the phone together was akin to being thrown back into the domestic scene I had recently left. My mother was in their bedroom; my dad in the kitchen. They had listened to my recorded message on the day I arrived. My mother was grateful to know I was safe; Dad simply wanted to know why I had not called earlier. What had I done on Sunday? Was it safe to be cavorting around at night? Who was Anne Stirling?

"Simon, listen to you," Mother finally interjected. "She's not twelve years old."

The conversation with them got worse when I jokingly alluded to the fact that, not only was I boarding in the Galsworthy's son's room, but I was invited to visit the family at their villa in Italy in the summer.

"Where in Italy?" Dad asked.

Before I could answer, he asked more questions. When were they going? Who was Lucia?

"I'd like to go, too," Mother finally said. "Can you finagle an invitation for us, Isadora? Wouldn't that be a lovely idea, Simon? We could visit them before going to Switzerland."

He sounded positively horrified.

"What's the matter with you, Simon? Don't you want to visit your old girlfriend?"

Now my parents really had me confused. I knew that Dad had gone to university with Antonia, but was she actually an old flame? Was Mother provoking him with her teasing? Was Dad being defensive with his hesitancy?

In an abrupt change of subject Mother started to tell me about my grandmother, as if I cared to hear about her shenanigans. Showing restraint, I remained silent. By the time I hung up I was ready to disown them all. All through dinner I looked differently at Antonia. How well did my father know this woman with her awful hair and gaudy lipstick? The longer I contemplated my hostess, the more my mother grew angel wings. I was beginning to feel sorry for Rufus whom I hadn't even met.

Watching big, affable Clive carving the leg of lamb, I had thought he was a wonderful counter-balance to the adults sprouting horns in my imagination.

Now, stopping in the middle of the bridge, I looked over the side and imagined climbing on top and taking a plunge. It wasn't that I wanted to commit suicide. I just wanted a normal life like other people, like all the students I saw going about their daily business at university. But what could I do to fit in? I had a Canadian accent. Mostly, though, I wasn't used to the hustle and bustle of large crowds on small streets, or narrow streets with historic sites, or throngs of self-absorbed faces not making eye contact or smiling.

By the time I reached Radcliffe Square I was breathing heavily, not from the exercise, but from my confused thoughts. I stood in the center, surrounded by the buildings that made up the Old Bodleian and gazed heavenward. The rain had stopped leaving thin clouds in the blue sky. A tower with statues too high up to identify with the naked eye dominated the square. There were numerous doors. I walked closer to one and read the Latin inscription on the blue panel above it, Bibliotheca Bodleiana.

"Good morning, Isadora." Startled out of my reverie, I turned and found myself face to face with Lewis who, recognizing my interest, led me around the square, explaining that each door represented the subjects originally studied at Oxford.

"Come with me," he said, after we'd made a three-hundred-and-sixty-degree tour. "We'll sign you up, and then I'll take you to Radcliffe Camera where you'll be working." Lewis smiled. I followed.

Inside the Old Bodleian a female librarian asked me if I understood that the library was closed stack: none of the material was available for borrowing; everything was for library use only. I reassured her that I understood the conditions. When my membership was confirmed, Lewis lightheartedly welcomed me to the Bodleian as a Reader. The librarian frowned at his frivolity. I wondered if she was jealous of the deference he was showing me. She was closer in age to him, so maybe she'd had earlier aspirations thwarted by his inattention. Was I making too much of all of this? Maybe, but love is always in the air.

Leaving the building, we walked across the square, and threaded our way through the hordes of tourists. Around the corner we squeezed through a mob of students and up the front steps of Radcliffe Camera where Lewis left me saying he would see me later.

"Thank you, Lewis, for all your help," I said. Once everything arrived and I began my work, I would have no further need of his services I thought, but he seemed to think differently. He wasn't going to let me go.

Within two hours I had identified and requested ten items. "That's your limit for now."

I thanked the librarian. With all the material I had selected, I could continue on my own for a full year if I wanted to. My original plan was to work until the end of the summer, then join my parents in Switzerland where my dad was going to spend some time on sabbatical leave. I wasn't sure I needed that much time. Was it a good idea to leave Oxford in the summer to go to Italy? Was it a good plan to spend time with my parents after that?

Lewis found me outside. "Most of the material will arrive within twenty-four hours, but some of it may be in use and take much longer," he said. "You'll have to come back tomorrow."

"Yes, I will do that. Well, goodbye for now and thanks again." I shrugged my shoulders.

"You needn't go. Would you like to join me for a cup of coffee?"

"Sure," I said eagerly. I was beginning to like his attention.

"I like to avoid High Street." Lewis guided me through Radcliffe Square. "We can go somewhere on Broad Street."

"That sounds fine." I wondered if he had to return shortly to the library to work. Was he entitled to extended breaks?

"Have you been to the covered market yet?"

"No."

"Let's go there, then."

Keeping up with Lewis's long stride was challenging. Although not tall, he had disproportionately long legs. He pointed out Walters of Oxford clothing store, but I was unsure if he thought I might want to go shopping there, or if I was to note that it was where he bought his clothes. On closer examination I decided he was dressed as if he did shop there. Inside the market he pointed out Brown's Cafe, remarking that it was used in the filming of the Inspector Morse episodes.

We laughed in recognition as he showed me to a seat in the coffee shop. Conversation came easily now that we felt comfortable with each other. He told me about his family. He had no brothers, only sisters who seemed to adore him.

"You'd like them. Alice is a writer and Heather a dancer." I wondered if I would have the opportunity to meet them, but they lived some distance from Oxford.

"Where do you live? I only ask because, after you disappeared so quickly last night, Clive said you don't like to drive in the dark."

"No, I seem to have lost my sight vision. I mean night sight. I'm sorry, night vision. I live outside Oxford near a village called Little Chesterton. You must come and visit me." His eyes never faltered, only his speech.

"Sure. Are you an Oxford grad?"

"No. Cambridge." He chuckled.

"Really?"

"Yes, that's why Antonia likes me. I'm not an Oxford man. I come from that other venerable university."

"Is she a snob?"

"You could say that."

"I could and I do. I think there was more between her and my dad than he ever let on."

"It's a ticklish subject. We were all young once."

"I still am."

"Yes. You, yes. You are." Lewis looked down and drank his coffee. We were silent, either unsure of broaching the age taboo, or embarrassed about talking so frankly. I was beginning to think we might not be able to keep up our acquaintance when Lewis lifted his head and, looking into my eyes, asked, "Would you mind if I photograph you sometime?"

"Photograph me?" I sputtered.

"I do portraits. I have been invited by the owner of a local gallery to put on a show of my recent work. I would like to include you."

"I guess I could." So, this explained why he looked at me so much. "It might be good for me to have some pictures."

"Could you come to my studio on Saturday?"

"Where is your studio?"

"In my back garden. It was once a gardening shed; now it is my studio. If it is nice weather, I can take pictures of you in the garden, too. Do come for lunch?"

"How lovely, I'd like that. Is it like Antonia's garden?"

"It is a getter barden, even if I do say so myself." Lewis sputtered. "It is a better garden."

"Then I look forward to seeing your garden, Lewis."

"You can get to my place easily on the bus." Lewis took out a pen and pad of paper and proceeded to write down the directions to Little Chesterton from Oxford. "The bus stops in front of my cottage." Putting the piece of paper in my pocket for safe keeping, we parted after returning to "Rad Cam", as I was to now call it.

I had the whole afternoon to myself. It had stopped raining, and the weather was now glorious. Wanting to savour our conversation, not wanting to go immediately indoors, I walked down Rose Lane off the High Street and wandered around Christ Church Meadow. I lost myself amid the activity of football games, bicycle riders, and people walking their dogs. After a while I sat on a bench and thought of brothers and sisters. Clearly Lewis liked his sisters.

This time last year, I had grudgingly attended the high school commencement of my cousins with my parents and grandmother who was overly proud of her grandsons. The principal was hilarious. He told the graduates they were not special and proceeded to cite statistics supporting his claim. I recalled the part about them not being the center of the universe because astrophysicists knew the universe had no center. I thought how that statement applied to all of us. When he mentioned jocks, I glanced over at Matthew and Sebastian. The twins were exchanging looks. The principal proceeded to deflate any notions the graduates might have about being important just because they had shelves full of trophies. Their wins were fleeting. Upon graduation those accomplishments would diminish to zero. Other boys would fill their shoes.

Maybe it was the distance of time, or the good weather, or the influence of Lewis, but I suddenly felt I should treat my mother's family with more kindness, despite their unimportance in my life or their complete indifference to mine. We seemed to come from different stratospheres. They were into sports, especially hockey. Next time I spoke to my parents, I would ask after them, learn if they had even succeeded in passing first year. That thought took me aback. I would obviously have to work really hard at ridding the long-standing cynicism I held toward them.

On my return to the Galsworthy's house, Clive told me I was just in time for supper. "Leftovers from Sunday's roast." He then wondered where I had been and how I had spent my day. Clearly my appearance showed I had been doing more than visiting Rad Cam.

"I fell asleep in the meadow," I said, pondering if it was the sun that had overcome me or the residue of jetlag. I watched Clive prepare three plates. It was a cold meal, with few dishes. The Galsworthys did not have a dishwasher. Clive did them by hand because it saved on water and energy consumption. I had helped Clive with the cleaning up after the Sunday Roast and had told him I didn't know anyone who did their dishes by hand in the sink anymore. Everyone I knew had an automatic dishwasher. He had simply said that I probably found them old fashioned. I was learning that they were also frugal.

"Would you please set the table, Isadora?"

"Gladly," I said. Since I now knew where things were, I went to the dining room. Above the sideboard was a grouping of family photos I hadn't noticed yesterday. When I examined them closely, I saw they had been taken by Lewis. There was his signature, scrawled on the corner. I assumed the portrait of the young man was Rufus. He was strikingly handsome, an amalgam of all the best traits from his mother and father. His face was strong boned with pale, clear skin and ruddy cheeks. His dark, deeply set eyes seemed to reflect his black hair. He was smiling for the camera, showing straight white teeth between thick lips. I was smitten, but I knew he wouldn't admire me. I had my father's intelligent but sad eyes, my mother's round cheeks and chin, and my own unruly brown hair. A woman would have to be beautiful to turn Rufus's head. How did I ever get anyone's attention except by saying my name was Isadora Duncan? It was my best feature and not everyone even recognized it.

"Lewis took those."

"Yes," I said, turning to face Antonia. I didn't tell her he wanted to take my photograph and had invited me to his place to sit in his garden.

"Here we are," Clive said cheerfully, carrying all three plates like a skilled waiter: one in his right hand, another in his left, and the third balanced on his left forearm.

"Have you had a nap? I didn't hear you come in?" Antonia asked.

"She fell asleep outside," Clive said, speaking up for me. "Isn't that indicative of what glorious weather we're having, Toni?"

"I suppose it is," Antonia said dryly. "How did you get on this morning?"

"Perfectly, thank you." I did have her to thank since she was the professor who had signed my nomination papers. I had her to thank since she was the one who had introduced me to Lewis. I suspected there would be more to thank her for in future, but somehow, I wasn't comfortable feeling beholden.

Facing the sideboard, Antonia raised her eyes to the group of family photographs. "Lewis takes wonderful pictures, doesn't he?"

Since it seemed a rhetorical question, I said nothing, but Clive responded. "Yes, he does. Jolly good. Nice fellow, too."

Antonia's face was pinched. Evidently neither Clive nor I had given her the desired response. "I'm so glad his next show is before we leave for Italy. I'd hate to miss it."

"Is he having an exhibit?"

"Yes, Clive. I told you. Don't tell me you've already forgotten?"

"Are you going to come to Italy with us, Isadora?"

Antonia sighed. Determined to please Clive, annoy Antonia, and meet their handsome son, I said, "Yes, I think I will take you up on your generous invitation before joining my parents in Switzerland." Did that sound snobbish enough?

"Your father is taking a year off to be in Zurich, I understand."

"Yes, Antonia, he is." She knew more about him than I had guessed.

"Why don't we invite them, too?" Clive asked, turning to his wife. "What do you say, Toni?" Before she could answer, he turned to me, "I've never met your father, but over the years I have heard so much about him. He and Toni were close friends at college."

"I'm sure they'd like to come to Italy." I couldn't wait to tell my mother how easily I had scored an invitation for them.

"Yes," Antonia said, without raising her head to either me or her husband. "Do."

Did she mean me? Or Clive? She couldn't mean Clive because he didn't know my parents. After dinner, I sent my parents an e-mail, telling them to plan on coming to Europe early because they were invited to Italy. Antonia may have expected them to visit later during the upcoming year while they were in Switzerland, but I wanted to arrange things my way. Without consulting Antonia, I suggested to my parents they could join us at the villa in Vignolo and later we could travel together to Switzerland. If things went well, we could visit again. And again, and again. Clive and I could have a jolly good time together, and I could seduce their son.

Somehow, I would transform myself into a beauty in three months. I pressed "send," pleased with my fanciful world.

Chapter Six

U nder the vaulted ceiling of the Bodleian, I spent the next three days with my nose in two books delivered to my carrel. The more I read, the more I craved to know. There was no doubt in my mind that Lucia Joyce was a fitting subject for my studies, and I was already looking forward to many more months of inquiry. Maybe I could go to Paris before spending the summer in Italy?

The Joyces' fortunes changed in Paris with the advent of a new benefactor whom Lucia had called "Saint Harriet." Lucia had lived with her parents in a flat at 5 Boulevard Raspail, and her brother, Giorgio, joined them at Christmas. Other family friends had been supportive too, and Lucia had made a great friend in Helen Kieffer. The two young women had both been at loose ends, separate from their peers, but not part of the Parisian teenage social life either. Together, they studied dance.

The idea that I could engage Dad in all things Joycean and Mother in everything related to dance made me feel as if I was giving myself a whole new life through Lucia. My enthusiasm grew by the hour. The more my enthusiasm grew, the more independent I felt. The more independent I felt, the more secure I felt in my own studies. No one had ever doubted my abilities to become an academic. Now, I was confident in my desire to fulfill that destiny.

"You have dark circles under your eyes," Clive said one evening as I was helping him in the kitchen, drying the dishes.

Clive did all the domestic chores, leaving Antonia free to totally immerse herself in academics. I was only too willing to help him as he was such good company. I told myself I was helping her too, in the same way her husband did.

"Are you working too hard, my dear? Own up, now. I think, rather you are."

"No, I'm not working too hard, but do I look so awful?" That night in bed I tossed and turned. Suddenly it struck me that I didn't want dark circles under my eyes for the photographic shoot with Lewis on Saturday. What had happened to my plan to transform myself into a beauty in three months? Academia had replaced vanity. How could I do both? Spending all my time in the library was making me restless. Here I was, twenty-four years old with no prospects of hitching up with a man, studying the life of a girl who discovered her own body through dance, music, and pantomime. What was I doing? Studying her. Reading all day about Lucia. I needed some balance in my life and resolved that on Friday I would not return to Rad Cam but spend the day outdoors to put some colour into my cheeks, tautness on my muscles, and oxygen in my lungs. Get rid of those dark circles!

Early the next morning, I stepped into the garden. The scent on the breeze was intoxicating. They were coming from flowers, the buds on blossoming trees, and the petals falling off nearby bushes. After three days of working hard, the soft wind filled me with craving. I wanted to satisfy my restlessness and told Clive I was not going to the library to study. "Today, I want to be outdoors," I said.

"Well, what about visiting the gardens at Rhodes House?" Clive suggested. "You don't have to leave Oxford to be outside. I could take you there this afternoon if you would like. You can join my tour again; I am meeting a group of botanists at two."

"That's a very kind offer," I said, realizing that Clive was trying not to act like a controlling parent, "but I was thinking of something more vigorous, at least for the morning."

"Would you like to take one of our bicycles and go for a ride? I'm sure Antonia wouldn't mind if you used her bicycle."

"Can I? Oh, that would be perfect." Clive really was a dear. I felt like giving him a peck on the cheek but restrained my enthusiasm. After breakfast, I collected a hat and shoes with rubber toes from my room. Before retrieving the bicycle, I secured a pair of sunglasses under a headband. Then I took off toward St. Hilda's, past the Music Building, through the playing fields of Magdalen College, and along to the copses to the west. Everything was a blur, but I was sure I could find my way back.

It was joyful to be focused on my surroundings and not on words on a page.

After an hour, I felt my heart beating loudly, and slowly applied the brakes. Dismounting, I planted my feet on either side of the pedals, keeping the bicycle upright. Hearing a bell, I shuffled off the path and watched an older lady wearing a skirt pass. Her bicycle had a large wicker basket filled with groceries which reminded me that Clive had said he didn't have to go shopping today. On Fridays, Antonia and Clive eat at a local restaurant. They invited me to join them at Pierre Victoire, a French bistro. As I rested on the grassy verge, I decided I would pay the bill since they hadn't asked me for any rent. Or maybe I needed to be more direct and simply ask about paying rent as I didn't want to abuse their hospitality. I wondered if Dad had made arrangements. He did seem eager to underwrite my doctoral thesis, although Mother had hinted that I should think about applying for a scholarship or two. Yet I doubted they had made any arrangements with the Galsworthys because they were surprised to learn I was staying with Clive and Antonia.

In front of me on the clipped grass was a small, brown shape. Squinting, I looked closer and realized it was a little bunny. It was facing the path, sitting perfectly still. Twitching its nose, the rabbit turned, and pushing off with its hind legs, disappeared into the tall grass along the edge of the meadow. I was filled with delight at seeing a creature in the wild. If I hadn't stopped, I would have missed it.

When my heart rate had slowed to normal, I climbed back on my bicycle and started back along the same route. It seemed I was going uphill. The path was along a river valley that must descend to the Thames. I was heading away from the major river and along its tributaries and canals. Certainly, I was not flying along effortlessly. My calf muscles started to burn; my wrists and forearms began to ache; my pace became sluggish.

Was it my exhaustion, or the name Shire Lake Ditch that precipitated my fall? Whatever the reason, it happened too quickly for me to prevent it. I was on the ground, the bicycle pinning my right leg into the earth, my nose against the cool metal of the handlebars, and my body raised up awkwardly. I grunted, unable to move, and realized I was alone. Although

I had encountered many people going happily along the banks and through the woods, suddenly there was nobody around.

I loosened my grip and freed my left hand, pushing my head away from the handlebars. With my right hand on the ground, I pushed my upper body off the bicycle and pried it off my right leg. Somehow, I managed to stand up. The bicycle tottered and I righted it onto its two wheels, thinking people aren't meant to balance on two wheels; two legs yes, but not two wheels. It had been a foolish idea to go for a bike ride alone.

Serves you right, I could hear mother's voice tell me. I was the clumsy one, the one who usually fell, the one with two left feet like my dad. Not like my mother, not that she was athletic enough to become a professional dancer.

I pushed the bicycle all the way back to Cowley Place. After hearing of my escapade, Clive suggested I attend to my wounds and gave me a bottle of Dettol to disinfect the cuts. Then I plastered bandages over them. Clive served me soup for lunch, treating me as if I was sickly, not simply injured. When he reminded me of his earlier invitation to join him on the afternoon tour I balked.

"Best thing you could do," he said, "is get back up on that bicycle. Why don't you come along and ride over with me?"

This time Clive had insisted I wear a helmet, but I doubted it would keep me safe. Nervously I followed him down the street and across the busy intersection. We cycled over Magdalen Bridge. What if I fell in front of oncoming traffic? Although motor vehicles and two-wheelers shared the roads in Oxford, I was uncomfortable. I noticed not all bicycle riders wore helmets. Clive didn't. There should be a law, I thought, to protect people like me who don't know any better. In Canada, we had laws for cyclists to protect their heads.

By the time we turned up Parks Road, I was starting to feel more relaxed. This was familiar territory. When we entered the grounds at Rhodes House and dismounted, I felt utter relief. Clive said we didn't need to chain or lock the bicycles; supposedly they would be safe unattended behind the building.

We met the botanists in the rotunda at the front of Rhodes House. Only four of the six on Clive's list were present. None of them were Rhode's scholars, but all were Fellows of the Royal Society. Clive told the one from Canada that I too was Canadian. He was a professor at the University of Toronto, like my dad. Of course, they didn't know one another. Why would they? A botanist and a Joycean. Worlds apart. Finally, the two latecomers arrived. Only one other person was a woman. The men seemed to range from my age to Clive's. The young one certainly held no appeal for me. He was rather sickly looking, and I figured he must be an indoor botanist. However, the woman intrigued me. Seeing my plasters, she asked if I'd had an accident.

"I fell off a bicycle this morning."

"Poor you. There must be more bicycles in Oxford than in all of Holland," she commiserated, extending her hand. "I'm Helen."

"Isadora."

I learned she was from Vermont, via Spain, where she went every spring studying certain plants. "Are you training to become a guide?" she asked, gesturing with her chin to Clive.

"Oh, no," I said, laughing, not surprised by her presumption. "It's a long story."

We turned our attention to Clive's booming voice, welcoming us and asking us to follow him outside. We gathered under the front portico. "You are all probably aware that these are award-winning gardens." Clive began. He listed the numerous awards bestowed on the gardens of Rhodes House.

Helen whispered to me that she had been a judge for one of the competitions.

"You've been to Oxford before?" I asked.

"Yes," she replied, "we all have, at some point in our careers."

If they'd all been to Oxford before, I wondered why they were taking a tour with Clive? Goodwill gesture? Surely, all six of them knew more about plants than Clive could tell them. That truth became apparent at our first stop in front of a formal garden. Clive and I ended up on the perimeter of the group, like weeds cast onto the pavement to die a slow death under the hot sun. The botanists huddled like an American football team, with Helen in the middle. Soon they dispersed into small groups, talking enthusiastically about the petals and leaves, using Latin names. I knew some Latin, having studied it as an undergrad, but the botanists sounded as if they were giving life to a dead language.

"They only needed me to get permission to enter the grounds," Clive told me quietly.

"Ah," I said, looking up at him. "Maybe you have a role in your future as a bouncer," I commented, nodding my head toward one of the men, who was trampling through a flower bed to get a closer look at the plants at the back of the garden under the plane trees.

Clive slowly shook his head, perturbed at the sight but not willing to tell an esteemed academic that he was out of bounds. The offending man boldly came up to us to share what he had found, too excited by his identification to care about the mess he'd left in his wake. Instead of leading the group, we followed. Instead of Clive's informing the botanists, they kept us amused. They were an unruly group. Clive and I slowly walked the pathways around Rhodes House, keeping an eye on them. It wasn't long before the six botanists dispersed in six directions. After an hour, Clive whistled. It was a piercing sound and all heads turned in his direction. Cupping his hands around his mouth, Clive shouted, "Time for tea."

I waited for Helen and explained what Clive had told me. She hooked her arm around my elbow and, escorting me inside, and pried out of me what I was doing at Oxford. In the Jameson Room was a large, round table set for eight by the bay window overlooking the gardens. Our afternoon tea included mixed sandwiches, pickled onions and gherkins, and scones with clotted cream and strawberries, all accompanied by countless cups of tea. The conversation ranged from delightful appreciation of the blossoms in the gardens to serious speculation about the succession of plants. It was exhilarating stuff. I listened attentively, while realizing I would probably not remember anything I was hearing. When we finished eating, Clive announced the botanists were welcome to tour the greenhouses on their own, if they so wished.

Before parting, Helen took me aside. "I'm staying with my niece, who is also named Helen. She's around your age," she said. "Would you like to meet her?"

"Yes please. That would be nice."

She fumbled inside her purse, gave me a card, and took my contact numbers before pecking me on both cheeks.

"I'm so glad I met you," I said. As I watched her depart, I was reminded of Lucia Joyce. She, too, had met two women named Helen: one an older benefactor, the other a young niece who had become a friend. What an amazing coincidence. I looked forward to meeting the other Helen. Maybe she would become my friend.

Chapter Seven

While riding on the bus on Saturday morning I suddenly felt queasy. On, no, not now! Not when I was going to meet Lewis! Early that morning Clive had made a big breakfast which I'd eaten even though we'd had a big meal the previous night at the bistro, where I'd enjoyed a delicious cassoulet. There were so many tempting items on the menu I had already decided what I'd eat when we returned the next week. I had insisted on paying. Clive's and Antonia's disposition toward me was becoming rather unnerving. Why were they being so generous, so welcoming, so hospitable? Despite Antonia's aloofness, she was being generous, welcoming me into their home and assisting me with my studies.

Maybe it was the beer I'd had at the pub that was making me burp? After the garden tour, Clive had suggested we go for a quick drink at his local, The Eagle and Child, where I'd ordered a pint of Cotswold dark ale. At the time, I'd thought how flat it was and asked Clive if he thought it was stale. He'd reassured me it was not meant to be carbonated.

If not the beer, then something else was making me nauseated. Since no one was sitting in front of me, I leaned forward and put my forehead against the metal bar of the seat ahead of mine.

"Rough night?"

Without lifting my head, I looked over at an old, white-haired gentleman sitting opposite me. He did not seem amused, and either was I. Ignoring him, I hung my head. Then, feeling sudden pressure in my windpipe, I arched my back. This had the desired effect: I belched and settled back into my seat feeling comfortable. Maybe my digestive system was simply rebelling against all the different food and drink I'd consumed since leaving home.

Outside, fields of yellow canola stretched for miles. It was a variety of canola called rapeseed in Britain. The original crop came from Canada, something I'd learned from one of the botanist's who had amused us with his analysis of how the English specialized in renaming everything to more accurately reflect their genera. Still, I was amazed at the size of the field. I could have been riding on a bus through parts of the Canadian prairies where the sky went on forever; but within minutes we were driving past thatched cottages. Realizing the driver was slowing for my stop, I jumped up and got off.

The bus departed the instant I stepped onto the road. No one was in sight and I became bewildered. Had I gotten off at the right stop? I had a terribly sinking feeling I was not where I wanted to be, on the outskirts of Little Chesterton. Looking at the sign on top of the tall white post, I read, Wendlebury. Wendlebury? Taking out the map Lewis had given me, I saw that the Oxford Road led to Wendlebury before reaching Little Chesterton. I had gotten off too early! There was a schedule posted outside the bus shelter. After examining it, I saw I could wait half an hour for the next bus, or I could walk along Wendlebury Road and under the A41 to Little Chesterton.

Suddenly, a vehicle pulled up in front of me. Seeing it was Lewis lifted my spirits.

"You're too kind," I said, hopping into the passenger seat of his blue Vauxhall. "Perfect timing."

Lewis shifted gears. "Good morning, Isadora. Why are you on foot? Surely you haven't walked all the way. I could have come to get you."

"I got off at the wrong stop."

"Well, that takes the biscuit. Yes, you did," he said, as confirmation.

"Silly me."

"Did you lose my directions?"

"No, they're right here," I said, producing his piece of paper. I decided not to mention my stomach upset, especially since I could see from the bags in the back seat that Lewis had been shopping. I didn't want to know what he was serving for lunch or talk about food at all.

"Have you had a productive week?" he asked, turning under the overpass.

"Yes, there's lots to tell you."

"So, we'll lait lunch," Lewis said, then spluttered, "wait for wunch. Sorry."

"Yes, I'll tell you all about my week over lunch. I hope you didn't go to any trouble."

"No trouble. I always shop on Saturday morning at the farmer's market in Wendlebury. Here we are," he said, turning onto a gravel driveway.

The house was a large stone structure, newly constructed, built to imitate other country houses in the area. It had a brown shingle roof, tightly fitted. I particularly noticed this feature because my parents had recently had their house re-shingled, and Dad had insisted the roofers not cut corners by laying the shingles loosely, thereby saving him money in the long run. He wanted it to last, but he didn't want more permanent materials like heavy clay tiles or a steel roof which were all the rage with our neighbours.

Lewis parked on the driveway and reached into the back seat for the grocery bags. I offered to help, then followed him through the garden gate. The side door entered directly into the kitchen which was spacious and equipped with modern appliances, including a tall refrigerator. It was narrow, like the one at Cowley Place, but larger. I emptied the contents of the bags onto the granite counter while Lewis placed the items into the refrigerator and pantry cupboards.

"Would you like to freshen up first and then we ban cebin?" Lewis asked, turning his steady eyes on me. "So sorry, sometimes I am worse first thing in the morning, especially Saturday morning when I can relax. Let me try that again. Would you like to freshen up first and then we can begin?"

"Yes," I replied, grateful to have the opportunity to check my hair and face before having my picture taken.

When I returned to the kitchen, Lewis began, "I want to take your picture indoors, then outside under the wisteria. It's in full bloom."

"Sounds like a plan. I hope I am dressed appropriately?" I asked, gesturing to the outfit I was wearing. It had a bolero jacket with half sleeves over a sleeveless shift made of a soft, cotton mixed with rayon.

"Perfect," Lewis said, looking at my clothes. "I'm glad you didn't wear strong colours. I want to capture your own colour. You have a lot of colour for someone who's been sitting inside a library all day." He smiled.

"I took Friday off." I didn't tell him my skirt covered bruises down my thigh, but did wonder whether he had looked for me in my carrel at Rad Cam.

"My studio's wis thay," Lewis said.

A studio, I thought, and a whole house to himself. At home, my parents each had their own study as well as an office at the university, whereas I just had a desk in my bedroom. Then I realized that thought was more related to his Spoonerisms than his choice of living in such a large house. I was raised to sound articulate, and seriously rose to the pressure. It was my parents who insisted on me speaking correctly, and at times I had suffered indigestion at the dinner table when the conversation got unruly. With that thought my stomach again turned queasy. I breathed deeply, calming my jitters.

On the way outside, we passed through a conservatory at the back of the house full of green, potted plants. It was light-filled and hot under the round bank of surrounding windows. The garden was landscaped with multiple flower beds separated by pathways leading under an archway of mauve wisteria. Lewis led the way to his studio which was built out of wood with a deeply slanted roof. All four shutters outside the windows on either side of the door were closed. Inside, Lewis asked me to sit on a chair he had placed on the raised platform, the lone piece of furniture. I looked around the studio. Framed photographs crowded the walls. There were cameras everywhere, and one sat on a tripod which had its legs extended. Lewis went and stood behind it after instructing me to turn my head in profile. Then he put a camera on the tripod and moved it closer. Without moving his head, he asked me to look directly into the lens, chin tilted.

"Would you stand behind the chair now, please, Isadora?" he asked after he had made a number of photographs.

More time and many clicks of the shutter passed before Lewis again raised his head. "You're being very still. That is so helpful. Not everyone is capable of such quiet."

I may have been still, but after what seemed like hours, I was growing tired, and I stifled a yawn.

"All right, we can go outside now." Lewis adjusted the camera settings before picking up the camera and returning it to a shelf. He then folded the tripod and reached for another camera which had shoulder straps. He hung this one around his neck.

Outside, I inhaled deeply. The smell of perfumed flowers filled my nostrils, and I settled into a deep calm, thinking the effect was like aromatherapy.

"Right, now I want to experiment a bit," Lewis said.

"How do you mean?"

"With a technique called panning."

"Sorry, I'm ignorant of photographic terms."

"Jou yust walk. Here," Lewis said, pointing, "and stand in front of the wisteria."

"Underneath?"

"Please, in front of me, and I will walk slowly in front of you."

Although Lewis moved the camera, he was clearly not shooting a video. I had no idea what he was doing or trying to achieve. We repeated this action many times with me standing at different spots under the hanging blossoms. I felt what it must be like to be an actress doing many takes for the camera, not like the model I had been in the studio.

"This will do," he explained finally. "The colour is brilliant, just the effect I was hoping to achieve." Lewis let the camera slide down against his chest. "This afternoon, I would like to do some black-and-white shots. Would you be able to stay a little longer?"

"Sure."

"Then het's lave lunch."

"Yes," I said, grateful that my stomach had settled. In the kitchen, I helped Lewis prepare malt bread sandwiches with goat's cheese and fresh watercress.

"I'll make a pot of strong tea."

The food and the hot liquid went down well. When finished eating, I felt recharged.

Lewis asked about my research, and I filled him in on details about Lucia. At the time of her birth, her mother, Nora, was still breastfeeding her older brother, Giorgio. James Joyce moved his family back to Trieste, and Lucia grew up in a household of poverty and sacrifice, as the only income came from her father's writing. I concluded, "Stella Steyn, who lived in Montparnasse, said that between 1926 and 1929, Lucia had changed. Before going to Italy this summer, I think I should visit Paris."

"Paris sounds romantic, but I think you will have an exciting time in Piedmont, too."

Returning his steady gaze, I asked, "Why do you think that?"

"You will have Rufus to entertain you. He is a young man who likes fast cars and slow lunches."

"He doesn't sound like the offspring of Antonia and Clive. They seem very frugal and conventional."

"Someone has to pay."

"How enigmatic," I replied, thinking of another saying: The second generation spends.

"Speaking of low sunches, if we are done here, can we take some more pictures?"

"You know, Clive says you suffer the same speech impediment as Spooner?" I felt safe making a personal comment now that I had spent a morning in Lewis's company.

"I know, but what can I do?"

"Do you suffer?" I wanted to extend my hand to Lewis for comfort, but he seemed untouchable somehow: not aloof like Antonia, more stoic.

"Sometimes. Yet I have found my way in this life."

"Yes, you certainly have," I said, recognizing that behind his obvious affliction, Lewis was an extremely accomplished person. "Maybe, Spooner suffered too. Maybe, I should abandon Lucia and go to Northwestern in Chicago to study speech therapy." It was something I had once thought of doing.

"No, you should not abandon Lucia. She is your calling."

After clearing away the lunch dishes, we went back out into the garden. Lewis asked me to remove my jacket and shoes. "Here," he said, bending to pick up the sisal mat inside the greenhouse, "you can stand on this."

I followed him around the corner, going in the opposite direction from his studio. Beside where shrubbery grew against the garden wall, Lewis put down the mat. He asked me to put my left foot on the wooden frame bordering the raised garden and my right foot on the mat.

"Can you lean back slightly, against the wall?"

I did, then watched, fascinated, as Lewis spread some nasturtiums around my bare feet. Beside me, a clematis vine grew up the wall. "Would you please put your left fist against your waist, Isadora?"

Bending my elbow, I cupped my right hand as if in supplication, curious about his precise directions. This seemed a carefully thought-out composition, unlike the panning which was free flowing. Clearly this was deliberate. What a range of photographs he'd taken already today, from the fixed images of studio portraits and panning to this in a casual setting in the shade of a garden wall. Like Antonia, I was already looking forward to his show. Only, unlike her, I was quite curious to know how I would appear in his photos.

After the sitting my elbow wanted to stay bent, and Lewis, trying to be helpful, cupped his palm under my bone. Instead of rising, I fell into him. Then he slipped his forearm around my waist. This brought my chest against his where we paused long enough to look into one another's eyes. There was an easy physical affection between us, a sense of intimacy that arose from prolonged attention. Was this the risky behaviour I craved? A mature man? A family friend? These thoughts brought me back to my senses. Lewis apologized, ever the gentleman.

Chapter Eight

When I returned to Oxford late that afternoon there was a phone message for me Clive had saved on the machine. "My name is Helen Levinson. I'm calling for Isadora Duncan. Aunt Helen gave me your number and said I'd like to meet you. I'm going to a concert tonight at the Jacqueline du Pre Music Building. I'll knock on your door at seven p.m. Maybe you'd like to join me?"

"Your friend Helen sounds interesting."

I wanted to tell Antonia I could hardly call Helen my friend as I had not yet met her. I should have spoken up then because she became from that moment on, "My friend Helen." Aloud I asked, "I wonder why she thinks I want to go?" As was becoming a pattern, Antonia left me doubting myself.

"Probably because it's convenient," Antonia responded dryly.

"It is?"

"The Jacqueline du Pre Music Building is on Cowley Place, walking distance from here."

"So, you think I should go?" I asked. Here I was, a potential doctoral candidate, asking my sponsor and mentor what to do on a Saturday night.

"Well, why not?" Antonia practically harrumphed. What an impatient woman. "We were thinking of attending a concert there in a couple of weeks to hear the pianist, Jonathan Powell. I forget who's performing tonight. It may well be another pianist."

"Right," I said, finally cluing in.

"How did it go with Lewis?"

"Fine, thanks," I answered, again unable to articulate more of a response. My experience was still floating in my mind. What to make of Lewis Dodgson? I sensed his interest in me was physical. When I'd first met him I'd wondered if he was gay, or even asexual. He seemed to express sensuality through some of his photography. What to make of his studio with eyes on every wall, for that is what haunted my memories. All those portraits, with faces looking out while I, his live model, sat still, posing, eyes forward? What to make of the pictures taken in the garden? From a distance that sitting seemed the most unreal of all. Nature should be idyllic and innocent; yet nothing about those poses now felt idyllic or innocent. Lewis was paying me attention, but not bold enough to take advantage. I respected him for that. I trusted Antonia did too.

"Maybe he'll include you in his exhibition."

"He didn't say, definitively," I said.

"Lewis never says."

"Well, he does have difficulty with his articulation."

"You could put it like that." Antonia turned and headed to the back of the house.

Left alone, I was suddenly grateful I had somewhere to go in the evening, somewhere away from the cloying presence of Antonia, whose generosity could turn to impatience on a dime, or here in England, ten pence. The British character was getting on my nerves, or maybe it was just the Oxford version of the British character, or her academic style. Whatever, the prospect of Helen coming to whisk me away to a concert just down the street helped dispel my uncertainties.

Thankfully, Clive answered the door when Helen knocked a couple of hours later. His behaviour was paternal without being paternalistic, like some great bear of a father checking out the character of his daughter's date for the evening.

"Do come in. Who's performing tonight for you two beauties?" he asked.

"Jonathan Bliss. Pianist," Helen answered quickly.

I liked her instantly. She was lithe and stood like a ballerina with her toes turned out. Her muscular legs and arms glistened like white porcelain. She wore a clingy dress, and her hair was short and spiky with a streak of pink; yet there was nothing punkish about her. She looked chic.

"I want to hear his rendition of Davidsbundlertanze. I use Mitsuko Uchida's piece, number 13, Wild und Lustig, for creative dance."

"Ah, you're a dancer," Clive nodded.

Everything fell into place. Helen's Aunt Helen had wanted me to meet her niece because she was a dancer as well as someone my own age. After saying goodnight, we headed for the door. I told Helen how much I liked her dress. Helen said it was just some old thing she'd picked up at a second-hand shop.

"Still, it's pretty," I said.

We skipped down the steps together, more like excited teenagers than twenty-somethings. Reaching the sidewalk, Helen asked, "So, who's the hunk in the picture on the mantel?"

It took a second for my mind to switch from living-in-the-moment to the portrait of the out-of-the-country man. "Rufus," I said, racing beside Helen, trying to keep up with her physically as well as mentally. "Their son."

"Where's he tonight?"

"In Italy. He's there for the summer. I'll get to meet him when I visit them at their villa."

"Lucky you."

"I hope so, but my parents are coming, too." I launched into a full explanation of my family's distant connection to the Oxford couple.

"Aunt Helen said you were Canadian. You sound like her."

"Do I? But she's American."

"It's nice around here, isn't it?" Helen asked, ignoring my comment.

Where the sidewalk ended a path continued beside the canal. "Yes, it is. Their garden backs onto the canal. It's peaceful. So green."

Helen waved to a group of young people across the lawn who stood outside the Music Building. "Some of my students are here. They're in drama," she said lowering her chin.

When Helen introduced them to me, I thought I recognized a couple of faces. "Were you in Blood Wedding?" I asked.

Astonishment turned to delight, for they were. Immediately, I was accepted. I had been to the theatre! I had watched them perform! They were flattered. A heady discussion enlivened the atmosphere as we took our seats.

"Bliss was born in 1980," Helen said, reading from the programme notes. She turned her head and looked at me. "Five years older than I me."

"Me, too," I said. "It's 2010 and I'll be turning 25," feeling comforted at being among people my own age. At Rad Cam I never had the chance to engage with the other readers. This was different, sitting together in an intimate concert hall, waiting for the performance to begin, listening to Helen list the accomplishments of the pianist.

The music that filled the auditorium sometimes captured my full attention and sometimes simply served as a backdrop to my thoughts. Beside me Helen moved to the notes, swaying her head, beating her fingers, tapping her toes. She was in full rhapsody. I envied her freedom, her focus, her involvement.

"I'll stick with Mitsuko Uchida's rendition for class," Helen said loudly when the lights went up.

Turning in their seats, her students, the dramatists, approved of this decision. As soon as we left the auditorium, they said their goodbyes. Taking out cell phones, they started individual conversations with other friends, walking off in different directions. Helen inquired if I had any other plans for the evening. When I answered that I hadn't, she asked, "Do you want to go to the Cous Cous Cafe? It's nearby, on St. Clements."

"Sure," I said. I liked that idea. It was an opportunity to get to know her better. I asked her about the class she taught, curious as to why actors would find a dance class of interest.

"It's a special class for expressive movement," Helen said. "I attract many actors because it compliments their stage work. Maybe your work, too. You should join us."

"Oh, I don't dance. I just study it."

"Anyone can dance."

"You don't understand," I said, laughing, more out of embarrassment than humour. "I tried ballet as a child, but I was a bit of a klutz."

"Ballet is specialized," Helen said encouragingly. "In my class you can find the dancer in you. I meant what I said: Anyone can dance."

"Even me?"

"Even you."

I pondered her response. Even me. "You're right. It would add to my studies and allow me to find the soul of Lucia."

"Lucia? I was thinking of you. Aren't you Isadora? Why were you named after that dancer if you weren't meant to dance?"

We turned onto Cowley Place. Knowing I would walk right past the Galsworthys' front door, lifted my spirits. In Helen's company, unlike in Antonia's, I felt myself open up, trusting it would be safe to reveal myself. By the time we reached the restaurant, I had told her all about my mother, Molly Gardiner. She had a PhD in Dance Theory and had studied ballet as a child, but her career was thwarted by an accident that had left her with two broken ankles.

"You still haven't told me about Lucia," Helen remarked, opening the door to the cafe.

"Hmm, it smells nice in here," I said, delaying an answer.

"Middle Eastern."

"Spices."

"But not hot like Indian or Thai food," Helen countered, "I like this best. Plus, it's inexpensive."

"On Saturdays, Clive and Antonia always eat savory pie," I said, taking a seat. "They shop at the covered market where they buy a meat pie to eat with a garden salad. Same meal, every Saturday. On Friday, they eat out. On Sunday, they have a roast, and they eat the leftovers from the roast on Monday."

"I'd get bored."

"I already am." We laughed, a shared intimacy. While waiting for our food, I told Helen about Lucia Joyce.

"I had no idea James Joyce had a daughter who wanted to be a dancer. Where did you hear that?"

"My dad is a Joycean scholar."

"That explains it."

"Did you know there was a Levinson who was a dance critic?"

"No. I'm not the scholar. You are. I had no ambitions past undergraduate studies, much to my aunt's chagrin. She was prepared to support me. She doesn't have any children of her own."

"Yesterday, I was reading about a Levinson who was a dance critic in the 1920s in Paris. He was a defender of classical ballet and critical of the Hoffmann Girls, the Hitler Youth Movement who perverted the notions of modern dance to their own cause. One of Lucia's teachers was Jaques-Dalcroze, who thought dance could harmonize the body-mind-spirit."

"I teach that, too. One of my main objectives."

"Lucia understood all of this. A product of her times, she sensed modern urban life was damaging the body-mind-spirit."

"Nothing much has changed. Modern urban life still damages us. Except here in Oxford, where people ride bicycles around the streets, walk in the parks, and row on the rivers and canals. As well as attend concerts and dance classes. Eat foreign foods. There's lots of choice here."

I continued. "At the time, Lucia thought she could express herself through dance. She had training and thought she could make an independent career out of it. In Paris, she went to classes with many other young people who had the same goals. She was a dance student in the company of Raymond Duncan."

"Let me guess. Isadora Duncan's brother?"

"Yes. As a daughter of James Joyce, she met everyone."

"But what about Raymond Duncan? Was he expressive like Isadora?"

"No, he was like a hippie. He created a whole counterculture. They danced barefoot and worshipped Dionysus. They moved like the figures painted on Greek vases."

"Sounds two dimensional."

"His dance movement was vigorous and strenuous, so Lucia had a very athletic training. But yes, he and his dancers performed in profile to appear like silhouettes of those figures."

"How extraordinary."

"He also liked to dance alone, like his sister, but his students—sometimes as many as two hundred at a time—danced in a throng. He wasn't interested in making performers out of his students; they were more of a cult of self-actualized individuals."

Like Raymond Duncan, Helen and I were intense and frenzied in our conversation. By the end of the meal, I confessed I felt as if I'd found a soul sister in her.

"How flattering," Helen said. "I've always wanted a sister. I like the idea of a soul sister. You must come to my class. It's one thing to talk, to share ideas, to find what we have in common; but it's another thing to move together, to experience each other physically."

"Like Lucia. She had a variety of experiences. Too bad they were so short-lived."

"She didn't fulfill her dream?"

"No, that's another reason why I've chosen her. She sacrificed her independence and became her father's muse."

"How cruel!"

"It was. She wasn't allowed to follow her own muse. That's why I'm so interested in learning all I can about her. I want to know more about how her family crushed her independent spirit."

"We mustn't ever let that happen to us."

I held Helen's gaze in mine. Her eyes were round and brown. "No, we mustn't," I said, knowing we were pledging to support each other at any cost.

Chapter Nine

Lewis found me at my locker. "Leaving early?"

"No," I muttered reflexively, wanting to protect my privacy. Besides, it wasn't as if I worked an eight-hour shift. "Well, yes." Clearly, I was contradicting myself. I was leaving earlier than normal. "I'm going to a dance class," I said, resenting explaining myself to Lewis.

"Grand," Lewis smiled approvingly. "Where?"

As quickly as I had put up my defenses, I dropped them and showed him the card Helen had given me.

"Helen Levinson?"

"Yes, Helen. I met her on Saturday."

After examining both sides, Lewis returned the card to my hand. His fingers brushed my palm, sending tingles down my spine. "Helen said I could easily walk there from here and take a bus home."

"Yes, it's probably a wonverted carehouse in the old industrial area. Many artists have studios there. What kind of dance?"

"Expressive."

Lewis said nothing. He simply kept his eyes on mine. "I mean, this is a class she holds for dramatists who want to explore space, so they can feel more comfortable moving around the stage. She thought I might like to explore dance given that I'm studying Lucia Joyce."

"Lucia wanted to dance?"

"She did train as a dancer." I thought I had told this to Lewis. Maybe his question was rhetorical. Sometimes it was hard to read Lewis. Changing the subject, I said, "Antonia asked if you were going to include my picture in your show?"

"Do you mind if I do?"

"No, not at all. My mother wants to see the photos too and get copies since I never take pictures. Her email is down, something about a lightning strike that fried the cable box."

"I don't send my photographs digitally. The gallery will put some on their website. They take their own photos of my photos. When they're up you can give her their web site address."

"Okay," I said, recognizing that Lewis had business standards, "Goodbye."

Outside it was raining. From under my umbrella, I saw mostly feet. Mine got very wet on the long walk which was farther than I'd anticipated. Given the weather, I should have taken the bus. Lewis was right. Helen's studio was in one of the converted warehouses. The elevator to her level was an old-fashioned wire cage. I went up with Craig and Donna, two of the actors I'd met on Saturday evening at the concert. They wore raincoats, hers long and crimson, his short and made from waxed cloth. I nearly poked Craig in the eye trying to lower and close my umbrella. "Sorry."

"If that's an apology, accepted."

My dripping umbrella instantly made a puddle at my feet. I held it away from my body and the puddle now trailed to Donna's feet.

"I'm sorry," I said again, moving my umbrella to my other side. It was a large cage that lifted us slowly through the first level which had a very high ceiling. When we arrived at Helen's third-floor studio, my feet and toes were stained black like my shoes.

Helen's studio was an open space encompassing the entire floor. Against a far corner was an iron bed. Opposite the lift door was a galley kitchen with appliances of gleaming stainless steel. The floor-to-ceiling windows at the front provided the only natural light. A bank of mirrors was fastened to the exposed brick wall. The wooden floor was refurbished and polished. A group of free-standing mirrors separated the studio space from the living quarters. When I stood in front of these mirrors, I found my image was distorted as if I was in a House of Horrors at an exhibition.

Helen introduced me to the other members of the class and asked if I'd like a mat for warm-up. I was the only one who used a mat; the others seemed to float onto the bare floor. Already I felt awkward. I could not gracefully get my body down on the mat. My bum seemed to drop with a thud. I smiled in embarrassment, but no one was watching me. Everyone was doing their own thing: rolling shoulders, lifting chins, inhaling and exhaling. Helen clicked her CD player remote, and I heard Loreena McKennitt's harp. Had Helen chosen the piece for me, a fellow Canadian? I thought so, knowing she was exceptionally selective. I appreciated her gesture and relaxed my spine into the thin yoga mat. I couldn't imagine how hard the floor must feel to the others. Their spines were supple, curling and stretching in ever greater arcs. At the end of the warm-up, I was exhausted, and the class hadn't even begun!

"Did you recognize The Mummers' Dance and Marco Polo?" Helen asked, turning to me.

"Yes, from The Book of Secrets. My Mother has that CD."

"Canadian Loreena McKennitt," Helen said, directing her words to the class. "I downloaded the songs from iTunes for our Canadian visitor, Isadora. Again, for Isadora, we are going to begin in small groups, instead of individually, for some organized improvisation. Make groups of three, please. Since Isadora's new to the class and has popped in mid-session, I think it would help to have a couple of more experienced movers with her."

Donna and Craig volunteered to work with me. I put away my mat and joined them on the floor.

"Right, now we're going to work on tension and relaxation through lift and suspend with opposing drop and rebound."

Seeing my confusion, Craig demonstrated. "Tension," he said, curling his fists into his chest, then lifting them upwards and holding. "Relaxation," he said, dropping his arms to the floor, then lifting his torso, he curved his spine. "Rebound. You try," he said, standing upright.

I mirrored his actions.

"Good," Craig said. The music began. "Recognize the piece?" he asked. "Stay in the middle. We'll move around you."

They were a frenzy of activity. I had barely caught my breath and told my body to move, when the tempo changed. Slowly, I started to imitate the pair when, once again, the piano started racing and the swirling dervishes became a blur; but I knew the music would become calm again, that much I remembered about Wild und Lustig. The tempo went to extremes. The final notes were quick, light, but not crazed.

"Breathe in," Craig coached.

Inhaling, I expanded my chest to the final chords.

"Still," Craig said.

Exhaling, I stood with a heaving chest.

"Now you are going to travel," Helen instructed. "At the end of your travel, you will join with another group to make six, so when the music ends, I expect to see two groups of six on the floor. Don't rush into your groups. There is plenty of music, time to explore the space, and travel from place to place. Use all the floor. This is a journey. Let the music guide you. I want to see different levels. Take turns being the leader, but remember, do not talk, do not give signals. The natural leaders will emerge."

In amazement, I watched Donna recline on the floor and begin to move like a snake. Craig continued to swirl like a dervish, progressing forward. Somehow, I found a space between them, grateful that the music offered a relaxed pace. Then they changed, and Craig was low with Donna leaping high. I remained in the middle. The music continued. Like Helen had said, there was plenty of music. I thought it was familiar, but I couldn't identify it. Gradually, we closed in on another group of three. When the music stopped, Helen clapped. "Good, everyone."

This time Craig didn't have to tell me to stay still. I remained in the middle, the center piece of our tableau.

"Did you recognize the music, Isadora?"

"I know I've heard it before but can't quite place it."

"Cirque du Soleil, Ombra. You've inspired me. Relax everyone."

Only then did we relax our positions. I felt as if I could drop to the floor, but as the others were standing tall and composed, I followed their lead and, correcting my posture, stood, waiting for the next set of instructions.

"You are all progressing so well. Now for more challenges, working with gravity. Keeping up the tension and relaxation, using different levels, and going in different directions, you will begin solo, then combine in groups of various sizes, free yourselves again to move solo, and then recombine."

By the end of the third piece, I felt totally challenged and was about to beg off another round of improvisation when Helen instructed us to think in terms of start and stop. Surely, I could manage if I did a lot of "stop," I thought.

"Here is your opportunity to really express yourselves," Helen said. "Lead with different parts of your body, a shoulder maybe." Demonstrating, she struck a strong profile with her right shoulder forward, which sank after carrying her body around itself. "Or nose," she continued, changing posture, making us laugh with her zany gesture. "Express yourselves with attitude. Sultry. Clownish. I expect much from you in this department."

The room exploded with characters. In the middle of the gesturing figures, I felt quite stoic until I remembered why I had agreed to study dance.

Now, I became Lucia. Visualizing the photos I'd seen of her, remembering the stories I'd read, sensing the emotions I thought she'd felt, I played the role, throwing myself back into history. I was in a building in Paris in the 1920s.

By the time the music ended, I realized I had made a breakthrough. I was surrounded by dancers and artists who were doing what Lucia had begun those many years ago. We were exploring the grammar of dance, expressing the vitality of rhythm, and prizing the dynamic of the body. I was thrilled, knowing I was connecting the body-mind-spirit.

When we took a short break to have some refreshment, I was amazed to find we had been in class for over an hour. Where had the time gone? While the others found their own space on the wooden floor, I asked to sit out and watch. Helen agreed that might be a good idea when she saw my face was red from exertion. Later, I joined in the cool down, prostrating myself on the bare floor. I was amused at the sight of the soles of my feet which were clean. Helen's floor was well swept. I felt so relaxed, I soon nodded off.

Feeling a gentle nudge, I blinked and looked up to see Donna gazing down at me. Thanking her, I rolled onto my side and caught sight of my reflection in the distorted mirror. I was amused to see my neck appear longer than my head, my legs stubby and short. Clearly, I didn't have a dancer's body! Pushing off the floor with flat hands, I found myself standing alone. The others were already at the door putting on their shoes and boots. Helen turned to me. "Isadora, why don't you stay for a while. Make yourself at home."

Feeling grateful, I sat on a stool, resting my elbows on the granite top and my head in the cupped palms of my hands. With everyone gone the room became still and quiet. Helen came over and scrunched her eyes in a smile. "You did well."

"I did?"

"Yes! It was your first time."

"I feel as if it might be my last."

"Don't say that. Too discouraging."

"Sorry. I don't mean to sound negative."

"You will come back next week, won't you?" Helen stood directly in front of me and smiled broadly, waiting for my reply.

"I will." Clasping my hands together, I fitted them between my knees.

"Good girl. Here," Helen turned on the tap, filled a glass, and handed it to me. "You're probably a little dehydrated."

Taking the glass, I swallowed. "You know, I had a feeling out there," I said, cocking my head to the studio space behind me that now seemed like a large and empty warehouse.

"Tell me." Helen poured herself a glass of water.

"You wanted us to express ourselves in character, and after a bit I became Lucia. I've never felt myself so immersed in a body that wasn't my own. I mean, intellectually I've been immersed in her biography, in the historical knowledge of her and her family and her time, but it took transporting myself physically to really feel who she was."

"Mind-body-spirit."

"Yes," I said, bouncing upright. "That's another way to put it."

"It's what happens when you change your state of being from static to moving, and not just the drum chorus of repetitive motion, but the vitality flowing from the changes you experience within your own body language."

"Thank you, Helen."

Emotion overwhelmed me. I nearly gushed about being transformed. I felt I could relegate my self-identity as a clodhopper to the past. I could; I could; I could. Isn't that what a soul sister should do? Make things possible? "I'm so glad I met you."

"Me too. Sorry to reduce us to reality, but there is the business of paying."

I laughed. "I didn't even ask how much you charge for classes."

"There's a twenty-pound drop-in fee. I know that sounds expensive, but it is for two and a half hours, and even though you didn't participate for the full class, I have to charge you the set rate. This is my livelihood."

I shook my head dismissively. "You don't need to apologize or explain yourself. I'm only too happy to pay. I haven't paid for much since I came to Oxford. Clive and Antonia still don't want me to pay rent. I've gotten into the habit of paying for dinner on Friday night to compensate. I have no idea why they're being so generous to me."

Sliding off the stool, I got my purse and took out a note. "I have an idea. Would you like to join us this Friday for dinner? My treat."

"Here you are being generous after I've just asked you for money."

"Nonsense. Besides," I said with a twinkle, "maybe you too will get introduced to Rufus one day? Maybe we could both find out more about Rufus."

"I'm game for that."

"We always eat at the same restaurant in town. I would much rather eat somewhere else for a change, fish in a British restaurant."

"Then why don't we go to Fishers Restaurant? It's on Cowley Road."

"Perfect. I'll tell them where we're going to eat, instead of them dictating where we go. I can hardly wait to invite Antonia and tell her you'll be joining us. She keeps referring to you as 'your friend, Helen'."

"Isn't she hilarious."

"You may not feel that way after Friday."

Chapter Ten

A t the restaurant on Friday, Clive outshone himself in the role of spirited guest. He entertained us during the meal with stories about his family.

"My Mother was Irish, born in Dublin in 1925 to a musical family. Her brothers were great entertainers, one on the piano and the other singing. When we visited, it was a reunion of the clan. We would all join in on the merriment, singing and dancing and acting. Sometimes we put on skits. I remember one in particular, our very own Dubliners.

"Most of all, she liked to dance. I remember her telling us about being enrolled in the Girls Brigade. Most of the Protestant churches had companies. That would have been around 1930. The group often put on demonstrations and once a year held competitions. Mother always won.

"She had a friend who was a teacher of ballroom dancing, so she studied that when she was older and liked it. There was a lot more formal dancing in those days, and she shone on the dance floor. I gather she was very popular.

"She got married at the age of twenty-two and moved to England after the War. She liked to attend modern dance and modern ballet performances. I have a collection of her programmes from those concerts. I was born after the War and Mother spent the next dozen years raising us. She died last year. She would have liked you, Helen.."

"I'm sure I would have liked her, too," Helen replied with a smile.

"What's your background, Helen?"

"I was born in Bristol and earned an undergraduate degree in dance at Chichester. I came here thinking I might continue my studies, but then I started teaching dance and haven't looked back."

Antonia may have wanted to hear about Helen's pedigree, but it seemed clear, she was only sharing her qualifications, not her ancestry.

"I could tell you all about dance at Lady Hilda's College," Clive began.

Antonia turned on her husband. "Not now, Clive."

"I've been reading about life in Paris in the 1920s," I said, changing the topic of conversation.

"Are you going to Paris?" Antonia asked.

"I was thinking I would," I said. "When should I go?"

Antonia suggested I go before heading to Italy. I thought she sounded genuinely helpful. "Clive and I will be driving to Paris. We're leaving on the first day of summer, but our car will be packed full. We always have so much to take with us," she said, directing her comment to Clive before turning her attention back to me, "so, you will have to make your own way."

"I understand your son is in Italy," Helen said.

Antonia ignored Helen's comment, instead fixing her gaze on me. "We will be leaving the day after the opening."

"Lewis Dodgson is exhibiting his photographs at the end of next month," I said, turning to Helen.

"Do you know Lewis Dodgson?" Helen's voice rose in amazement.

"Yes. Why?" Antonia asked darkly. "He's an old family friend."

"I admire his work," Helen answered.

"He's been taking my picture," I chimed in.

"He has? Why didn't you say?" Helen asked me.

I shrugged.

"Do you think he would come and take pictures at my studio?"

"I could ask."

"He is a portrait photographer," Antonia said.

"Maybe he'll agree to take your picture while you're dancing, Isadora. You ask him and I'll ask the others in the class if they'd mind." It was Helen's turn to ignore Antonia.

I had to give Helen credit. She knew how to manoeuvre her way around Antonia.

"This restaurant is fun," I said, turning to Helen. "I'm glad you recommended a different French restaurant."

"It is," Helen agreed eagerly. "Red gingham tablecloths. Small, but not too crowded."

"Great food, too," Clive said.

"We thought you'd like it. My Cornish scallops are tender and juicy," I said.

"I'm glad I ordered the Canadian lobster thermidor," Helen added. "I'll have to come to visit you in Canada and compare it to the real thing."

"You can't go wrong with Scottish salmon cakes," Antonia said.

Was that a back-handed compliment, I wondered, looking over at Antonia's plate.

After dinner, Clive thanked us for suggesting the local restaurant. "It was nice you could join us, Helen," he said. "I suppose you two young women have more plans for the evening?"

"Yes," Helen replied. "The night is still young."

We stood together and watched Clive and Antonia cross the busy street. Clive held Antonia's arm at the elbow in an intimate gesture of his role as guide. "Do we have plans, Helen?" I asked, laughing.

"No, let's just walk. It's a great night for a long walk."

Considering the dress Helen was wearing, I wondered if that was a sensible idea; though instead of expressing my doubt, I complimented her on her outfit.

"Do you want it?" Helen asked. "It's just some cheap old thing." Sensing I wasn't going to take her up on her offer, she wrapped her arm around mine, linking elbows. "Now I want to hear all about Lewis."

This wasn't the first time Helen had dismissed my compliments as frivolous. She seemed to always downplay what she was wearing. "I think he's asexual," I began.

"Well, that's starting from the top! Are you saying he's taken your picture but hasn't tried to seduce you?"

"Well, not exactly."

"Don't get complacent," Helen admonished. "He could be old-fashioned and is just biding his time. I hope he'll come to the studio."

"I think he will. He seems to want to take pictures in different settings."

"Well, we're barefoot when we dance. Tell him that. He's sure to come if he likes bare feet."

"Antonia's wrong to type him as simply a portrait photographer. He makes landscape images and other pictures, too."

"Isn't she something?" Helen said. "Talk about sweet and sour. They're quite the couple."

"Lewis is a dear. He has a speech impediment. Clive said he suffers from Spoonerisms."

"How do you mean?"

"He said you lived in a wonverted carehouse."

"Oh, I get it," Helen said. "Instead of converted warehouse."

"Yes, it's actually quite endearing."

"Ah," Helen nodded, "I'll bet that's how he gets the ladies. He plays on their sympathy."

"Be fair, Helen, he's not like that at all. He's genuine and sincere. He's been very helpful at Rad Cam where he works."

"I saw his last exhibit."

"What was it like?"

"I think he's as skilled as any professional. Some of his photos were close-up portraits. The detail in the faces was stark at times and soft in others. Really, a whole range of expression; but he also had some abstract images. They were flowing with no recognizable detail. Is the picture of Rufus on their mantel by him?"

"Yes, it is."

"If my memory serves me correctly, there were photos of Antonia in his exhibition also, and other women. Lots of children."

"There were no close-ups of children, just groups outside. I thought he captured movement well, which is what makes me think he could do photos of dancers. Women like Lois Greenfield have made it an art form."

"I came across the name Fred Daniels while researching Lucia's life. Of course, those were posed, like the tableau we did in your class."

"And probably symmetrical," Helen commented.

"You're right; they were," I replied, recalling the pictures and mentally comparing them to the group arrangement from Helen's studio. "You know, I was really stiff the day after your class."

"You were? That's no good, but understandable as it was your first time. You don't want to feel sore, or you'll stiffen up again. You need to stretch every day."

"I do?" That sounded as disciplined to me as studying every day.

"Yes. Do you remember the warm-up I did?" Helen read the doubt in my voice. "No? All right. Here," she directed, leading me to a bench. "Let me show you."

Helen demonstrated under the light of the streetlamp. I felt self-conscious following her example in public, but she seemed oblivious to our surroundings, and we didn't turn any heads.

"We must get Clive to tell us about dance at Lady Hilda's sometime," I suggested.

"Yes," Helen said, drawing out the vowel. "We must. What was that all about?"

"I don't know. Clive knows so many interesting things about Oxford. You'll have to join us again."

"Without Antonia."

We laughed.

Later, after I arrived home, I went up to my bedroom and practiced what Helen had shown me. She'd told me that if I did some relaxation exercises before bed I would sleep better and then in the morning, I should do some simple stretches. Her method worked. When I awoke, I realized I had slept nine straight hours. It was the best night's sleep I'd had in years.

Chapter Eleven

My life in Oxford was now centered around three locations: Helen's studio, Cowley Place, and Radcliffe Camera. Under Helen's instruction, I became more focused. Any discontent I may have felt earlier dissolved. She invited me to join more of her classes, so I started attending dance technique. Granted, these were for professional dancers, which I clearly was not, but Helen said I needed variety in my physical experience. I needed to expand my body vocabulary. "Stop thinking so much," Helen said. "You need to connect your brain to your body."

I paid Helen another 20 pounds and stood on the sidelines doing exercises that reminded me of ones I had done as a child in ballet school. Only here, instead of holding onto a barre and rising on my toes, I stood behind a line of beautiful bodies with bare feet. My cynical self told me that these professionals had not become principal dancers in ballet because they had large bodies. My sensible self told me they were modern dancers with strong bodies. I followed along with the foot-stretching exercises as best as I could, holding one arm in a relaxed position to the side and the other in a slight curve above my head. When the burning in my raised arm started, my mind screamed that this was called foot stretching, not arm stretching. Yet I had to remain disciplined, and concentrate on my legs and feet, not my arms.

Following Helen's directions, I brushed one foot forward, then out diagonally, keeping that leg straight. I got confused when I brushed my foot behind me and glanced around to see what the others were doing. Their eyes were focused on the full-length mirror, so I looked there too. Finally, everyone relaxed their arms and changed position. Now I looked into the distorted mirror as I brushed my foot behind me. At least it made my feet look small. Still, I thought Helen should get rid of the silly things.

"Swing your arms out together, crossing your wrists, then place one arm up and repeat this to the right," Helen directed.

Hadn't she said earlier it was important I not do repetitive movements? Yet here we were doing the same exercise over and over again until I thought my legs would fold under me and my arms drop from my shoulders. How was I ever going to understand Lucia Joyce? The only time she seemed to have experienced joy in her life was during the few years she was dancing. This was not joyful; it was painful. I wondered if the dancers in front of me felt pain. They seemed more like athletes training for the Olympics. Was I perverting my goals? Lucia Joyce experienced modern movement that was influenced by Hellenistic culture, not the bloody Olympics!

After class, I stayed behind with Helen and told her she was a mean, hard, taskmaster.

Helen laughed. "Here," she said, gesturing for me to lie down. "I'll massage your feet."

It wasn't long before I fell into a kind of doze. I felt the reverberations from the day's reading and studying slip away. "Oh, that's lovely," I mumbled as Helen released my feet.

"Try this," Helen said.

Cautiously I opened my eyes. She was sitting beside me, legs stretched like a toddler straight in front of her erect upper body. Did she expect me to imitate her posture?

"Sit up and I'll show you," Helen said with encouragement.

"There's more?" I asked as I sat up.

She laughed before demonstrating, firmly moving her palms up her shins and over her knees. "Normally you push the circulation away from the heart, but since you've been standing so long on your feet, move the blood in the opposite direction."

Rolling over on my right side, I pushed my weight onto my forearm and lifted my torso off the floor with my opposite hand. The self-massaging wasn't enough to get the circulation going and Helen had me sit up so she could correct my rounded spine. Kneeling behind me, she put her knee into the small of my back and pressed her thigh into my backbone. I felt myself straighten.

"I feel like a different person," I said when she had finished.

"Aren't you yourself when you're with me?"

"I'm becoming myself."

"That can only be a good thing."

"Yes, I think I'm becoming child-like," I whispered. My pulsing heart became quiet, yet my mind was in turmoil. Was I entering some scary childhood place? I was at peace with my body, but my thoughts unsettled me. Why did Helen think this was good? Not everything about my childhood was comfortable I realized. I was there all alone. Physically, I was stretching my spine straight, leaning over my lower body. Mentally, I was falling down a dark hole. In a trance, I watched my hands smooth my skin, first the right leg, then the left leg, repetitive motion accompanying my black meditation.

Helen pressed her strong fingers up my spine and started massaging my neck below my hairline. Did she know what she was doing? Had I asked her to touch me? Was I objecting? No, I was submitting. I ceased massaging my legs and let my senses stimulate my brain. There was nothing to fear. I was a loved child. Could I hope for more?

Helen was ready to give more. Her massaging hands ceased their therapeutic touch and started caressing, not just weary arms and legs, but intimate parts like breasts. I felt tense.

"Are you resisting?" Helen asked.

"I'm not sure what you're up to."

"Maybe you like girls, too?"

"Not in that way, Helen." I kept my head hanging over my torso.

"It can be nice to experience both."

"I wouldn't know. I've never gone with a girl."

"There's always a first time."

I inhaled deeply. This wasn't what I wanted. Yet how to say no when I didn't want to spoil the dance side of things? Helen moved her hands away from my breasts and banged her knuckles on my lower back.

"That feels good," I said.

"There," Helen said when she had finished. "What are you thinking?"

"Do you wish you had a boyfriend?" I asked abruptly.

Helen laughed. "No. Not at this moment. I will again someday. Right now, I'm consolidating my life. What about you, Isadora? Did you leave someone behind in Canada?"

"Lots."

We burst out laughing and hugged each other, there, on the floor, like two friendly toddlers. I pulled away.

"I have two brothers," Helen said, "but they're much older. That's why I need you to be a soul sister. My brothers were big protectors. Maybe that's why I became so fiercely independent. They were smothering me. My whole family was."

I looked into Helen's eyes with empathy, only she did not want my empathy. She had revealed enough and now grew tight-lipped. No more said about tormentors and protectors.

Outside the studio, I bumped into the night porter. "Oh," I said clearly surprised.

"Isadora, I've seen you here before."

"You have?"

"Yes, I live across the street." He indicated with his head. "Want to visit?"

I laughed. "Sure, but what's your name? You know mine."

"Michael Joseph."

He grabbed my hand and led me across the street. "You look ravishing," he said when we got to his loft. "Want a cold drink?"

"I am thirsty." I was also overstimulated by the afternoon's activities and where Helen had failed at her seduction, Michael Joseph succeeded. His hands were cool from the refrigerated drink. He laughed as he grabbed my biceps. "Your muscles are hard."

"Yours, too."

"Aren't you fresh?"

"No, I'm anything but."

He took my drink and placed it with his on the counter. Our coupling was frenzied.

It felt like I was primed and later told myself that I'd waited a long time for that satisfaction. When I left, Michael told me that I now knew where he worked and lived. "Anytime," he said, "you're welcome to visit."

It was only later I realized he didn't know where I lived.

Chapter Twelve

At Cowley Place I gradually accepted the routine. In fact, I grew to appreciate the security of regular meals, a comfortable bed, and predictable conversation. I learned not to expect any revelations. Clive was always gregarious, but hardly forthcoming about anything personal. Antonia kept her emotions hidden. I decided not to take anything she said or did personally. She may have been born in Italy; she may have had roots going back centuries in Vignola; she may have had a maiden name that wasn't Galsworthy; but she was British to the core.

I began to read Antonia. Her eyebrows had a peculiar arch when she was critical. She was cerebral, not at all impulsive. First the arch, then the thought, finally the spoken words. I speculated that even her suggestion that I visit Paris before joining them in Italy was thoughtfully considered. It may have come out at the restaurant as spontaneous, but now I knew better. What was she controlling? At the time she seemed helpful, but upon reflection I decided she was being canny; so, I decided to pursue the subject.

It took some days before I found the right opportunity. When at home, Antonia was always in her study. At mealtimes, she barely acknowledged our presence because her mind was totally absorbed in her work, even while away from her desk and the college. My chance came one afternoon when I happened upon her walking home.

"What a coincidence," I said cheerily. "It's a wonder we haven't bumped into each other on the street before."

"Is it?" Antonia's brisk retort matched her pace.

I quickened my step, much like I did when walking with Helen. Yet Antonia had short legs.

"I'm glad you suggested I visit Paris before going to Italy. I had been procrastinating with my plans."

"Let us know when you get to Torino. Rufus can pick you up at the airport."

"He can?"

Antonia's eyebrow arched. "He has his own car."

I refrained from saying Lewis had told me Rufus had a car of his own and had described her son as liking fast cars and slow lunches.

"Isadora, when I came to England, I learned that my generation, well, Clive's, treated sex with prudery. In Italy we treated it with religion. Either way sex was unexciting at best and frustrating to say the least. It was difficult for any female at ease with her body. That posed a challenge for me. I've seen you come into your own, Isadora, over these past few weeks."

I grew conscious of my own discomfort. Was she assuming the role of advisor? Did it show that I'd had sex with a handsome man and resisted the temptations of an older man? None of this was a mistake. I'd have had to be intoxicated or reluctant.

"It has," I answered. Walking too quickly was leaving me out of breath. I thought how I hadn't arrived in England as a virgin but didn't blurt that out. "I mean, I was always inhibited by my mother." Were we talking about dance?

"Yes, so I've heard. My son, Rufus, is free with his morals. We're not practicing Catholics or the Church of England, but I'm warning you before he catches sight of you. He can be charming." Antonia smiled. "What I'm saying is, you have my permission to enjoy him if it comes to that. We're very relaxed in Italy. We're on holiday."

I was taken aback and let my mind digest her candid offer. "I'm still thinking about what I should do in Paris besides visit the bookstore."

"There's the bibliotheque as well as the usual tourist sites. I can recommend a hotel where Clive and I stayed last year. We always make a detour on our way to Italy to visit somewhere. This year I've decided we should spend a couple of days in Salzburg. You don't want to arrive before us."

"No," I said hastily. Of course, she didn't want me to arrive too soon. "I've been thinking I might also visit Trieste, but it's far."

"The opposite side of the boot. I'm sure Rufus would take you."

I nearly stumbled over my own feet. Had I heard correctly? "Maybe we should all go to Verona? It's on the way." I had heard correctly. Did I want to go to Verona? "Do you like opera? Every summer we make at least one excursion to the Verona Arena. Maybe we should wait for your parents? They might like to join us."

"I don't know whether they would want to go to Trieste." Would I get any research done accompanied by two sets of parents?

Again, the arched eyebrow. "I don't mean we should all go to Trieste. I recognize that you want to go there to work on your thesis proposal. Your father's been there. I'm merely suggesting that we visit the historical ruins of Verona and take in an opera."

Again, the impatience. I felt idiotic. "I'm sure my parents would like that." What was I thinking? I couldn't get to the villa before she and Clive arrived, yet I could go to Trieste with Rufus. Nothing was making sense. We turned down Cowley Place.

"Lucia Joyce was born in Trieste in 1907."

"Yes, I know.

"I share a birthday with James Joyce, February 2nd. Not the same year, of course."

I smiled. Was this her idea of humour?

"That's how your father got interested in James Joyce."

Dumbstruck, I followed Antonia as she walked up the outside steps. The germ of my father's lifelong interest in James Joyce came from Antonia's shared birthday with the great author. Was Antonia my father's muse? Gregarious Clive met us inside the house. End of conversation. Beginning of wild speculation.

Inside Radcliffe Camera I sought out Lewis and asked him to join me for lunch. "I have two questions to ask you," I said as soon as we were seated at the covered market.

"You make this sound like a business lunch," Lewis said.

"Friendly business," I said. "Remember I told you about Helen?"

Lewis nodded, fixing his eyes on mine.

"She was wondering if you would like to photograph the dancers at her studio?"

"Why?"

"Why? She just wants you to do this," I repeated. Did I sound like her emissary? "Helen's got this artistic tendency to seek out what inspires her. You see, Helen went to your last exhibit and saw the photographs you took of children. She thinks you are very skilled at capturing movement and would take good pictures of dancers."

"How flattering. Your friend is perceptive but let me consider first. She thinks I can make poving mictures from still photographs? Oops, sorry," Lewis said, scrunching his lips as if he were biting into a sour lemon, "photographs showing movement."

"You, too are perceptive, Lewis." He got the gist of my simple request. "She asked the people in her class if they would mind, and they all agreed to have you come. She didn't say it was you. I mean, she didn't tell them your name, just that she was thinking of asking a photographer to take some pictures."

"I am very busy right now getting ready for the exhibition."

"Yes, I understand, Lewis."

"This is my last week at work."

"It is?"

"Yes, next week I will be taking holidays to focus on my photography, preparing for the show. Was it Monday that you went to her class?"

"Yes. That's the day she teaches expressive movement. I've been going to other classes as well, like dance technique, but I think it is the Monday class when she wants you to come. The dance technique is not too picturesque. I can't think there's much to photograph there. It's so stoic. Monday is, well, expressive."

"I could manage that. Monday it is, then. Maybe I can drive you there. I'll have to come into Oxford with my equipment."

"That's very kind of you. Let's plan to do that then."

After a quiet interlude while we both ate Lewis looked up at me. "And your quecond session? Sorry," Lewis said, swallowing, "your second question?"

"This is a little more personal. It's about my father and Antonia?"

"Not about your dad?"

"Pardon?" I asked confused.

"You always called him your dad. Now you say father. Has he taken on something of a new role?"

"Yes, he has." I nodded my head slowly. "With her."

"Antonia?"

I continued to nod my head. "She said something to me the other day. She gave something away."

"What did she say?"

"Do you know when her birthday is?"

"Yes, in February. I've often been invited to dinner to celebrate with them. It's a good excuse in the middle of a long term when it's very dull outside, to eat and be merry."

"Antonia told me the reason my father got interested in James Joyce is because her birthday is on the same day as the author's, February 2nd."

"That's correct. There are always student and staff celebrations among the James Joyce Society then too."

"So, maybe they were at one of these celebrations when they were students here, at Oxford, and maybe when my father learned it was her birthday too, he took an interest and one thing led to another."

"One thing led to another?"

"Was she his muse?"

"Mis huse? I do not know."

"Perhaps she was more than his muse?"

"Perhaps. These things happen at university. It is only natural. Many things happen at university. The students are young. They are serious and vulnerable. Why are you so worried about this, Isadora?"

I shrugged. "Because I'm there, living with Antonia. I mean, does my mother know?"

"What is there to know?"

"I'm not a puritan."

"About your parents. Do you think they were never intimate?"

"Of course. You don't know my parents. They're all lovey-dovey, joined at the hip."

"Isadora, this bothers you?"

"No, just the thought of my father with Antonia. It makes me uncomfortable." I wanted to scream at Lewis.

"This is bot your nusiness."

"Not my business!" If Lewis sensed I was correcting him he didn't say. Now I felt as if I was interfering, getting myself in way too deep. Unseeing, I stared at the remains of my lunch.

"You must focus on your thesis," he said quietly.

"Yes," I said, recognizing that he was only being helpful. He was right. I needed to focus on my research. Helen was right too. I needed to focus on my body and not let Antonia and my father mess up my mind.

"I would like to spend more time with you, Isadora, but you have your studies and I have my work."

"Yes," I said mulling over his words which were banging around at the front of my head, not deep in the recesses of my brain.

"If I was not so much older than you would you find me attractive?"

"Oh Lewis," I said. "You are a very attractive man. Yes, do you wish we could be closer?"

"Very much, Isadora. I think of you all the time. For so long I have accepted living alone. It is fy mate." He shook his head, then laughed. "Not so mixed up. I imagine you as my mate."

"Lewis."

"I'm sorry, I have shown you my heart."

"Don't be embarrassed, Lewis. Love is in the air."

Lewis remained serious. "Yes, Isadora. Love is in the air, but I will never speak of this again if you will keep my secret."

"Of course." I reached for his hand and squeezed it. That night I couldn't sleep. During my time in Oxford, I'd had one older man fall in love with me, one woman had tried to seduce me, and one young man had succeeded. I'd not seen Michael Joseph again. Try as I would he was not at home when I rang and never lurking in the street.

Chapter Thirteen

A fter lunch on the first Monday in June, I helped Lewis carry his equipment from his car to the lift. At the top, Helen met us.

"This is my friend, Lewis," I said, carefully setting the tripod on the floor. I'd never seen Helen greet anyone with such spontaneous warmth. She really was excited about having a photographer present. I asked her if she was wearing a new outfit.

"It's Lululemon."

Lewis, with both hands full, bowed his head. "Isadora has told me much about you."

"I'm so glad you agreed to do this," Helen enthused. "Do come and meet everyone."

Lewis said he would try to remember everyone's name. He commented on the light, noting the large expanse of windows. "Let me just orient myself first. You go ahead and start."

Helen turned to the class. "We'll begin our warm-up."

Smiling at Lewis, I forewent taking a mat and joined the others on the bare, wooden floor. I found myself distracted by his presence. Everyone else in the class seemed to carry on as if he wasn't there. Maybe because, as actors, they were used to being under the lights? Why was I so self-conscious? Was it because, unlike the others, I knew Lewis?

Helen looked stunning in her white top and black tights. These weren't her usual thick leggings, but stockings made from a thin and shiny material. Today, her hair shone. Usually, by the afternoon, it was a bit straggly from hours of exercise. She must have brushed it just prior to our arrival. I didn't dare look at myself in the mirror. I probably had black bags under my eyes from hours of reading. As I passed Helen to take a spot at the back of the group, I caught a whiff of the elegant scent she was wearing. Compared to Helen, the rest of us appeared like a motley crew. She was the prima ballerina.

After the warm-up, Helen asked us to turn to face the mirrors. "Today we're going to do something new, improvisation using the mirrors. Usually, I don't like to stand with my back to the class, but I will be in front so you can follow my movements. Please position yourselves so you can see me in the mirror. I will also be using some props."

With that, she strode over to a large trunk, from which she pulled out a top hat and tails. This outfit certainly got a reaction from the group: oohs, whistles, and cat calls. She clicked on her iPod, then returned to her position. Appropriately, the music was Puttin' On The Ritz. We followed her choreography like a bumbling chorus line. Helen was magnificent in her role, sliding her feet along the floor in a soft-shoe parody, shifting her weight from side to side with the lightness of a tightrope performer, twirling her body like a principal ballerina. At the end, we clapped. Lewis kept the camera rolling to capture our responses.

"I hope you're clapping for yourselves too, Craig," Helen said. He followed her to the trunk. As she fitted a poncho over his shoulders and put a sombrero on his head, he asked, "My turn to lead?"

I didn't recognize the music. It had a long introduction, giving Craig an opportunity to find his role as an Hombre. Then the music picked up and the lyrics began. "*No Parlo Americano.*" Craig did some fancy footwork, which I found too quick to follow. He also kept changing direction, so it was hard to see him in the mirror. Sometimes, I did what the person in front of me was doing. At the end, we all laughed at our own efforts.

"Thank you, Craig. Donna, would you please take a turn?"

"Certainly," Donna said, going with Helen to the trunk. Helen pulled out a hat, so elaborate that royalty could have worn it to the Ascot. She put a matching shawl around Donna's shoulders. As Donna took her place in front of the mirror, Helen said, "A gavotte played by Pablo Casals."

We all seemed to have an easier time following Donna as she acted the part of a lady swaying gracefully to the strumming guitar. After Donna's number, Helen invited the rest of us to choose an outfit. In front of me, someone pulled out a clown's hat, complete with bulbous nose and a colourful jacket with puffy sleeves. I surveyed the remaining items and was happy to find a Charlie Chaplin hat and fitted jacket. Just that morning I had been reading about Lucia Joyce dressing up as Charlie Chaplin. Here was my opportunity to fit into her character once again. I wasn't just a star in silent film; I was Lucia acting the part. Even before the music began, I started imitating the exaggerated walk. Thrusting my arms down at my sides, I flexed my wrists and rocked from side to side.

Lewis was right there, snapping pictures. As the room filled with characters, he moved around with a hand-held camera. Sometimes he took close-ups while the actors posed and made faces; sometimes he let the dancers move around him with the camera following them. When the music ended, he asked if he could take a group photo.

Helen stepped up and arranged us in a group. In consultation with Lewis, she placed each of us in a position to best display our colourful characters, then inserted herself in the middle of the back row.

A few seconds later, Lewis asked, "Now that I have a formal shot, can everyone strike a pose? Break out a bit into your characters."

"Can a few at the front go down on the floor?" Helen asked.

The clown sprawled in front of me. I remained standing in my Charlie Chaplin posture with straight arms and flexed hands.

"Good," Lewis said, "you're towing sheeth."

"Showing teeth," I said loud enough for the others to hear, hoping Lewis did not. Everyone laughed, signaling they had heard me and fortuitously guaranteeing Lewis what he wanted, mouthfuls of teeth.

"Hold it!" Lewis said. Looking at us from over the camera, he said. "Thank you, ladies and gentlemen."

"Thank you, Lewis," Helen said, clapping her hands together. We joined in a round of applause. "Can we put back our costumes neatly, please, and assemble for a cool-down?"

After class, Lewis asked Helen if she would grant him a favour.

"Well, of course," Helen replied.

"I would like you to attend the opening of my exhibition and perform at the gallery. It is a space set up for art shows, but there is a small area where we sometimes have some entertainment, usually musicians. This time, though, I would like you to compliment my photographs with your dance moves."

Helen beamed. "I'd be honoured."

Lewis grinned. "That's kery vind of you. I mean, very kind of you, Helen." Reaching into his pocket, Lewis pulled out his business card and wrote on it. "Please save the date. I will have the gallery send you a formal invitation."

"I look forward to it," Helen said, reading the card. "Thank you so much."

"Could you perform a snippet from all four numbers and wear the appropriate costumes?"

"All four pieces?" Helen asked.

"Putting on the Ritz, *No Parlo Americano*, the gavotte, and *Atmadja.*"

"And what four costumes were you thinking of? What I'm wearing, the poncho and sombrero, the hat and shawl," Helen started, listing the obvious.

Lewis gestured to me. "And the Charlie Chaplin costume."

"What about Isadora doing that piece?" Helen asked, spinning on both feet to look at me.

"Oh, no, I couldn't," I interjected quickly.

"Yes, that's a good idea," Lewis said.

"Well, only if I can share some notes on Lucia Joyce," I said, capitulating.

"What does she have to do with Charlie Chaplin?" Helen asked, not hiding her impatience with my request.

"Lucia loved mimicry," I said, fiercely defending my role. "I was thrilled to improvise in class as Charlie Chaplin because that was a role Lucia favoured. After seeing The Kid, she raided her father's and brother's closets to make a getup of baggy trousers, a cane, a bowler hat, and shoes that were way too big for her. She was only fourteen at the time when Charlie Chaplin went to Paris to promote his movie. Europe was in love with the Tramp. It was like, uh," I said, trying to come up with an analogy, "like the craze for the Beatles. Even at that young age, Lucia already saw herself as an artist. Like many children of that era, she liked to imitate his droll walk and buffoonery."

Lewis suggested I put what I had said in writing and asked Helen if she too could make some program notes for the event. "Just a few words about your background and what you do as a teacher."

"I suppose I could," Helen said, before turning once again to me. "You could help me with that, couldn't you, Isadora? You're good with words."

I agreed to.

The following Monday, when I arrived for class, I found Helen at her computer, surrounded by the others leaning over her shoulders to get a good look at the screen. She had brought up the web site for the gallery. Helen clicked on Enter, then Upcoming Shows. "There!" someone said excitedly.

I read from the script, "Images viewed on the web sites tend to be less sharp that they are in their original form. The upcoming show will feature recent works by photographer Lewis Dodgson using a range of techniques to show people in everyday activities, together with many of his celebrated formal portraits."

"You look gorgeous, Helen." There was a photograph of her lifting her top hat with extended arms while positioned in a half split, one leg extended with her knee touching the floor, the other knee fully bent.

"You, too, Isadora."

"Thanks," I said. The photograph of me was a formal, but very flattering, profile taken in the studio. I was at once humbled and impressed. I pointed to the picture under it, a colourful blur of mauve and green. "That's me too, under the wisteria in the garden."

"It's very effective," someone commented, "even if you aren't recognizable. It looks like an abstract painting."

"It's a special effect Lewis uses," I said.

"I got my invitation in the mail," Helen said, looking up at me. "Did you?"

"Yes, so did Clive and Antonia."

"Even if the rest of us aren't invited to the opening," Donna added, "we'll have to go see the show. What are the dates?"

Helen pointed to the dates at the bottom of the screen.

"It runs for a month," I noted, calculating the dates.

"I wonder who that is?" Craig asked, pointing to a full-face portrait of an older man with white hair and undisguised wrinkles. "He looks familiar."

"I think that's Professor Winchester. You've probably seen him in posters advertising the talk he's giving on Dickens. Might be interesting."

In all there were six photographs posted on the gallery's web site. The other two were group pictures, one of rowers on Oxford Canal and the other of a family picnicking beside the canal. That evening, when I returned to Cowley Place, I told Clive and Antonia about the web page and immediately Clive downloaded it.

"Look at you," Clive exclaimed. "Don't you look lovely."

"Lewis does justice to his subjects," Antonia said. "He always finds the best angles and he knows how to use light for effect, even if not always flattering. Poor Winchester."

"I don't know, Toni, I think it's rather becoming. Old Winnie is getting on."

"We should send the link to Rufus," Antonia put in. "He'd be interested in having a look at what Lewis is doing, even though he's not here to see the show."

"Could you send the link to my parents, Clive?"

"That's a jolly good idea," Clive said, his hands on the keyboard.

"Lewis certainly seems enthralled by Helen," Antonia said.

"She's smashing," Clive affirmed.

"I didn't know she posed for him."

"She didn't, Antonia. The whole class did," I said, explaining that Helen hadn't gone to his studio like I did; it was the other way around. "He took pictures of everyone in the class. They're actors she teaches expressive movement to on Mondays."

"Remember, Toni?" Clive said. "Helen asked Isadora at dinner about Lewis taking pictures."

"Is that why she's in costume?"

"Yes, we all dressed up," I said, defending Helen. "I was Charlie Chaplin. Someone else was a clown. Another dancer looked as if she was going to the horse races."

"Lewis doesn't usually take pictures of clowns," Antonia said drolly.

"Always a first time, my dear."
I smiled at Clive, and mentally told him he was a dear.

Chapter Fourteen

Three weeks later, Helen and I left her studio early to reach the gallery well before the opening. I carried the bundle of costumes and Helen brought her music. We each wore two hats, which was easier than putting them under our arms. I wore the top hat over the bowler, and Helen wore the sombrero over the lady's hat. Granted, we were a sight, and garnered lots of attention on the street. By the time we got to the gallery, I was suffering stage fright and felt I couldn't possibly appear in the Charlie Chaplin getup, let alone perform in front of strangers. Helen was oblivious to my predicament. She was ecstatic, pumped with anticipation, excited about the event.

When Lewis saw us arrive, he unlocked the door and held it wide. Once we were inside, the gallery owner greeted us with open arms, willing and ready to relieve us of our packages. This was the man in the photo, Old Winnie.

"I didn't realize you owned the gallery," I said. "Someone said you're a professor."

"Retired from Oxford, but not retired from life. You must be Isadora?"

I nodded.

"And you're Helen."

"Yes, Professor."

Old Winnie laughed. "That takes the biscuit. Just call me Percy, please. Here, ladies, let's take your things to the back."

We followed Percy into the storage room, where we hung up the jackets and laid the shawls on an empty table with the hats. Lewis handed us programs.

"I'm sorry I didn't get back to you with the final edit. I hope this meets with your approval," he said.

I was relieved to note that I was on last, at four o'clock, near the end of the reception. Helen was appearing three times, on the half hour. I felt like asking her to do my number, too, but decided to bide my time. Maybe by the end of the reception everyone would have seen enough and would just have me read the program notes rather than perform, like I wanted to do in the first place.

"May I get you ladies something to drink?" Percy asked.

"Not for me, thank you," Helen said. "I'll wait until after my performance. Nothing to eat or drink until then."

Seeing the table outside the storage room laden with bottles and glasses, I asked for white wine, deciding that I needed fortification. Percy poured wine for me and for Lewis before excusing himself. "It appears people have arrived. That's a relief. Don't disturb yourself, Lewis. I'll send them your way."

I watched the back of Percy Winchester as he retreated. He was about the same size as Clive, a large man but more stooped with age. He was their "dear friend" and I thought he projected something familiar that I couldn't quite put my finger on. Sometimes family friends ended up looking like family.

Inside the storage room, Helen was testing her equipment. "Can you hear it?" she asked. "The volume isn't great on this machine."

"It is wonderful, my dear," Lewis said. "Come along now and mix and mingle."

Within minutes there were twenty people at the drinks table, greeting Lewis. I stepped aside, then saw Clive and Antonia arrive and gave a little wave, but they were engrossed in conversation with Percy. Now I saw a clear likeness between Percy and Rufus. Maybe he was family, some distant cousin.

More people kept coming behind them and soon they filled the gallery, examining the photographs on the walls. I decided to do the same and looked at the ones hanging on the interior wall in front of me, a group of eight, all showing the same technique of blurred colour. One I recognized as the image on the web page, the one taken under the wisteria. A couple beside me were discussing the effect. I listened but made no comment. I didn't point out that they could also find me in a garden in one of the photos.

Above the din of conversation, Clive used his tour guide's voice to ask for everyone's attention.

"Welcome," Percy said. "I want to introduce Lewis Dodgson. Many of you know him personally, but for those of you who don't, please make yourselves known to the man of the hour. Two years ago, Lewis held a show on these premises, and the public greeted his work with great admiration. I am happy to be the new owner of this esteemed gallery and to oversee Lewis's return with a whole new show from this talented man."

Lewis was still boxed in at the drinks table. Excusing himself, he stepped forward. "Thank you, everyone, for coming. I am delighted to be exhibiting here again, and especially to know the gallery is in such good hands. Please don't hesitate to ask me any questions you have about my work. If you don't get the opportunity today, I will be here every day while the show is running at the same time as today, between two and four.

"Now it is my great pleasure to introduce Helen Levinson, who will perform for us this afternoon. You may have seen her photograph on the web site. Please take a look at the original which is hanging on the back wall with other pictures of dancers. These are my most recent work and I hope to continue doing 'moving pictures' in still life."

Polite, but appreciative applause followed. Helen had disappeared into the storage room and shut the door. Percy indicated the small corner that was roped off as an impromptu stage. Helen now reappeared in top hat and tails, having removed her flowing skirt. Earlier, she had instructed me on how to use the remote control, and I stepped up to turn on the music. I was impressed by her well-choreographed performance. Clearly, it was not expressive improvisation. Helen received enthusiastic applause. Afterward, people gathered in front of the photographs taken at the studio, but there was also a noisy crowd in front of another group of pictures. I went over to investigate.

"Iconic," was the first word I heard somebody in the crowd say.

"What imagination Lewis has."

I stood back, peering between heads. The first photograph was the familiar one from the web page of a family picnicking on the banks of the canal. It was very large, making the faces recognizable, and in the middle was Percy Winchester, patriarch of an extended family. Next to this were three more large pictures showing the same family group but superimposed with creatures from nature. The second picture had a mouse the size of a rat. The more harmless rodent with its long tail was crawling out of the water. The next picture showed a gigantic eaglet, a baby bird grown super large, flying above the heads of the family group. The last in the series had a menacing magpie perched on a branch in the trees behind the group. The bird virtually filled the sky.

These were pictures deserving the description of imaginative. The ones people were describing as iconic were of me. Four black-and-white photographs of me standing barefoot against the garden wall.

"I'm not myself," I said, unaware I had done so audibly.

Those within earshot turned their heads to look at me.

"Then who are you?" a woman asked.

"Aren't you the dancer in the Charlie Chaplin outfit?"

"Yes," I answered, not realizing the pictures of the dancers from the studio included me in that costume. I had not yet seen them. "I'm Isadora Duncan," I said, feeling pressured into introducing myself.

"Are you related to *the* Isadora Duncan?"

"No," I said.

"Isadora died young, remember? I doubt she had any children," someone said testily.

I felt small. As those in front kept their eyes turned on me, I felt as if I were growing smaller and smaller. In a little voice, I told them it was just a coincidence. What did this barefoot pose in the garden mean?

"Fascinating, aren't you?"

Recognizing his voice, I asked Clive, "But what does it mean? Someone said it was iconic?"

"It reminds us of the photograph of six-year-old Alice Liddell."

"Who?"

"Alice in Wonderland."

I returned my gaze to the four pictures. "Alice in Wonderland? They don't look like any illustrations I've ever seen of Alice in Wonderland."

"Taken by Charles Dodgson, a.k.a. Lewis Carroll," Clive said, explaining away my confusion.

"Really? Is Lewis related to him?" I asked, unable to take my eyes off the photographs. These were not pictures of me. These were of me in the role of Alice Liddell, a.k.a., Alice in Wonderland!

"Distant," Clive said. "Charles Dodgson was a lecturer in mathematics at Oxford who became interested in photography. In his time, it was a new technology. I believe the original is in the collection at Princeton University Library. Too bad. We should ask for it back."

Trust Clive to make light of the circumstances. Turning, I smiled up at him just as he raised his arm and examined the time on his wristwatch.

"Excuse me, Isadora. I believe it's time to announce another performance by your friend."

Helen performed a lighthearted choreographed piece, this time to No Parlo Americano. She included some clapping, which I found very effective; also telling, because recently she had us clapping in class. Many people left after her three o'clock performance, but a few loyal supporters remained, including Clive and Antonia. Three or four stragglers arrived, but now there were only a dozen guests mingling around the gallery, conversing, as well as drinking and eating.

My earlier relief about not being personally recognized, or on view, was short lived because through the door came him! What on earth was Michael Joseph doing here? In that instant I half hoped he had come to see me. Evidently, he was invited because he placed his invitation card on the table inside the front door. I watched him as he picked up a program and read it. He must have sensed me gazing at him because he raised his eyes and looked directly into mine.

"Hello, Isadora," he said, coming over to me. "I see you're going to dance for me later."

What conceit! "Hello. I'm sorry, I didn't know you were invited," I said curtly, feeling deflated by his attitude. What a stupid thing to say, as if I had drawn up the guest list.

"Percy Winchester was my professor a long time ago," he replied.

"Are you an Oxford man?" I asked, stumped that his name revealed nothing about his origins.

"You could say so. Percy was my tutor when I first came up to Oxford."

"Now the owner of the gallery." I stated, too tongue-tied to sound clever.

"I thought I recognized your picture on the web site."

My heart flipped, then dropped. Was he saying he had come specifically to see me? "There are more here," I said, leading him to the iconic photographs.

"Interesting," Michael Joseph observed.

I explained what Clive had told me about the iconic nature of the black-and-white photographs.

"A dancer and an actress," he observed, smiling at me. "Playing both Charlie Chaplin and Alice in Wonderland. Is someone else dancing?"

"Yes, my friend, Helen. Would you like to meet her?"

We made our way easily through the diminished crowd. I found Helen in front of the group of photographs taken at the studio. Michael immediately recognized her from the web page, too. "And I believe I live across the road from you? I recognize you from the street."

What an idiot I was. Of course, he had also seen her picture there. Did I actually believe he had come to see me? He had recognized me, but now I realized he wanted to meet Helen. Why not? She looked so sexy in that photograph and now she was clearly flirting with him. I felt like the third wheel, standing on the sidelines.

"You two know each other?"

I was about to open my mouth to speak.

"Excuse me," Helen said. "I have to prepare for my next dance."

"I'm looking forward to seeing it," Michael replied with a glint in his eye.

"It only lasts a few minutes," Helen said, departing with a grand gesture, already assuming the role of an aristocratic lady.

I pointed to the picture of Craig in a shawl and sombrero. "Helen wore this outfit for her last dance."

"Did she? I'm sorry I missed it."

"You didn't miss much," I said cattily. "As Helen said, the pieces only last a couple of minutes. I looked for you when I went to her studio, but you were never home."

"Are you in this picture?" Michael asked, ignoring my question, and leaning closer to the group photo. "Here you are." He pointed to me standing behind the clown.

I was made to feel that I was being rude, yet it was his rudeness that was irritating. "Let me show you some colourful photographs," I said, attempting to redeem my dignity and leading Michael to the interior wall. "They're very artistic." I began to explain the method Lewis had used to achieve the effect when Percy once again invited us to turn our attention to Helen. Damn Helen, I said to myself. Here I was being so clever, getting Michael's attention by telling him about the art of photography by Charles Dodgson and his distant relative, Lewis, when once again Helen appeared to rain on my parade as she made her entrance.

"She looks as though she's dressed for Ascot," Michael said admiringly.

"Foolish, isn't it?" I muttered. Should I tell him that she's bisexual? Wasn't that a potential turn-off? Mayne not.

What was I trying to do? Minimize the effect Helen had on everybody? Reduce her talents to mimicry? Whatever I was trying to achieve failed miserably. Michael was enthralled by her. I was so discombobulated by my emotions that I forgot to help with the remote. Clive jumped in and did it. My services weren't needed. Helen swirled about in her shawl and hat.

Turning back to the abstracts, I immediately realized that one of the photographs was of that costume, its colours sweeping across the picture frame. I refrained from pointing this out to Michael as he clearly was not interested in my observations. He was mesmerized by Helen. That's why he'd come. Not for me, but for her. Was I just the ruse for him to get to her? He wasn't even interested in photography.

More people left after Helen's three-minute performance. Thank goodness I wouldn't have to put on my own getup to perform in public. Percy and Lewis were preoccupied with the departing visitors. I introduced Michael to Clive and Antonia, since they were the only ones left standing around the almost empty drinks table.

"Where do you know Michael from?" Antonia asked.

"Keble College," I replied, quickly. Could she read that we'd been intimate once? Only once. Hopefully not.

Helen reappeared. "There's nothing left now that I'm ready for a drink."

"Then let me take you to a pub," Michael offered.

"That sounds like a splendid idea," Helen said. "But I have these costumes to carry."

"Put it all in the storage room," Percy said, joining the group. "Thank you so much for your participation this afternoon, Helen. Everyone commented on how wonderful it was to see you in person. You young people run along and enjoy yourselves."

"Isadora," Michael said, turning to me, "will you join us?"

"I think not, thanks," I answered, swallowing my pride. "I have to get ready for my flight tomorrow. Besides, I've had plenty to drink this afternoon."

"You're going away?"

"Yes," Helen said, "she's going to Italy."

While I was jealous that she was leaving with Michael, I sensed that Helen was jealous too. This felt like revenge. Absence makes the heart grow fonder. Could I count on that? Did I even want to? He had asked me, but twos company, threes a crowd.

"We're joining Isadora later at our ancestral villa in Italy," Antonia chimed in. "Tomorrow Isadora is going to Paris."

"What a jet-setter," Michael said.

"Hardly," I said, "it's for my research." I felt triumphant. Even glamourous.

"Well, nice to have met you." Michael said to Antonia and Clive and, taking Helen's arm, he led her outside.

I watched the two of them walk down the sidewalk, blinking tears of vexation. Had I done the right thing?

"I never did like your friend Helen," Antonia quietly said, for my ears alone.

Chapter Fifteen

At the airport arrivals lounge in Turin, Italy, I caught a glimpse of Rufus. He was holding a large sign above his head with Isadora Duncan printed on it, looking more like a male cheerleader brandishing the name of a favourite player than a man offering a woman a ride. Coming to a standstill behind the congestion of disembarking passengers, I was not visible to him or anyone waiting in the crowd.

My pulse quickened. There's no logical explanation for the first blush of love. Plenty of theories abound to describe that blush as well as other physical responses, including a softening of the mind, a collapse of the knees, and a weakening of the heart. I felt none of those. I felt a twinge in the pit of my stomach and a sensation below that warmed my inner core.

A second time his face briefly appeared, too briefly for me to acknowledge him, but not too briefly to send my heart aflutter. It seemed I was going to react in typical fashion. Rufus was better in real life than in his picture. He was flawless, so beautiful I was certain he would turn out to be arrogant, or insensitive, or both. I hoped he would be. Then I could dismiss him, which would protect me from his charm. I was feeling vulnerable after Oxford. Helen's and Michael's betrayal had left me doubting myself, my judgment, and my motives. Practically the entire time I was in Paris, I was in tears, unable to eat or focus on anything. What did I care about researching Lucia Joyce when my own world was falling apart?

Before leaving the gallery in Oxford on that fateful last day, Percy Winchester had told me that Michael Joseph was quite the ladies' man, a dabbler. His judgment only shocked me into a deeper sadness. Those first tears were the beginning of an avalanche. I felt sorry for the person sitting beside me on the plane to Paris. He must have thought there was a death in my family. How could I begin to explain? I'd put my faith in finding Lucia, my hope in revealing her agony, only to find myself undone. Now I told myself, no more tears. All that was behind me. Grow up, Isadora, I told myself. Be bold.

Ahead of me, the crowd thinned. I restrained myself from running. Don't run. Walk. Stop. I looked into his deeply set eyes. "Hello. You must be Rufus?"

"I am." A smile spread wide across his face. "You must be Isadora?"

"I am," I breathed, drowning in his look.

Rufus lowered his sign. "You don't look anything like your portrait."

"Portrait?"

"The one my parents bought."

"They did? You mean, a photograph?"

"Yes, the one that Lewis took of you in his garden. You're barefoot in it." Rufus looked down at my feet. I was wearing a new pair of shoes purchased in Paris. They were fashionable, not sensible like the rest of my footwear. I had managed to do some shopping, or rather, Parisian salesladies had knowingly taken me under their wing to flatter and dress me.

"Alice."

"Alice?" Rufus asked, looking into my eyes.

"Lewis had me pose to look like Alice Liddell of Alice in Wonderland fame, except she was only eight when her picture was taken."

"And you're a grown woman."

"I am."

We stared at each other in silence. I had not realized that Clive and Antonia had purchased the photograph, let alone brought it to Italy with them.

"Here. Let me take your bag," he said, reaching across me to grab the extended handle. At the car park, Rufus apologized that he had come in his family's vehicle and wasn't driving his own sports car. "More fun, but it only has two seats. Too small for both of us and a large piece of luggage. I'll take you for a spin tomorrow if you like."

"I'll look forward to that. We could go to lunch."

Rufus winked at me. "We could. We could go to Monte Carlo."

"We could?" How quickly I had fallen into my habitual gullibility. "I mean, are we close enough to Monaco to drive there just for lunch?" I asked, trying to sound sophisticated, and failing miserably.

Rufus slammed the trunk lid closed. He brushed my forearm before holding open the passenger door. "Yes," he said into my ear. With his other hand he touched my shoulder, guiding me into the seat.

As he drove, I watched Rufus out of the corner of my eye. He was concentrating on getting us out of the airport and out of the city. My palms grew clammy; I had butterflies in my stomach; I was light-headed. I was beginning to see myself through Rufus's eyes. The thought of arriving at the villa in my present state gave me chills. What would Antonia say? She would see I was transformed. Antonia had acute powers of observation. In a matter of days, I had completely altered my physical appearance. The crying had purged the dark bags under my eyes. Not eating had left me thinner. The ladies in the shops in Paris who had selected my new clothes knew how to dress me better than I did.

Suddenly, I laughed out loud. Rufus glanced sideways at me. He'll think I'm mad, I thought. I am. I'm madly in love. I had imagined a crush on Michael Joseph after only one glimpse. At university I had taken sexual satisfaction with others who infatuated me. Whether imagined or real, they all disappointed. None had the effect on me that Rufus did. After nearly an hour of intense driving, he seemed to settle behind the steering wheel.

"Was it your first time in Paris?" he asked.

"Yes."

"Did you like it?"

"Not really. I guess I was a bit preoccupied."

"You had work to do. Still, brave of you to travel there alone."

"Was it?" Then I did become brave. "Everything went more smoothly than when I arrived in Britain."

"Why? What happened? Was it your first time there, too?"

"Yes, and I arrived in Reading with only a confirmation, so I had to buy another ticket at an exorbitant price, but even without it I managed to get through the gate and onto the train."

Remembering my earlier situation and how discombobulated I was then, made me grateful for having an easy time now. Through the window I could see the rolling hills of Piedmont where stone villas dotted the landscape and tall Cyprus bordered the narrow roads. I thought Italy was beautiful and said so.

Rufus smiled at me. "I'm looking forward to hearing all about your studies. Mummsy said you're working toward a Doctorate in dance theory."

"I hope to. What about you?"

"I've taken a year off to think and write."

"Ah, so you're not completely idle in Italy?"

"Completely, utterly, and foolishly idle. Italy inspires me."

"Inspires?"

Rufus laughed. "I write poetry. I will write poetry for you, and you can dance for me."

"You think so?"

"You have to earn your keep."

"Are you offering to be my keeper?" He was teasing, and so was I. It felt delicious to be engaged in the foreplay of love. I kept my eyes on Rufus. His eyes were on the road.

"I doubt you need a keeper. I would never stoop to that. We can do better. Will you be my muse? I think you would make a good one. I must warn you, though. You have competition. My cousin, Lucia, likes to think of herself as my muse. She can get very jealous."

"You have a cousin named Lucia?"

"Yes, didn't Mummsy tell you?"

"No. Is she your muse?"

"No, she's a married woman."

"That's never stopped a writer."

"You'll understand when you meet her. Lucia Ricciuti is doted on by her mother, my Aunt Augusta, a spoiling that did not end with her marriage. Octavio also dotes on his wife. One spoiled, two doting, equals a force for reckoning. Those three live together at Octavio's farmhouse with three chickens and two cats. The cats are called Rex and Regina."

"Do you like pets?"

"I do. My cat is called Dinah. She sleeps with me." Rufus smiled sideways at me, a broad smile that lit up his vibrant brown eyes with a flirtatious twinkle.

"Does she?" I turned to look out the front windshield, thinking how I could change that situation. We sped along the motorway heading south past Carmagnola. "I got the feeling that your mother likes opera."

"Do tell. Has Mummsy talked you into going to the opera?"

"She suggested we go to Verona in August when my parents arrive, but my parents aren't opera fans. They go to the theatre. They like ballet. I didn't want to disappoint your mother."

"Don't worry about her. She's a schemer. My parents can take Uncle Stuart and my cousin, Ed, to the opera when they visit."

"So, you have other visitors?"

"They're coming next week. It's the first time they've come to Italy to visit us at the villa. Papa has been trying to persuade them to come for years. Uncle Stuart is recently widowed, which explains why they've finally agreed to visit. Mummsy never got along with my late aunt. Mummsy can torture my uncle and cousin with a trip to Verona."

"I'm sure the opera is very good."

"Oh, it's a spectacle."

"So, you're a regular?"

"Every year. It's de rigueur. And I mean that literally. We dress for it, even though it's outdoors, for God's sakes. The tourists don't dress up. Just us old Italian families."

"What's the name of this old Italian family?"

"Spano."

"I don't have formal attire."

Rufus glanced my way. "Well, you won't fit into Mummsy's clothes. She's a lot smaller than you. Or Aunt Augusta's. Or Lucia's. They're both big women. I guess you're out of luck."

"I felt big in Paris, trying on clothes."

"French women are petite." Rufus turned off the motorway.

"Are we going to Fossano?" I asked, reading the sign.

"Cuneo."

"It's not far now," Rufus said, as if sensing my growing wariness.

"It's beautiful here," I said, telling myself to relax and enjoy the present moment.

"Like I said, inspiring."

Turning to face Rufus, I smiled. "Yes, inspiring." I was smitten. He was charming. He was sensitive. He was a poet, for God's sake.

Chapter Sixteen

I felt like the luckiest woman alive when we arrived at the villa. Recognizing my excitement threatened to over-spill and turn me into a giggling schoolgirl, I concentrated on keeping a sober face when Rufus drove up the driveway and stopped in front of the single car garage that was attached to the house. I didn't wait for him to turn off the motor before getting out of the car. Curious about the other vehicle parked outside, I walked over to the sporty Fiat. It was red with black leather upholstery. The top was down which stimulated my imagination. I pictured Rufus jumping into the driver's seat like some male lead in the movies, and me sitting beside him with the wind streaming through my hair.

Dear Clive appeared. I put my lips on both his cheeks, giving him two quick pecks.

"Kiss one cheek gently. Kiss the other softly."

Together, Clive and I turned to look at Rufus who was standing with his head tilted at a fetching angle.

"Don't mind Rufus, Isadora. He's a poet. I'm sure he's already told you that."

"He did," I said, dropping my arms, "but he didn't appraise me of his talents until now."

"Flattery will get you everywhere."

"Rufus, make yourself useful and bring in the lady's luggage. Would you like some refreshment, Isadora? I'm sure you're tired after your journey. How was Paris?"

"Wonderful," I lied, flicking my chin and turning my back on Rufus, "once I figured out the spiral pattern of the *arrondisements*. I'm used to cities laid out on a grid. You know, streets going north-south or east-west and crossing at right angles."

"Is it really that monotonous?" Rufus asked, breathing down the back of my neck.

"Yes." I savoured the heat of his breath. "Not like here, either," I said, thinking of our approach. We had driven the corniche out of Vignolo and climbed up a private road to a gated area that was unlike any gated community I'd ever seen. The compound sat on a ridge in the mountains on the outskirts of the village. There were twelve houses on an oval shaped cul-de-sac, set well apart from each other with trees and vegetation surrounding each house.

Inside the front door, a cat glided up to Rufus and wrapped her silky body around his ankles and legs. "Dear Dinah, have you missed me?" he asked, dropping my luggage.

Dinah was a big puffball with long white hair. Bending down, Rufus picked her up and stroked her behind her ears. "Do you want to come with me to park the car? Is that what you want? You must make yourself useful."

While observing this encounter, I immediately concluded that Rufus took a highly anthropomorphic view of his pet. We had driven past the private driveway that led to the separate garage where Rufus and Dinah now took the car. I followed Clive into the kitchen.

"Benvenuto! Look at you," Antonia said, coming over to give me a quick, but welcoming hug. "It seems Paris did you the world of good."

"Yes," I said, catching my breath. I was flabbergasted by her behaviour. Although I had anticipated that Antonia would notice the change in my physical appearance, I was amazed at her warm hospitality.

"*Andiamo,* please, sit," Antonia said, gesturing to a chair.

I took a seat on a comfortable chair at the round table where there was a window overlooking the private backyard and saw many painted birdhouses dotted the garden. The room was renovated to take advantage of its position with lower cabinets along both sides. Clive handed me a cup of coffee. Clearly, we were in a different country. I was being served coffee, not tea.

"Antonia painted those," Clive said.

Shaking my head, I thought how some things weren't always the way one expected.

"Clive brought the gong back from Bali," Antonia said.

"Ah," I said, catching sight of the huge Asian gong that was hanging in the center of the garden. "It's not as dry here as in the hills."

"No, not in the mountains," Clive said, sitting opposite me. His large hands hugged his mug as if anticipating a good cup of coffee.

"I'm surprised to see evergreens and hardwood forests."

"We have cold winters and get a lot of snow. You'll have to come back to go skiing," Clive said.

"Actually, I'm not much of a skier. We live in the flat part of the province. We don't have any hills or mountains, but sometimes we go to New York State to ski."

"Much of a muchness," Clive said.

"Oh, right," Antonia said, "all part of North American culture. Nordamerica!"

Together we turned at the sound of Rufus coming into the mudroom before entering the kitchen. "*! Una vista che mi riempe di gioia.*"

"Are we being too domestic for you?"

"*Niente non potrebbe essere oltoe dalla verit.*" Rufus sat beside me, placing Dinah on his lap. "You don't speak Italian, do you?"

I hardly knew what to say. "No, sorry."

"I'll teach you."

"Leave poor Isadora alone, Rufus," Clive said.

"Are you poor?"

"Don't mind Rufus," Antonia said. "He's a tease."

I quite liked the witty way Rufus teased, thinking how he was unlike my twin cousins who could be cruel in their teasing. "I hadn't thought of learning Italian, but since I'm here, I guess I should. What about Dinah? Does she speak Italian?"

"Of course," Rufus said, tilting his head at that fetching angle of his and giving Dinah a quick peck between her eyes. "You should learn, too, Isadora. You don't want to be seen as one of those conceited Americanos who think everyone should speak their language, but not bother to learn the others'."

"No," I said, recognizing that Rufus knew how to place his head to gain maximum effect. I could have called him conceited but refrained.

Turning to Antonia, I said, "Rufus told me you bought the photograph of me as Alice." I hoped I didn't sound conceited.

"Yes," Clive said exuberantly, butting in. "I insisted. I find it imponderable."

"As in difficult, or fascinating?" Rufus asked.

"Both," Clive said.

"Your parents bought the one of you in profile," Antonia said. "We brought it along with us, too, for them to take when they visit, saving on postage."

I wasn't sure if that was Antonia being frugal, or my parents, or both.

"You can hang it up in your room for now." Clive said.

"Or I can hang it in my room," Rufus said.

"Why would you want it in your room?" Antonia asked. "Rufus, do behave."

"I'll take your luggage up to your room now and we can decide."

"Give Isadora a minute to catch her breath. She's only just arrived."

"Actually, I could use the washroom," I said.

"Come," Rufus said. "Dinah and I will show you to your room."

Excusing myself, I followed Rufus who put Dinah down on the stairs. Then he picked up my piece of luggage and carried it upstairs where there were four large bedrooms and two bathrooms. The staircase continued up.

Rufus said. "You entered on the second story. There's a lower level and an attic." He turned his back on the bedrooms. "But you want the washroom."

By now I was desperate. "I don't know why your mother served coffee. In Oxford, they always served tea."

"I won't ask you to guess why because you're in such a frightful hurry, and besides, you never could guess, so I'll tell you straight out." Rufus gestured in the direction of a bathroom.

"Afterward," I said, shutting the door. I wondered if he intended to tell me through the closed door, but he was silent which only made me self-conscious of the tinkle sound my pee made.

"Tell me," I asked, rejoining him in the hallway.

"We drink coffee in Italy. The water here is better for coffee, not so good for tea." Rufus stroked Dinah behind her ears. Dinah purred.

"That's nonsense," I said. "Surely the quality of the coffee is in the beans and the quality of the tea in the leaves." I stared back at Dinah who was watching me intently with her deep, dark eyes.

"That's only part of the recipe," Rufus said, turning on his heels. "Follow me."

I peered inside one of the large bedrooms. "Is this your room?" I asked.

"Yes, do you want to see it?"

Rufus changed direction at my bidding. I followed him. When I entered the room, I had an uncanny feeling I had been in it before which I attributed to having stayed in his room in Oxford, although there was nothing similar between the two rooms. This one was spacious. The other was small and cramped. This one had a private view while the window in his other room looked out on the street. The walls at Oxford were covered in wallpaper. Here photos and framed documents covered the walls. One with a small, framed fabric underneath caught my eye. I peered closely at the stitchery.

"Mummsy embroidered my haiku."

My graduation
A diploma with a seal
The future unfolds.

"How unique," I said, after reading the haiku. Then I looked up at the Oxford diploma.

"I'm sure I am," Rufus said. "At least Mummsy would like everyone to think so. Don't all mothers feel that way?"

"Only about their sons," I said. "Fathers adore their daughters."

"The voice of experience." Rufus looked down to Dinah. "Did you hear that, Dinah? Mothers adore their sons. And what about you, girl. Who adores you?"

"It seems you do."

Rufus smiled over at me. "It seems I do. Someone has to like you girls. Come, I'll show you to your room."

My room was the guest room beside his. Here, too, framed photos crammed the walls. There was also another small framed embroidered poem. I read,

Time marches on
Beginning, middle and end
Nonsense illusion.

"See what I mean? Mummsy so wants me to become a famous poet."

I looked above to a striking photograph. It was taken by Lewis Dodgson.

"He did it using a second exposure."

"Of your parents?"

"Yes. They're walking in the garden."

"Yes," I said, recognizing the pair. "They're recognizable because they're coming toward the camera, whereas the background is spread out with the slow-timed focus."

"You are an observant, bright critic."

"I've learned a little having my picture taken by Lewis using various techniques."

"Do you want me to write a poem to your portrait photo?"

What I really wanted was to roll and roll about with him on the double bed, but I simply smiled and said, "Yes."

Chapter Seventeen

When we retired to our rooms, I lay down and fell asleep at once, still feeling airborne from my flight. It had been a long journey from Oxford to Italy with a short trip to Paris. In my dreams, I found myself back in Oxford at the gallery with the distorted face of Helen mocking me. Panicked, I fled only to find I was walking upside down upon the sky painted on the ceiling at the opera house as if I was someone in the Chagall mural. The land below me was scattered all about with markers from my visits: the formal gardens behind familiar houses and buildings; the narrow paths through meadows and city streets beside rivers; the winding roads travelled on bicycle and in cars. Sunshine shone through the mysterious weightlessness of clouds, and I felt changed. In the moment I returned to my body on earth I started falling down a well. The earthen tunnel shot past my vision in blinding speed.

Suddenly I woke up and remembered other dreams of falling when I awoke before crash landing. I was shaken but consoled. What if I had stayed asleep to the end? Would I have died?

Somewhere in the bowels of the villa, a chime sounded. It rang every hour and on the half hour. When I first heard it ring, Clive said it was over a hundred years old, a gift to his grandfather for services rendered during a lifetime of work as a foreman in a factory at the beginning of the industrial revolution.

My waking thoughts returned to my dream. I felt marked by my recent experiences. The landscape of my mind was changed by where I had been. I was conscious of integrating all that I had witnessed and done. Soon, the chimes rang four times. I had been awake alone with my thoughts for one half hour.

As I slowly emerged from the medley of my dream state, I became anxious and started to question what I was doing at the villa. Was I becoming part of a surrogate family? Or was my future unfolding like the message in the haiku Rufus wrote? I smiled in the darkness, picturing the stitched lines and trying to remember the last line of the framed poem, but I couldn't. I was touched by Antonia's gift to her son and by the sensitivity of his words, yet I could not recall them, so I quietly got out of bed and turned on the lamp.

My window was open and the breeze from the night air blew softly into my room, tickling my feet and stirring the hem of my night shirt. Cautiously, I walked across the floor and stood in front of the haiku. Nonsense illusion.

Was my life but a dream? I felt it could be. I returned to bed and to darkness.

Later I was woken by a commotion. The sun on the window shade told me that dawn had arrived. I got out of bed and poked my head around the door where I saw Clive talking to Rufus at the open door of his bedroom. "I have to warn you. Augusta is here and she's in a state."

"What's new?" Rufus asked in an aloof tone, blinking his eyes.

"There's a reason," Clive said seriously. "Lucia miscarried."

"Oh, sorry," Rufus said.

I sensed he was embarrassed at having behaved coldly. I was about to retreat, but Clive's next sentence caught my attention. "She has the fetus with her."

"Good God," Rufus said. "Why?"

Clive turned away from his son. "Just be prepared for the sight."

Rufus raised his eyebrows at me. "Good morning, Isadora."

"Good morning. Should I stay in my room?"

"We couldn't possibly keep family dynamics hidden from one so astute as you. I'll see you downstairs," Rufus said, throwing a robe over his shoulders.

Following him, I descended the stairs. I did not have to be formally introduced to Augusta to recognize Antonia's sister. They were the same height, but Augusta was wider through her hips. She wore a faded dress made shapeless by over-washing. Earlier, I was told she was two years younger, but she seemed decades older. In her arms she held what seemed like a small package. It was swaddled in a rough linen material. I was horrified to recognize that this contained the dead fetus.

Rufus made a beeline to her. "*Mi dispiace, tanto!*"

Augusta lifted the baby bundle. "*Sepoltura,*" she said, pleading with her eyes.

"She wants us to bury it?" Rufus asked, turning to his mother. "Is it a boy or a girl?"

"*Bambina piccola.*" Augusta began to wail. She handed the swaddled fetus to Rufus. He rocked the fetus in a state of distraction, as if it was alive and needed comforting. "*Non È stata colpa mia,*" she cried, turning to Antonia.

Antonia went to her sister and tucked Augusta's head into her shoulder.

"*La bolent di Dio,*" Augusta said, between muffled sobs.

"Can we go outside?" Clive asked. "Should we take her back to the farm?"

"*Non sono affetti sicuro che sia una buona idea,*" Rufus said to his mother.

I started to get the drift. Rufus did not think it was a good idea to go outside with the fetus he was now carrying.

Augusta raised her arms, shaking them to the heavens while speaking a diatribe.

"Lucia is distraught, and Octavio is comforting her," Rufus said. "What are we going to do?"

"We could use the wooden cheese box as a coffin," Clive said.

"I suppose that will have to do," Antonia said. "It's not as if she can bury her in the cemetery," Antonia said to Rufus. Again, Antonia comforted her sister, reassuring her that they would help her bury the baby in the ground.

"But not here, at the villa. Why did she bring it here?" Rufus asked. "We'll have to take it back to the farm."

"*Bambina piccola.*" Augusta lifted her head and wailed more loudly. "It's a girl, Rufus. Stop calling her that."

"Sorry, Mummsy," Rufus said, clearly exasperated. He returned the bundle to his aunt, telling her that we would all get dressed and go with her to the farm.

Not wanting to impose on this most intimate family function, I stayed in the background, although still curious. I recognized that the family could not bury a fetus in a churchyard, but wondered if this was a custom in Italy, or only in Piedmont, or just in Vignolo? Maybe it was some bizarre personal request to have the aborted fetus set in ancestral ground? Why did Augusta think it was her fault? Was this guilt, superstition, or witchcraft?

As he passed by me, Rufus took my hand and led me away from the kitchen. I followed him upstairs. "Can you join us?" he asked quietly.

Although not sure why he made the request, I agreed and dressed quickly, then followed the procession outside. Clive carried a spade.

We passed through the gate and followed the road down a steep descent. I felt like we were running to keep up to our feet that were moving too quickly underneath us. Shortly we reached the farmhouse. To the side of the wide yard was a stone table surrounded by chairs. It was a shaded spot, underneath an arbor of hanging vines that were mostly withered, nothing like the profuse wisteria in England, though there were blossoms on a tall border of bushes beside the table. These were a stark white colour, and I thought they might be Rose of Sharon as they seemed similar to what my mother grew at home. In the middle of the yard were small trees that looked like willow, but I couldn't imagine that variety growing here. Maybe they were birch?

The family headed to a structure that seemed built into the stone wall that ran along the eastern edge of the property. Rufus gave his father the swaddled fetus to hold and took the spade. Antonia stood with her arm around Augusta's shoulder. Shuddering with each sound the spade made, I hugged my shoulders, then turned when I felt a presence behind me. There stood a young man whose eyes welled in tears.

When Rufus gestured that he was done, Clive put the box into the shallow grave. Augusta crossed herself and threw a handful of loose dirt on the lid. Antonia followed suit, and the father stepped forward to do the same. "*Mi dispiace, Octavio,*" Rufus said.

Octavio took the spade from Rufus. "*Gracias,*" he said, and piled the remaining dirt on top of the little box.

After Rufus introduced me to Octavio Firmino, who invited us to come inside. Following him, we walked across the yard to the stone house and entered the courtyard.

"*Che pazzia!*" Octavio said, looking up to the second floor of his farmhouse.

"Lucia," Rufus called.

Lucia leaned further out the second-floor window, holding the sill with one hand and a small puppy with her free hand. "You like him?"

"*Si*," Rufus said with laughter that dissolved the tension in the air. Augusta started muttering in Italian.

"But Mama, I will love this dog like I love Rufus." She held the puppy to her nose and sniffed, leaning precariously further out the window.

Augusta flailed her arms in protest, all the while mumbling, "*No amore. No amore.*"

"What is wrong with loving my cousin? He is so handsome. He is the handsomest man in the world. If he weren't my cousin, I would have married Rufus."

I looked over to Rufus. I could not agree more, but I wondered at Lucia's use of English. Was she deliberately speaking a language he understood, but her mother didn't?

"You will make Octavio jealous," Rufus shouted.

"Octavio is never jealous. He gives me whatever I want. Even you."

"I am not his to give."

"You hear that, Mama? Rufus is a poet. I am Juliet. Can you climb up here, Romeo?" Lucia leaned further out the window. With her free hand she pulled on the vine growing on the outside wall as if examining its strength. Her action caused a shower of little pebbles to come rattling down on the courtyard. The puppy started barking. A few pebbles hit Octavio and Rufus in the face. Alarmed, Octavio disappeared into the barn.

"Be careful, Lucia. The wall will crumble underneath you," Rufus called.

Octavio ran into the courtyard with a ladder.

"Look, Octavio, Rufus is panting for me," Lucia said, looking down at the puppy whose tongue was lolling over its chin.

Rufus folded his arms over his chest and watched the drama unfold.

Augusta started pulling at her hair. Her braided coils fell behind her ears. Antonia patted the loose coils in a soothing gesture.

When Octavio perched the ladder against the stone wall, two doves fluttered off their lazy perches and started to flap and coo at the activity. The ladder wobbled under Octavio as he climbed to the height of the second floor where he offered his right hand to his wife for support while holding the ladder tightly with his left hand. "*I sta' attento, caderai alla tua morte.*"

Once she was safely indoors, Lucia stood at the window and blew a kiss to Rufus. Then she started laughing hysterically.

Octavio climbed back down the ladder, and as soon as his feet touched the ground, he too started mumbling to us that he would never forgive himself if his wife perished before his eyes on his ancestral land.

"*Torta.*"

We all turned our gaze up to Lucia who was still framed in the window.

Again, Augusta started to fret. Rufus turned to me. "She wants us to go in for cake."

"And why not," Antonia said, leading her sister indoors.

In the kitchen, Rufus bent down and picked up the panting puppy. "I think you should change its name," he said, stroking the animal under its chin.

Octavio agreed. Lucia glared at her husband. "Then we'll call him Octavio," she said, turning on her heels, not hiding her indignation.

"*Siedesi.* Sit, sit," Octavio said, pulling out chairs for everyone.

Augusta went to the counter and took down six plates from the open shelves.

"Let's call him Tavus," Rufus said.

"My poet," Lucia said, flopping lazily onto a chair. "Have a piece of almond cake."

Augusta put the plates and cake on the table. Then she sliced the cake into thin pieces.

"And espresso. Do you want coffee? I want an espresso, Octavio," Lucia called. Her voice was loud, as if she thought she was still at the second-floor window, and we were below her on the ground.

Octavio did her bidding.

"You will have to behave yourself, Rufus. Our parents are here."

"Lucia, I am the model of good behaviour."

Turning sharply, Lucia stared at me. "*Lei, si chiama?*"

"I'm sorry. This is Isadora. She will be staying with us this summer."

"Bella," Lucia said. "Isadora who?"

"Isadora Duncan," I said, finding my own voice in the bedlam. I stared at Lucia, thinking her facial features were like her mother's, but she was slight. She could have been a younger Antonia.

"Should I be jealous?" Lucia asked, looking me up and down.

"*Si*," Rufus said, "Isadora is not my *cugina*."

Liking his intermingling of English and Italian, I smiled. For a poet, Rufus had a calm and logical mind.

"You are spoiled," Lucia said.

"You too," Rufus said. "An only child." Rufus turned his eyes to me. "We are all spoiled."

I looked from him to Lucia. We had that in common. What else, I wondered, would I discover?

Chapter Eighteen

On our return to the villa, Rufus quickly told his parents not to bother with food for us as he was taking me to Monte Carlo for lunch. Antonia's immediate response was to apologize for her niece's harum-scarum behaviour.

I had expected Rufus would explain that yesterday we had made tentative plans to go to lunch today, but Rufus was not trying to set his family at ease. On the contrary, he seemed to be continuing the drama.

"Crikey," Clive said, shaking his head, "We've seen Lucia out-of-control before, but this morning's antics really take the cake. Still, I suppose she was traumatized."

Afterward, in my room, I, too, had something of a meltdown. To acknowledge this loss was foreign to me. Poor Lucia. And Octavio. I couldn't imagine the sense of loss. Poor Clive. And Rufus. The presence of mind to know what to do. Poor Augusta. And Antonia. I'd never witnessed such intimacy between women.

Sensing the passing time, I turned to practical matters. What to wear? That morning, I had quickly thrown on my clothes from yesterday. Now I had to choose something from my old wardrobe, and I was indecisive thinking I should have bought more clothes in Paris. In the end, I chose the same dress I had worn for the infamous photograph. I had a scarf that matched to wear on my head. Scrutinizing myself in the mirror, I pondered the wisdom of wearing a scarf while driving in a convertible sports car. Don't be silly, I told myself. I'm not going to be foolish enough to stand up in a moving vehicle like Isadora Duncan did.

It was a windy two-lane road down to Monte Carlo. Small villages clung to the sides of the mountains where houses set deeply into the terrain appeared cave-like. They were also brightly coloured. For many villagers the only access to their houses was up a winding path or staircase.

At the side of the road were small, arch-shaped shrines with statues of the Virgin Mary.

I was amazed by how many national parks and forests covered the area. Sometimes, it seemed we were going to drive straight into the mountain cliff, then rounding a curve on the road, it seemed we were going to drive off the cliff into the sea. I was thrilled by it all.

Rufus parked the car on a street along the sea cliff, and we walked down a steep path that was lined with palm trees and beautiful gardens full of blossoming rhododendrons. When we reached the sea wall, we continued to walk, passing marinas filled with very expensive yachts.

Rufus chose an outdoor restaurant where the staff knew him by name. He let me know that they knew his seating preference. "Not everyone gets to sit where they want in these places."

It all seemed very snobbish to me, but I wasn't going to spoil Rufus's claim to privilege, so I made no comment except to ask that I sit in the shade. Rufus sat in the sun, sprawling over his chair.

"It's very peaceful here," I said.

Together, we looked over the expanse of water.

"The light is so different. The sea seems to shimmer into the distant horizon," I said.

"The sky is the source of light in nature, and it governs everything."

"How observant."

"John Constable."

"Ahh," I said, recognizing the English painter.

Keeping his gaze ahead, Rufus recited:

"*Distances recede in blues*
Our gaze in precious greens
Follow like waves breaking
On shores we've never seen."

My poet, I thought. I didn't ask if he had just made it up, or even written it. I didn't know if he was quoting another poet. Maybe I was supposed to recognize the lines.

Turning his head, he looked at me. "For you."

"Thank you," I said, blushing.

"I recommend their Salad Nicoise."

"I'm in your hands."

Rufus smiled. "*Presto si spera.*"

Again, I blushed. Presto meant soon, that much I had already determined.

"That's the dress you wore for the photograph."

I looked down. "Yes, it is."

"It's very becoming, but today it looks like a whole dress. In the photograph, it doesn't."

"No?"

"In a sense, nonsense itself is a sanity-insanity inversion. Do you think my cousin Lucia behaved the way she did because it is the only way she can keep her sanity amid so much grief?"

"I suppose. Yet, she didn't lose a child. It was only a tiny fetus. Has she been trying for a while to get pregnant?"

"They want to have children."

"Yes," I said, feeling admonished.

"Do you want to have children?"

I was taken aback. "To be honest, I haven't thought that far. I'm still thinking about my education, not starting a family. Besides, I don't have a steady boyfriend."

"That will change."

I laughed. What a serious fellow Rufus was.

"Say what you mean. Not the same as meaning what you say."

"Did you study philosophy?" I asked.

"Imponderable."

If Rufus wanted me to ponder, I could not oblige. "I think you're metaphysical."

"Of course, I'm an English poet. That is the origin of the word."

"Sorry."

"Don't be."

"Lately I've been into body-mind-spirit."

"Tell me more."

I decided to keep Helen's name out of my telling. Over lunch we talked about the connections between body-mind-spirit.

"Maybe you'll make me less metaphysical," Rufus said, after paying the bill.

I had no idea what lunch cost as I had not seen a menu or any Euros pass hands. Rufus had paid with a credit card. "I wonder if that's good or bad."

"All experience is good. I can already feel you becoming a different sort of muse."

"A muse?" I had been Lewis's muse, too, but didn't remind Rufus.

"Only time will tell. Do you want to drive around?"

"Yes, I'd like that."

Our uphill walk was very slow, and I was happy to reach the car.

"We'll drive along the roadway they use for the car races."

Although we were not part of any car race, the traffic was busy and very fast. When we left the main city, Rufus warned me we were going to drive on some very fast toll highways. I had never experienced such speeds. The languishing metaphysical poet was a speedster, an incongruous man. Eventually, I removed my scarf because I felt it loosening with the force of the wind in my hair. I could imagine it becoming tangled in a tire spike. Thankfully, my hair was cut short and didn't blow into my eyes, but I felt strands swishing around my ears. Blinking away windy tears, I kept my eyes on the road and breathed the dead air between my face and the windshield. It seemed the only calm space. We climbed and climbed. Soon, I recognized we were heading east, away from the setting sun and on route to Italy. When we crossed the border, we followed a series of secondary roads before joining the same highway we had travelled from the airport. Now the road back to Vignolo was familiar.

Over a late meal, Clive wanted to know if we had visited Casino Monte Carlo. "I only ask because it's a Beaux-Arts construction with a formal garden, worth a visit."

"No, we didn't," Rufus said. "Next time."

I was still trying to distance Helen from my thoughts as she had sent me an email which I refused to open, but I remembered that she and I had wanted to ask Clive about dances at Oxford, so I inquired.

"Don't bother Papa with all that old history. He's on holiday here."

"Not a bother," Clive said, before starting into one of his spiels. "It was not considered desirable for students to go to dances. This sentiment came from a house rule of 1898 and continued in spirit for many years, but by 1912 dancing with each other was permitted under set guidelines. Every evening between Dinner and Chapel fifteen minutes was given over for music and dancing. By 1915, a folk dancing club was popular and well into the 1920s students gave displays at fund raising fairs.

"The signing of the Armistice in 1918 was celebrated by a dinner and fancy-dress dance, and this form of entertainment continued in popularity. It's even recorded, and you'll like this Isadora," Clive said, leaning his head closer to me, "a student sent a letter home in 1923 requesting a pair of Daddy's grey flannel bags and a cricket shirt for a fancy-dress dance at Somerville."

"Isadora dressed up as Charlie Chaplin in dance class," Antonia explained to Rufus.

"What's that, pray?" Rufus asked, turning to me.

"Like Lucia Joyce," I said, "that was a costume she preferred."

"As I was saying," Clive continued, "it is rather surprising to find on record the foundation of a dance club for members of the University in 1926, as at that time all undergraduates were forbidden to take dance instruction except from teachers licensed by the Proctors. The dons were not so enthusiastic, feeling that 'dancing was peculiar in its disturbing effect upon work.' Anyway, the club was dissolved in 1931."

"Good heavens," I said, as much enthralled by these revelations of dance history as I was by Clive's photographic memory.

"Let's take some night air," Rufus said, rising from the table.

"Yes, you two young ones go off and enjoy yourselves," Clive said. "We'll do the washing up."

I felt I should offer to help, but I had noticed that Antonia did most of the domestic chores at the villa. Besides, Rufus offered intrigue and he did not disappoint. Outside the night was dark and clear; the sky was black and full of bright lights.

"*Beautiful star, Beautiful star, Star of the evening, Beautiful star*."

Looking up, I asked about the constellations.

"My dear, I'm giving you poetry and you want science."

"Not really," I said, "I like your poetry."

He said:

You've waked me too soon,
I must slumber again
A little more sleep
And a little more slumber
Thus he wastes half his days
And his hours without number.

I caught my breath as Rufus stepped close to my ear and whispered, "Can I visit you tonight?"

I kissed his lips and felt a quiver up my spine. His hand held my head, and he fingered my ear lobe. Catching my breath, I said, "Yes."

Chapter Nineteen

In the morning after breakfast, Rufus suggested I join him in the garden. Saying I needed to do some work, he suggested I bring along my laptop.

"I too will work."

"Writing poetry?" I asked, in an upbeat tone, intending to dignify his aspirations.

"Followed by lunch in San Remo."

I was taken aback. Was he serious? Were we to repeat this pattern every day? Why balk at a little bit of work and a lot of luxury? "Today, I'll pay," I said.

Rufus turned up his nose at my suggestion.

"Please, I insist."

Acceding to my wishes, Rufus said, "San Remo is known for its focaccia and extra virgin-grade olive oil."

When I joined him in the garden, he had a few lines written on a sheet of paper in his notebook.

"Can I see?"

"Of course, it's for you," Rufus said, gently tearing off the single sheet. I read:

In dreams beneath a sunny sky
Sweet moments of lingering silence
An evening of love in July.

Returning the verse, I sat across from him and opened my laptop. Time to get serious. Yet, how could I? My mind was smiling. Totally conscious of his presence, I faked a serious engagement with the printed screen. On the tabletop was an abandoned sheet of his writing. Reading it upside down, I deciphered three words in the margin written in upper case letters: ALICE PLEASANCE LIDDELL.

"What's this?" I asked, picking it up, turning it around, and scanning the lines.

"An acrostic."

"A boat beneath a sunny day," I read aloud and continued reading all seven verses that spelled Alice Pleasance Liddell. "This is about the Alice in *Alice in Wonderland*."

"Yes, my dear, Alice Pleasance Liddell. Not my acrostic. This is mine," Rufus said, handing me the sheet again.

I read the second verse:

Dancing lovers who nestle near
Only care one for the other
Revive and sigh with willing ear.

"Ah," I said, "and the next line will begin with 'A'."

"My clever Isadora. Please," Rufus said, taking back the sheet. He scribbled, then showed me an acrostic of my first name:

In dreams beneath a sunny sky
Sweet moments of lingering silence
An evening of love in July.
Dancing lovers who nestle near
Only care one for the other
Revive and sigh with willing ear
As eager minds find memories.

"You must get to work, otherwise you won't have earned your lunch."

"But I'm paying, remember?"

"A footling gesture."

"Footling?"

"Trivial. Silly."

"Am I to understand you think my offer to pay is trivial and silly?"

Rufus tilted his head and looked into my eyes.

"And don't pull that cute pose on me."

Lifting his head and sitting upright, Rufus asked indignantly, "What do you mean?"

"You know what I mean?"

"No, I don't. Are we having a lover's quarrel? After only one night?"

"What's wrong with me paying? What do you mean, footling?"

"I simply mean that paying the lunch bill won't absolve you from having to get down to work. Nothing more."

"Easy for you to say." Yet I was mollified, and turning away from him, I concentrated on my laptop. As I worked, I heard familiar sounds: the clock chimed indoors; church bells tolled in the distance; somewhere a rooster crowed. Rufus was quiet except at one point when he crumbled a sheet of paper into a ball.

Before we departed for San Remo, Rufus handed me his completed acrostic to take to my room where I read it and pondered over the ending:

Die and fade that July
Under a long pallid sky
Never seen by waking eyes
Cares that still haunt me
And what is life but a dream
Nonsense illusion?

Why do I find this sad? I thought, looking up to the stitched haiku. Was it real; the love I felt?

Driving to San Remo, we passed hills covered with oranges, lemons, pomegranates, and olives.

"The A10 Motorway continues into Genoa," Rufus said, after turning onto the main road into town, "*Autostrada dei Fiori*, Freeway of Flowers."

"Can we drive there someday?"

"Tomorrow."

I laughed. My wish was his command.

"This is the City of Flowers, *la Citt· dei Fiori*."

Hand in hand, we walked from the parking lot to the coastal path where Rufus took me to his favourite restaurant for Torta Verde.

"I thought we came here for foccacia?" I said.

"That too."

"Let me guess, green tart, a pie made with vegetables. Is it like the Greek spanakopita?"

"Better," Rufus said. "Here they make it with Swiss chard, onions, potatoes, and eggs inside an olive-oil crust rolled very thin." He waved over the waiter. "*La signora pagler. Non si preoccupi delle spese.*"

"*Si, signora,*" the waiter said to me, laughing while taking our order. "Tell me about your work this morning."

"This is interesting," I said, ready to engage in a lengthy conversation like we had had yesterday. "After reading the biography of Vaslav Nijinsky by his wife, Romola, in 1934, Lucia's parents worried that her fate would be the same as his. He went mad, you know. It didn't help Lucia's case that the Joyces' friend, Harriet Weaver, shared their concerns. She thought his experience was prophetic. The family saw Nijinsky dance in George Antheil's Ballet mecaniqueî which was previewed in Paris on June 19, 1926, at Theatre des Champs-Elysees. The place seated twenty-five hundred and Ezra Pound had marshaled all his forces to attend and that included James and Nora Joyce and their two children."

"Well, if Lucia's long-suffering parents didn't want her influenced by the likes of Nijinsky, why did they take her to see avant-garde performances?"

"They were exposed to everything." Over the next hour I told Rufus about the domestic life of the Joyce family in Paris. Finally, I summed up, "Everyone in the arts knew everyone else in those days. The Antheils lived above Sylvia Beach's bookstore, Shakespeare and Company, for ten years. Initially she had helped James and Nora Joyce find a place to live in Paris, but they couldn't fit their family into her second—floor space with their two children. Still, Sylvia Beach did publish James Joyce's *Ulysses* in installments when his publishers refused the manuscript."

"And they were all friends?"

"Sometimes, they weren't," I answered, thinking of a historical situation that reminded me of my relationship with Helen. "Initially, James Joyce did support Lucia in her dance. They'd met Margaret Morris and she'd invited Lucia to come to her classes." I thought of my meeting Helen's Aunt Helen. "Lucia thrived in these classes. It was the happiest time of her life." I thought about how Antonia had observed my deployment after months of creative movement, but I thought better of sharing that with Rufus. "When the French version of *Ulysses* was published, her parents insisted she attend all the social functions in celebration which took her out of classes. Then she had to go with them for an entire summer while her father did research. In the end, Lucia lost opportunities to perform. By this time, her father scolded her for thinking that she could take dance seriously."

"How cruel."

"And I was reading this morning how George Antheil had a falling-out with Stravinsky that depressed him tremendously." I thought how I had overcome my depression in less than a week. Maybe I shouldn't compare myself to characters from history. "Anyway, it haunted his dreams for years, but his wife, Boski, was happy about the split because she thought her husband, George, worshiped Stravinsky too much. She wrote, even though we recognize the value of the innovations brought about by these men in our imbecilic age, we want nothing to do with them. I like that term, imbecilic age. George and his wife eventually went to Hollywood, so he was treated as a traitor by real artists for compromising himself to the almighty dollar, but, in the end, he didn't make much."

"Well, it's good someone has dollars," Rufus said as the waiter handed me the bill.

I smiled at Rufus and paid.

"Want to visit some sites?" Rufus asked. "Edward Lear is buried here in Foce Cemetery and there's a permanent exhibit at the villa where Alfred Nobel once lived."

"Edward Lear? The writer of nonsense? Here?"

"Yes, don't sound so surprised," Rufus said, taking my arm and guiding me in the direction of the tombstone. "You know he had a cat named Foss."

"Did he? He's sounding more and more like you with each revelation." I thought how I'd recognized at once that Rufus had an anthropomorphic relationship with Dinah like Lear had with his cat. His "The Owl and The Pussycat" included a cat, an owl, a pig, and a turkey.

"One story goes that he was on a train ride from London to Guildford when two small boys accompanied by two ladies entered his carriage, and one of the boys had a copy of his *A Book of Nonsense*. So being a practical joker, Edward Lear pointed out to them that it was the Earl of Derby having his own little joke on the public."

Rufus stopped at a corner and looked around in all directions. "This way. Let me fill you in; you also need to know that Edward Lear was invited to Knowsley Hall to make drawings of the animals in the Earl's menagerie. So, on the train he told the boys that the name LEAR is simply EARL transposed."

I thought of dear Lewis Dodgson and his Spoonerisms that were no joke.

"I think I remember *A Book of Nonsense*."

"I'm sure you do. Here's mine:

There was an old man from Oxford
Who had a large gong from Bali!
In the garden he hung it.
In the daytime he rung it.
Then jumped up and down with glee!"

"I've never heard anyone bang that gong."

"Silly, don't take me literally."

At the cemetery Rufus read the inscription:

Tomohrit, Athos, all things fair,
With such a pencil, such a pen,
You shadow forth to distant men,
I read and felt that I was there.

"From *On His Travels in Greece*. I didn't realize he was also a travel writer," I said.

"Yes, and an illustrator—a man of many talents. Did you know International Owl and Pussycat Day is celebrated on his birthday, May 12?"

"Well, no, sorry, I didn't."

"You can google it."

"And break the flow of my research?"

"No, I don't mean to distract you."

"You don't really. Tell me more about Edward Lear."

"Well, he wrote 'The Owl and The Pussycat' for the children of his patron, Edward Stanley, 13th Earl of Derby."

"How interesting," I said, thinking of Charles Dodgson writing for the Liddell children. "Do you know The Stanley Cup was donated to Canada by Lord Stanley?"

"What's that?"

"Spoken like a true Brit," I said, placing my fists on my hips. "It's awarded annually to the winning hockey team."

"You must tell me about this sport."

"No, I mustn't."

"Then I must kiss you."

Rufus put his arms around me. "Now, do you want to learn about the most important discoveries of the 19th century, including Nobel's research interests, or do you want to come back here another time?"

Leaning away from his close embrace, I said, "I want to return another day with you."

"Well then, let's stretch our legs before getting back into the car for the drive home."

"Yes, let's walk along the Italian Riviera," I said enthusiastically.

"I love your spirit," Rufus said, swinging my arm:

"And hand in hand, on the edge of the sand
They danced by the light of the moon,
The moon,
The moon,
They danced by the light of the moon."

"We'll do that tonight, shall we?" I suggested, snuggling up to Rufus.

"You dance. I'll recite."

"We'll see about that."

Chapter Twenty

My life at the villa was idyllic for one glorious week. Then Uncle Stuart and Cousin Ed arrived. Physically, Stuart was a smaller version of his brother, Clive, and Ed was an even smaller version of his father. Standing in a row, they looked like receding bowling pins. On the first day of their visit, the men invited me to join them on a day trip to San Remo.

"We're going to have lunch before visiting the science exhibit," Clive said in his usual optimistic and encouraging fashion.

"I'll stay behind with the women."

"You didn't get to see it on your last visit," Rufus said, pleading for my company.

"No," I said, not changing my mind. That morning Antonia said Augusta was coming to help her with the cleaning and cooking which was why she'd begged off joining the men. Even though I knew Clive would make the tour interesting, and despite Rufus's pleading eyes, I felt more comfortable remaining behind.

"It will give me an opportunity to catch up on my work," I said, then thought, "And to ponder my feelings and reconnect with my brain." Any heady bliss I may have felt earlier dissolved.

Clive chuckled. "Rufus has monopolized dear Isadora. He's taken her everywhere."

"I bet he has," Ed said.

Looking stoically at the "*cugino*," I instantly took a dislike to him and decided he was what the Brits called "a dodgy fellow."

"Jealousy will get you nowhere," Rufus said.

"We don't all get to enjoy whirlwind romances like you," Ed said, pulling his head back to see our reaction.

I sensed I was meant to feel in terrible danger with the likes of Rufus. The real danger lay with Ed. He seemed like many men I'd had the misfortune of knowing. Ed had probed an old wound, to remind me that I was missing the point of men, that my delicious limbo could not last. Rufus was right. Jealousy would get him nowhere.

Once the men left, domesticity reigned that day. Continuing my habit of working in the garden, I wallowed in the sounds and smells coming from the kitchen where Antonia and her sister were cooking the fresh chickens Augusta had brought from the farm. As if their activity was contagious, birds twittered and flew overhead preparing their second nesting of the season.

Despite my intention to work, I wasted half the morning. I kept thinking about what Clive had said when he quoted those Oxford dons. Dancing was peculiar in its disturbing effect upon work. Yet I missed dancing. Just like Lucia had while on holiday with her family in Torquay, the English Riviera.

On one of our outings, Rufus had quoted Cicero, "No one dances while he is sober unless he happens to be a lunatic." We'd talked about the Roman invasion in Italy. Like all our conversations we circled topics, probed history, and quoted sources. Rufus had said that Cicero was the greatest of Roman killjoys in a culture where one apologized for one's lack of ability to dance or play the flute well.

Quoting Cicero did not encourage Rufus in my attempts to get him to dance with me. He refused and unfortunately, I found myself growing more and more distant from my own physical enjoyment of moving to music. If I hadn't felt betrayed by Helen, I would have missed her, too; still, I missed her wonderful classes. I decided I needed to dance to reconnect my body-mind-soul. I was no longer starved for physical contact. I was more than satisfied with Rufus. Yet, why depend solely on sexual gratification? I needed to dance to express my emotions, to celebrate what I had.

Kicking off my shoes, I stood. Humming I swayed, easing my limbs into wider and wider arcs. My leg muscles were solid from walking, so I needed to loosen them gently. I started to pick up my feet and soon I was leading my movements with my knees rising and falling in figures of eight. My head and shoulders came alive. Then I started to twirl around the garden.

I stopped when I heard clapping. Looking up I saw Augusta and Antonia watching me.

"*Bravo! Bella ballerina!*" Augusta clapped enthusiastically.

"Please, don't let us stop you," Antonia shouted. "We are enjoying your free movement."

I curtsied. "Thank you. I miss dancing and thought it might get my brain moving again."

"Don't let us interfere with you. I know my son has taken up most of your time."

"But he's charming," I said. "It's been a working holiday."

"I'm glad you find him charming. I'm afraid his cousin is right. He's charmed his way through many whirlwind romances. Yet he does seem to be charmed by you. I hope for his sake you're not the whirlwind who crushes him."

"*Pensi che sono amanti?*" Augusta asked, clearly alarmed.

"*Forse, ma non È affare nostro.*" Antonia led her sister indoors.

What wasn't their business, I wondered. I was sweating slightly, but that was all. My heart was not throbbing; my pulse was not pumping; my lungs were not gasping. I could have continued dancing, but decided to return to my work, all the while thinking how I was going to turn the whirlwind romance into true love.

Lucia came for lunch. She told me she hoped I would treat her like a sister. She spoke English to me and refused to translate for her mother. "Yes, we all love Rufus," she said, "but someday he will find true love and happiness. Maybe that will be with you, then you can be my real sister. Would you like that?"

I laughed. "*Sì.*"

"You can ask me anything."

I knew she meant about Rufus, but I wanted to ask her about children. If she was really a sister, I could. Maybe, someday when we knew one another better.

The men returned late from San Remo. Octavio and Lucia joined us for the evening meal and were introduced to Clive's relatives.

"*Abbiamo alievato i polli noi stessi,*" Lucia said. "We raised the chickens ourselves."

"*Ceno, pollo casalingola,*" Octavio said, gesturing to Antonia and Augusta in thanks.

"*Saporissimo,*" Rufus said. Turning his back on his cousin, he spoke Italian to Lucia and Octavio.

"I'm starving," Clive said, rubbing his hands together. "We've been smelling the wonderful aromas since our return, haven't we?"

Rufus agreed. "*Niente come un pasto casalingola.*"

"*Pieno di erbe locali,*" Augusta said.

"I like pasta," Ed said.

"Ever the fool," Rufus whispered in my ear. Aloud he said, "Tomorrow we will go together to San Remo. I can share with you what papa said."

"I know he's a wonderful guide."

"*Posso venire?*" Lucia asked.

"*Sono amanti, Lucia,*" Augusta said, shaking her arms at her daughter.

"What have you been saying?"

I shrugged at Rufus. "Nothing. What are they saying?"

"Could we please sit down to eat before everything gets cold," Antonia suggested.

That night, the family prepared to go to church the following day which surprised me. There had been no offer of a church visit the previous Sunday, not that I would have wanted to attend. I was happy when Rufus excused us from this Sabbath obligation saying we had an early visit planned to San Remo.

In the car, Rufus carried on about religious hypocrites like his relatives.

"You're sounding like a typical intellectual," I said.

"Am I? Well, excuse me. Mummsy's relatives attend regularly and they're not hypocrites. Their religion is part of their culture, too, only they're dignified about it. Their faith in God isn't some spiritual mumbo-jumbo. It's deep-rooted and complex, more about using God to convince themselves that they're not alone on this earth and that their lives are not just hard work."

"Not nonsense," I said, trying to ease the tension.

"So glad you understand."

At the Villa Nobel, Rufus apprised me of everything Clive had told them yesterday about the science museum. I liked the elegant Mooris-style house and the personal history of how Alfred Nobel chose the riviera for health reasons.

"Nobel was able to install a laboratory here for the studies of dynamite."

"Did your Uncle Stuart and cousin Ed find all this interesting?"

"Indeed, they did. They're both men of science."

"Have you been close to your cousin all your life?"

"At home, we visited during the holidays. Like me, he has no siblings."

"But here, in Italy, you had your other cousin?"

"Yes, Lucia, who also has no siblings."

"Umm," I said, "no wonder you're close to them. I've always wanted a sister."

We had lunch at the same restaurant that we visited last week, only this time Rufus paid.

Afterward Rufus rhymed off his latest ditty:

"No girls can Edwin win
He has a skinny dick
What makes Edwin so thin?
The girls don't like his prick."

No use chastising him for being mean. I could have told Rufus he was behaving immaturely, but I felt empathy. "I think you have those lines in the wrong order," I simply said.

"At least he's an Edwin and not an Edward. That would make me really mad."

"You are mad, Rufus. And mean and brutal."

"Are you mad at me?"

"No, somehow, having a way with words excuses you. I'm sure even Ed will find someone to love him as there are still foolish girls who fall for the likes of him."

Rufus was gleeful. "You're on my side! He'll meet some pale-faced, up-tight virgin."

"Careful."

"Agreed," Rufus said, "enough of that."

That evening at dinner, the conversation centered on the topic of nineteenth century inventions. Ed shone light on his favourites, then expanded on nobelium. Apparently, if it was produced in any great quantity, it would cause a radiation hazard. Rufus did not endear himself to his cousin with his criticisms of how all scientific inventions posed risks.

After dinner, Rufus and I went outside to find some privacy, but Ed trailed after us. "The others may have found him stimulating," Rufus mumbled, laying on the grass with Dinah on his chest.

"Hear that," I suddenly said, walking further into the garden. "An owl."

"Yes."

Rufus sang:

"You elegant fowl!
How charmingly sweet you sing!
O let us be married!
Too long we have tarried
But what shall we do for a ring?"

"If you're proposing, that's pathetic," Ed said, taking a chair.

"Do you think I'm pathetic, sweet Dinah?" Rufus petted Dinah who purred.

Sensing the cat had scared off the owl, I took a chair across from Ed. "I think Rufus is just singing the lyrics from *The Owl and the Pussycat*."

Rufus kept singing.

"O lovely Pussy!
O Pussy, my love!
What a beautiful Pussy you are, you are, you are!
What a beautiful Pussy you are!"

"Then the lyrics are pathetic," Ed said.

"Do you remember rowing together in a boat?"

"Are you talking to me, Rufus?" Ed asked.

"Of course, I'm talking to you."

"Oh, I thought you were talking to your cat."

Touche, I thought, but didn't say aloud, not wanting to score points for Ed. After all, it was a competition.

"So, Ed, do you have a girlfriend? Have you proposed?"

"If I had, you'd be the last to know," Ed said.

"I'll come to your wedding."

"You can come, but not Dinah." Ed turned to me. "You can come, too."

"Can I?" I asked, wondering who would marry first. Ed? Who would marry Rufus? Suddenly I felt inexplicably sad, as if I was experiencing something I may never possess. My earlier excitement and euphoria at possibly finding true love became mixed up with this terrible and peculiar sadness, leaving me stranded.

Chapter Twenty One

Later that week, Rufus and I found ourselves again alone in the garden. Antonia and Clive had taken Stuart and Ed to Monte Carlo. They wouldn't return until late.

"Antonia is a very different person here than when she is in Oxford. She does nothing around the house there, except cook the Sunday roast. Here she does everything."

"In Oxford, she's a professional woman. Here, she's a country wife."

I laughed. "You're too droll."

"Besides, Papa owns the house in Oxford and Mummsy bought the villa with her inheritance."

"In Canada, as a married couple, they would own both properties jointly."

"Europe is different."

"It is," I acknowledged. "Aren't we lucky to have the day to ourselves? Can we just stay here? Let's not go anywhere today."

"My sentiments exactly. We could make love outdoors, in the garden."

"Later," I said, giggling. Snapping my laptop open, I said, "First, I'll get caught up on my correspondence. Look how many emails I have."

Raising his head to peer across at the screen, Rufus asked, "Who's Helen?"

I froze, my quietude shattered.

"She has a British address," Rufus said, sensing my agitation.

"Yes," I acknowledged. "Helen was my dance teacher in Oxford."

"How charming," Rufus said. "Maybe she could teach me to dance."

"No, you wouldn't like her."

"Wouldn't I? Yet you want me to dance. Pray, what else did Helen do? I get the impression you don't particularly like Helen?"

"Your mother didn't like Helen."

"No? Did Mummsy take dance lessons, too? I can't imagine that."

"No, you're quite right. She didn't. She did meet her, though. So did Clive. So did Lewis Dodgson. It was at Helen's studio that he took the photograph of me as Charlie Chaplin."

"I'm sure he did a fine job. Lewis knows how to capture movement."

"He does." Then I thought, *He did too fine a job; too flattering to some.*

"So, what's the problem?"

What to say? "She ran off with a man who came to Lewis's exhibition."

"Still, not a crime. Did you know this man?"

"Not really, although I introduced them."

"So, you were jealous?"

I looked over at Rufus. "No, that's not how I felt," not admitting that I sort of knew him in a biblical sense.

"Then how did you feel?"

"Betrayed." Turning away from Rufus, I examined my emotions. Why had I felt betrayed? Life's betrayal. "I was wrong about everyone and everything," I confessed, thinking about Helen, Lewis, my family, my work. "Even dance."

"But you don't feel that way now."

Smiling, I turned back to Rufus. "No, I don't."

"You must have met other dancers?"

"I did: dancers, actors, students."

"But you only made friends with Helen."

"Yes."

"Then you should answer her emails. Don't pay any attention to Mummsy."

"Thank you, Rufus." His support buoyed me.

I opened Helen's first email and read her apology for leaving me at the gallery without saying a proper goodbye. In her second email, she told me what she and Michael had been doing. In her third email, she asked if Rufus was as handsome as his photograph. I hit 'Reply' and wrote: Apology accepted. Sorry I haven't answered sooner. Glad you and Michael are hitting it off. Rufus is better than his photograph.

Then I sat back pleased with the contact I'd made. All was forgiven. She had apologized.

"Speaking of Mummsy becoming domestic, did you see her latest embroidery?"

Nodding, I looked up from my screen. Again, Rufus was interrupting me, but I was only too willing to let him. "Another haiku?"

"Yes, it's for the kitchen." He recited from memory,
"Encased in brown skin
Cutting gnarled ginger root
No longer wild."

"Why do you write them?"

"Well, it's something I do as a mental exercise, because the thing about haiku is it isn't strictly about counting the number of syllables per line. Japanese is a very different language from English as each syllable has more meaning in Japanese than in English. Haiku is spiritual, so the challenge is to try to invoke three elements: God and space and time."

"You do all of that,"

"Not really. It takes a lifetime to write the perfect haiku." Rufus twirled his pen above his head. "But what's a lifetime for, if not to achieve perfection just once?"

"Admirable," I said, returning my focus to my email list., *Enough of heads in clouds.*

"You know many Canadians have attended Oxford."

Clearly Rufus was not going to leave me to my own devices. "I'm sure," I said. At least he wasn't making me feel the fool for not knowing, or using a mocking tone as would his cousin Ed. His tone last night had been more taunting than enlightening. Unlike him, Rufus was not a bully. Yet, he was a ladies' man. Was that reassuring?

"For instance, take the Canadian diplomat, Charles Ritchie. He went to Pembroke College where he hung around with all the upper-class twits. The room he occupied was the same room Samuel Johnson held two centuries earlier."

Now I understood. "Did he now?"

"Yes, and the story goes that the day he lost his virginity on the sofa in his room, the porter brought around an American couple who wanted to view the room while young Charles was still in the first flush of relief, or release."

"Not remorse. Those damned porters," I said. Rufus, I'd decided, was the better catch. I continued to listen while Rufus wiled away the morning regaling me with more tales of distinguished Canadians behaving badly.

Later, we decided to make a lunch to eat outside. We brought plates of antipasto that included generous servings of green olives with pimentos, pickled onions and red peppers, bottled artichokes and mushrooms, and tinned tuna. We'd forgotten cutlery, so we ate everything with our fingers and washed the food down with gulps of Chianti. The wine bottle looked old-fashioned as it was encased in a straw basket.

Rufus raised the bottle to drain the contents and declared, "This fine wine is from *Provincia del Chianti, Rufina* to be precise."

"Is that the feminine of Rufus?" I asked, slurring my words.

Sticking the empty wine bottle under my nose, Rufus pointed to the picture of the black rooster on the label around the neck. "Gallo Nero."

That action started us giggling. Then we grew heated. I crawled over to where Rufus sat.

Tumbling to the stone floor we rolled over to the grassy ground where we spent the afternoon indulging our passions. Afterwards, we drifted off.

Later Lucia arrived. "It's tea—time," she said.

"Lucia likes tea," Rufus said to me.

"Then I'm glad you came," I said, mostly glad she hadn't arrived earlier to catch us in the act.

"I'll boil the kettle," Rufus said.

"I made these," Lucia said, showing me what was in the porcelain bowl.

"What are they?" I asked trying to sound enthusiastic. They looked very dull. I peered closer. "Oh, apricots!"

"Yes, from our orchard."

"Marvellous, apricot tarts."

"You like?"

"Of course," I said reclining. "Did you bake them?"

"No, my mama. She still won't let me do anything."

"I'm so sorry you lost your baby."

Lucia exhaled a full symphony of grievances. Before speaking, she inhaled. "Thank you. You are kind, Isadora. This is my first try. My mama tried many times to give me a sister or brother. *Mi sento svenire*."

I didn't know what Lucia was feeling. "Is that why she thought it was her fault?"

"Yes, all her fault. Everything her fault. Now my fault. What we women have to bear."

"Yet, it isn't your fault, Lucia. It's just nature."

"You think?"

"Yes, I'm sure."

"Maybe next time."

I squeezed her forearm. That explained why Lucia was an only child, not by choice, but by circumstances beyond the family's control. I suspected for Antonia the condition was by choice. "I'm sure a cup of tea will make you feel better."

When Rufus came with a tray of tea things, I looked up at him pleadingly. "I think Lucia is feeling sad."

"*Come sta?*"

"*Mi gira la testa.*"

"The tea will help," Rufus said to Lucia while raising his eyebrows at me confirming what we both knew. Lucia was here for our sympathy. We spent an hour together with Lucia and Rufus sharing funny stories of their childhood in Italy. "Remember when I dared you to go into the field with the bull?"

"That sounds dangerous," I said.

"It was, and Lucia had to save me."

Lucia laughed. "I loved summer when you came. We played together. Remember Rufus, how we would go exploring in the woods? And the goldfish. Remember the pond? And we would go swimming?"

"In the goldfish pond?" I exclaimed.

Rufus cocked his head. "No, silly, we went to the ocean to swim. You must swim because you're from Canada. Don't you have more fresh-water lakes than anywhere else in the world?"

"That's not why I can swim."

"If that's not why, then please tell."

I smiled at Rufus. "I took lessons as a child from a swimming instructor at a pool."

By early evening we sensibly retired to our separate rooms. We were both sound asleep when the others returned.

Chapter Twenty Two

The next morning, Rufus and I woke before the others. Quietly, we stole out of the house. During the night it had rained, and the air was laden with a heavy morning mist that hid the driveway from our view. Once we found our footing, I looked back to see if we had woken the others, but the fog obscured the house. Feeling disoriented, I reached for Rufus who held my hand.

We were like thieves, stealing away and taking our leave. There weren't even shadows of outlines to mark where buildings and structures stood. It was too dangerous to walk on the road. The thick air muffled all exterior sounds. Would we hear the roar of an engine if a car approached?

As we descended, the fog thinned which confused me as I figured it would be thicker in the valley, but what did I know of this mountainous terrain.

Soon we were safely at the farm and overheard voices before Rufus could announce our arrival, before he could make them hear him calling, "*Buongiorno.*"

Augusta and Lucia were kneeling on the ground, putting flowers on the grave site.

"Fresh *fiori*," Lucia said, standing to greet us, "*buongiorno.*"

Augusta remained bent in grief, not even acknowledging us.

"*Venite a noi per prima colazione.*"

I dreaded that I would once again have to listen to Lucia's mixed conversation. Although my Italian had improved, I distrusted the secretive and possessive way Lucia addressed Rufus in front of her mother.

"That's why we're here," Rufus said, "for breakfast."

"*Proprio come al tempo passato.*"

"Yes, like old times," Rufus said.

Lucia's face lit up, smiling as she turned to me. "Rufus and I always ate breakfast together, from when we were little, before I was married." Then she turned to Rufus and led us away. "I'm so happy you bring Bella Isadora. We can have a fresh *omelette di funghi*. What is that in English?"

"Mushrooms," I answered, stunned by her unexpected compliment.

"Mushrooms," Lucia repeated in her accented English. "I make for you with fresh mushrooms, fresh eggs, fresh milk, fresh herbs. You like."

Looking over to Augusta, I hesitated.

"Don't mind Mama," Lucia said, quietly. "She's like this every day."

"I guess she really wanted to be a grandmother," I said, walking toward the farmhouse.

"Yes, and I tell her, she will someday, but she keeps saying it is her fault. She's crazy with grief. She lost many babies after me."

"I didn't know that," Rufus said, holding the door open for us.

"No, we not talk about it. You were young." Lucia pinched Rufus's cheek. "My little *cugino*."

Now they had piqued my curiosity. Lucia had confided in me, but never told her cousin, Rufus. It was something you shared with women. I asked about her father, Augusta's husband. He too died when Rufus was young.

"Before Mummsy bought the villa we stayed with Aunt Augusta and Lucia at their home."

Augusta came into the kitchen and started to fuss with washing up. She did not speak, and I worried about her. Was she becoming depressed?

"We should go to the ocean to swim. Why haven't we done that?"

"I don't know," I said, returning my gaze to Rufus. "Let's."

"You'll have to take Cousin Ed," Lucia said, cracking eggs into a mixing bowl.

"No, we don't," Rufus said adamantly.

"I can tell you don't like Ed," Lucia said, taunting her cousin. "Can you?"

I appreciated they were speaking together in English which I surmised had more to do with Augusta's presence than out of consideration for me. They drifted into their own intimate world which I was happy to eavesdrop on.

"Am I still your favourite cousin, Rufus?"

"Yes, Lucia."

"Do you like Ed, Isadora?"

"No, not really. He lacks charm and regards me with disapproval."

"I thought he was trying to win you for himself," Rufus said.

Lucia laughed. "Rufus, are you jealous?"

"Hardly."

"He does not need to be jealous of a prickly prick," I said.

Banging the omelette pan on the counter, Lucia turned to me. "What did you say?"

Rufus was laughing.

"We shouldn't laugh at people behind their back," I said, sounding like my mother, "but ever since you wrote that limerick, I keep thinking of him in those terms."

"Righto, go and blame me." Rufus laughed loudly.

"Still," Lucia said, returning to her task of flipping the omelette pan, "he's more educated than you, isn't he, Rufus?"

"In a way."

"In a formal way," I said.

"Not in life," Rufus said.

"Not with women," Lucia said. She smiled and winked at me as if in a conspiracy.

"No, not with women," I said, agreeing, and I started to wonder about Lucia. Why did she not have an education?

Then I jumped up and grabbed a plate. "Can I help?"

"Yes, this one's for you," Lucia said, sliding the perfect omelette onto the dish.

"You two could be sisters," Rufus said. "You're exactly the same height. Same strong build, same shaped head, same short arms."

"Not the same hair or face," I said, looking from Lucia to Rufus and thinking how I was built like my father's side of the family.

Soon Octavio came into the kitchen from the barn where he had done his chores. He had eaten breakfast earlier but joined us for coffee and insisted on Augusta sitting down too.

Later, while walking back to the villa, I asked Rufus why Lucia had not gone to university.

"Augusta wanted her to stay close to home. She has been very protective of her all her life. Mummsy is the only one who left to get an education. She was the smart one in the family. When Augusta lost her husband, Mummsy became very protective of her sister and niece. She helped them through difficult times. In return, we got to have wonderful summer vacations here.

"I hope Lucia gets pregnant again. It is heart wrenching to see Augusta so saddened by what happened. She seemed mad, crazy even, but I can understand now that she is very saddened. She's probably remembering all the losses in her life. We think we have so much control over everything when we don't. Anything can befall us at any time."

"That was madness. Maybe we can sometimes allow people a little bit of madness in their lives."

"And grief."

"Italians do grief," Rufus said.

At the gates, we stopped and turned to look behind us at the panoramic view over the hills toward the sea. It had turned into a beautiful day.

"You know, your mother refers to this place as her ancestral villa."

"Trust Mummsy. As you can see, there's nothing old or ancestral about it."

At the villa, we found everyone up and having breakfast. We told them we had already eaten and were going swimming in the ocean. Rufus glared at Ed, daring him to invite himself to come along.

"We had a late night. None of us is up for much this morning," Clive said.

"We were surprised to find you two already asleep. 'Tis love that makes the world go around.'"

As Rufus strode past his cousin who was seated at table, he whispered into Ed's ear, "Somebody said it's done by everybody minding their own business."

"Cheerio," Clive said loudly.

"Don't forget we're going to Verona tomorrow," Antonia called.

"Eagerly anticipating it," Rufus shouted over his shoulder as he went bounding up the stairs.

In the car, I ruminated on Rufus and his antagonism to Ed. After the experience with Lucia that morning, I saw that Rufus was comfortable in Vignolo with her and his mother's family. His father's relatives didn't fit into the picture. They were eager tourists, but they were also house visitors, guests of the family, and so, required some indulgence. Rufus was treating Ed like a nuisance in the manner of an annoying adolescent boy. Was Rufus being spoiled, overly indulged, too entitled? Or was Rufus simply avoiding his family duty to spend more time with me? That was a flattering thought. Still, it was no excuse for bad manners. Tactfully, I tried to share those concerns with Rufus.

"Forget about all that. Now we're going to enjoy the sea. Tomorrow, I'll be the model of good manners. You will love me in Verona."

I loved him on the beach that day. After swimming in the Ligurean Sea, we lay together on the sand, and I told Rufus about seeing the play 'Blood Wedding' in Oxford. "It was written by Federico García Lorca. Do you know his work?"

"Known for his Poetic Realism," Rufus said. "A blend of music, movement, and dialogue. He suffered in Spain. Fought against Franco. Was arrested and shot dead."

"Yes," I said sadly, almost sorry I had spoiled our pleasure with the poet's tragic life. "He had a passion for the art of flamenco."

"Not the kind of dance you're studying," Rufus said, nibbling my shoulder.

"No." I thought how I wasn't studying dance since coming to Italy. I was studying my research notes on my computer files and taking pleasure in getting to know Rufus.

"He studied as a concert pianist before turning to writing."

"Yes, I remember reading that."

"We could make our own poetic realism," Rufus said.

"Could we?"

"May you dance through life
On the wings of a dove
Carrying you higher, my love.

May you dance through life
On the shoulders of Troy
Savouring moments of joy.

May you dance through life
Inspired by the muses
Greatness all she chooses."

I closed my eyes, listening. The warm sunlight felt like liquid on my face and glowed red against my eyelids. "You've a nice singing voice."

"I'll sing it again and you can dance."

I rolled over onto my stomach. "Rufus, I'm not a dancer. I'm a scholar. You're the creative one."

"Nonsense and silliness. Tap into your creativity, my love. I wrote a poem for you." Rufus turned over and sat upright. He repeated the first verse, serenading me and gesturing for me to move.

"Here? On the beach?"

Nodding his head, Rufus kept singing.

He was persuasive. Standing, I placed my feet firmly on the sand and probed my memory bank for inspiration. Remembering how Helen began her improvisation classes, I swayed until I felt my limbs float. Then I danced for Rufus while he sang, our paired act of romantic love. My body felt like flotsam thrown up by a high tide.

Late that night Uncle Stuart spoke. He had been quiet through most of his visit, so when he did finally open up to us, we listened. "The loneliness is hard. You've given me some relief from my grief." Tears crammed his eyes. "I'm afraid I've got myself in a right mess again. Everything Joan did was so precise; you couldn't fault her."

We all remained silent. Stuart gave a swallow that smacked the silence. "I don't know why I feel guilty."

"Give it time," Antonia said. "You'll find it helps."

"Can I brew a spot of tea?" Clive asked.

"Tea would be very kind," Stuart said.

"Jolly nice," Ed said.

In homage to his visiting relatives, Clive had resumed the practice of making tea.

"Enough of that," Stuart said. "Tell us about your day. I understand you went swimming?"

"We did," Rufus said. "We went to Laigueglia."

"A beautiful day for you. I wish I'd travelled more when young, but Joan never liked to go abroad. It's been frightfully good of you to have us."

"We have much to look forward to tomorrow," Rufus said.

"Knock my knickers, *cugino*."

"I promise, Ed, our last day together will be *fantastico*."

I thought Rufus was already playing his role well by being the model of good manners.

"Aren't you lucky to have found each other," Stuart said, looking at me and Rufus.

Clive chuckled. "Remember, Stuart, when we started 'going out'? That's what we called it back then," he reminisced. "We were never conventional at Oxford, although we were relatively private. At least we Brits were. Compared to the foreign students. We had ancestry. At least we thought we did. They were mostly from the colonies, so we thought they were more liberated. Yet we've always been gossips. Take John Aubrey, the supreme gossip. That was our history. We gossiped about Milton and Shakespeare. See what I mean by ancestry?"

I stayed quiet, but Rufus said, "Author of *Brief Lives*." I felt I was getting an Oxford education.

Chapter Twenty Three

After we'd checked into our hotel in Verona, Rufus told me some of the history of what was still the biggest open-air lyrical theatre in the world. The ancient amphiteatre was built by the Romans and had brilliant acoustics. In 1913, to celebrate the birth of Giuseppe Verdi, Verona restored its Roman arena and staged Aida. Rufus remembered his late grandparents telling him fantastic tales about seeing live elephants in a production. "That was in 1954."

We had arrived ahead of the others, agreeing to meet them later. The dress code for spectators seated in the stalls specified elegant attire, so we thought we would change our clothes after exploring Verona. Walking hand-in-hand with Rufus, I said, "I'd love to have an aerial view of this place."

"Look online," Rufus suggested.

"Good idea. Look at that," I said, pointing to hoarding outside the arena.

"Opera props," Rufus said enthusiastically. "Come, let me take your picture."

Crossing the ring road that circled the arena, we craned our necks and looked up at the gigantic props. Above the hoarding, we saw tall staffs with flags, a balcony with a circular staircase, and an armoured giant peering down at us through his metal face mask. A second ring of props stood behind barred metal fences. Rufus asked me to stand by one to take my picture in front of a twenty-foot king dressed in red robes with gold wings. Behind these props, the Doric columns graced the main entrance. It was all larger than life.

Along the marked route to Juliet's balcony, we passed a wall covered in graffiti where young lovers proclaimed their feelings in a torrent of hearts superimposed on top of one another. Beside a tall wall covered in vines, a crowd of American tourists stood outside listening to a guide.

Rufus stood in front of the two narrow arched windows underneath the stone balcony and started mimicking Romeo. He spoke incomprehensible Italian to me. *"Odorosi fioretti, rose porporine, bianchissimi gigli, me testa lunga, fiori di me."*

An American tourist asked me if Rufus was proposing.

"I don't know. I don't speak Italian," I said.

The guide laughed. "Your suitor is mad."

"Poet," Rufus shouted, pointing to himself to reveal why he had spoken nonsense.

Now that we had the attention of the whole group, they all joined in the hilarity, inciting a public debate about whether I should accept this ersatz Romeo. "A poet? You'll be poor." "Clearly, he's madly in love with you." "He's too handsome to resist."

Rufus smiled broadly. Pulling me close, I smiled in return as he placed his hand on the small of my back which he stroked. We kissed underneath Juliet's balcony. The crowd cheered. Silly Rufus bowed, then dragged me away and led me to a pedestrian area where the street opened to reveal Roman ruins. Here we sat outside at a table underneath a white canvas umbrella. When our order came, Rufus raised his water glass to me. *"Buon appetito."*

Thirstily, I raised my glass of Pellegrino and drank, soaking up the sparkling drink, the romance of Verona, and my poet.

"Let me tell you everything I know concerning Verdi's Aida."

"I'm all ears," I said.

"It begins with the story of an extraordinary French archeologist named Auguste Mariette who became fascinated with the figures and hieroglyphs painted on mummy cases. At the height of his professional career while travelling in Upper Egypt in the late 1860s he wrote a short story called *La Fiance du Nil*, The Promised of the Nile. This story he developed into the plot of an opera and in 1870 had four copies printed. Mariette's plot contained a romantic triangle. At its center was the Ethiopian slave girl, Aida."

I listened intently as Rufus described the love triangle. "Sounds like a classic tale."

"Yes," Rufus enthused, "a first-time author, in probing the past, had created a modern classic."

"Thank you, Rufus. I look forward to this evening's production."

"It will be *fantastico*."

"A spectacle," I said.

"Of course," Rufus said, "you saw the props."

We wiled away the rest of the afternoon then returned to the hotel just as the others were checking in at the desk. "*Ciao! Ciao!*"

Despite our enthusiastic and warm greeting, Ed looked at me with disapproval after a little natural hesitation. Yet, once again, he tried to impress by pontificating on Verdi even while we rode the elevator. Did he know he was telling these Italians about their greatest composer? We all grew silent listening to his fussy impotence of stupidity.

"You know, Isadora," Ed said just as the elevator doors opened at our floor, "Aida was written and performed to celebrate the opening of the Suez Canal."

"There, you're quite wrong," Rufus said, standing aside and blocking the elevator doors from closing to give everyone a chance to disembark with their luggage. "I must disabuse you of that misconception. Only this afternoon, I told Isadora the true story behind the opera."

"Chop! Chop!" Clive said, ignoring the sparring young men. He led the way, hurrying down the hall and encouraging us not to dally.

Following Clive's urging, I fled to our room and bolted the door shut with its double lock. "Your cousin is annoying."

"Manners, Isadora."

Looking at mischievous Rufus with his handsome head tilted to one side, I saw he was reminding me to behave the way I had encouraged him to do only yesterday. "Why is he like this?"

"Blame his upbringing. Mummsy said Uncle Stuart and Joan had a shot-gun wedding, only they tried to keep it a secret from him because they're Christian."

"That's no excuse. I find him invasive."

"Invasive. Hypocritical. Greedy. All the worst faults of Christianity, and none of its strengths. Certainly, he doesn't follow the dictum, 'Know thyself. Instead, he likes to know about everybody else. Not a good course; in fact, a road to personal ruin."

"Well, that's a bit dramatic, Rufus, but I agree," I said, thinking how as a poet Rufus was exploring his inner self, the nature of love, and the natural world. No wonder he was so appealing compared to his cousin.

"And, of course, he's jealous."

"Well, anyone can see that," I said.

"Not just normal envy of physical traits, but jealous that Mummsy supports my ambitions to be a poet."

"Why does she?"

Rufus raised his eyebrows. "It was what she wanted to do. Write. But she had to be practical because she came from a poor family."

"Yes," I said recognizing the syndrome of parents wanting their children to walk in their footsteps while they pursue our dreams. I, too, had the same kind of support.

Later, we gathered in the lobby, all suitably dressed for our GOLD seats. When handed my ticket I also noticed it was valued at nearly 200 Euros making the total cost for the six tickets at close to two thousand dollars. Clearly Antonia did not scrimp when it came to the opera. Earlier, Rufus had told me every season his mother had a standing order for the same six seats. When Lucia and Octavio were married, Antonia invited them to attend with Augusta. Lucia claimed it was her best wedding gift, and to this day she still pranced around the farmhouse belting out '*O patria mia*'.

At night, the amphitheatre stood impressively in the center of the ring road. Every arched doorway was lit, and above the ancient brick structure the floodlights from the interior shone against the dark sky. The excitement in the air was visceral. Behind me, Ed remained sober, sophisticated, and suitably unimpressed. His loss, I thought, as I grinned at Rufus in excitement.

When seated, we read our program out loud to each other.

"Conducted by the Israeli, Daniel Oren."

"Costumes by Anna Anni."

"Oh look, Ed," Rufus said, "the soprano is Amarailli Nizza, a blonde bombshell. Think you have a chance?"

"Do we get to meet her after the performance?" Ed asked gullibly. "Maybe an introduction is included in the price. Ask Mummsy?" Leaning my chin on Rufus's shoulder, I hid my head and giggled. He could be a polite bully and a juvenile tease, but I liked him anyway.

The evening was a spectacle, so larger than life its effect swamped all my senses. Verona was the apex of our affair.

Chapter Twenty Four

En route to Trieste, the sun torched our windshield making the skin on our faces burn; the scenery changed constantly and became a blur forcing our eyes to focus on the road ahead; sopranos graced our ears over the radio thrilling our hearts with Italian song. As we had to shout to be heard above the noise of the traffic and the roar of the little engine that was chugging along at high speed, Rufus and I did not talk much. We were content to feel our individual freedom and to thrill in our mutual abandonment. We had packed lightly for our long journey and our hearts were as weightless as our luggage.

Yet all was not frivolity as I had done some research online. Lucia Joyce was born in Trieste. Rufus may stir my senses, but I was narrowing my attention to my subject. Another person crowded my being with words, ideas, details, history. By the time we arrived at our destination, my imagination belonged to her.

Earlier, I had emailed my father that I was going to Trieste., He responded immediately saying he was excited by my prospects and reminding me he had been to The Trieste Joyce School in 2004 during the months of June and July. Since participating in the seminars, he'd hoped they would invite him as a speaker to their annual event, but so far that had not happened. Maybe next year, he emailed. I replied reassuringly that after a year in Zurich he would become well-known, and they would not overlook him again.

I could picture the poster from 2004 my father had framed and hung in his study above his filing cabinet. It was blue and white, showing a stylized profile of James Joyce that ran vertically, starting at the top with an outline of his hat. The number eight, which indicated the eighth annual event, was drawn on a slant to represent his mustache. My father was very proud of all his Joycean paraphernalia.

Our emails about Trieste were more prolific than any correspondence we'd had since I'd left home. I found it amusing that my father did not inquire about my travelling arrangements to Trieste, unlike at Oxford when I'd first arrived, and he practically accused me of being heedless about my personal safety. When I'd shared with Rufus that my father said I must go to the Hotel James Joyce, Rufus immediately booked us a room there. When we checked in, I emailed my father: Have arrived at Hotel James Joyce. Then I giggled like some excited schoolgirl with a secret kept from her parents. Unlike Antonia who gave me her blessing before I left Oxford, my parents said nothing about meeting anyone my own age.

Still, the emails continued. My father was clearly rehashing his own dissertation even though my focus was not on the literary scholarship of James Joyce but on the thwarted career of his youngest child and only daughter. I was curious why Lucia was born in a pauper's hospital. Why was the family poor when her father taught English to immigrants at the local Berlitz school? To that query my father dropped his own bombshell, describing in chronological detail the emotional upheavals James Joyce suffered with his wife and other family members; the financial woes of pursuing a literary career while raising a family; the erratic life of a man living in exile with his unstable family. There was more information than I needed, but I didn't say anything disparaging to my father in case he felt I didn't appreciate his support.

For his part, Rufus was fully supportive in every aspect of my investigative research into the famous author's daughter. The hotel was in a great location for exploring the Adriatic city. It was small, only twelve rooms, and quiet. The dining room where they served a simple breakfast every morning was intimate. It had a low wooden ceiling with thick beams. There was an assortment of small tables covered in white linen cloths and matching straight-backed wooden chairs. The entrance to the cobblestone pedestrian street was arched in stone like a vaulted church. We thought we had stepped back in time as it must have been the same a hundred years ago.

On our first day, we walked everywhere, soaking up the atmosphere along the streets in the old city where remains from the time of the Roman invasion surprised us at every corner. Yet there was more to the quiet city than history and architecture. When we strolled along the harbour we felt the place come to life with the animation of people from all over the world. Soon we came across a full-scale bronze statue of James Joyce on the low Ponterosa bridge over the Canal Grande. It had him wearing a suit with his signature brimmed hat and spectacles. I told Rufus the author would have trouble with his vision later in life.

"That must have been devastating for a man as brilliant and creative as him," Rufus said.

"It was."

Together we stood over the plaque at the foot of the statue reading about the letter the author had written.

Then we continued walking along the harbour, enjoying the area with its slim boats and glittering water. There was a wide selection of eateries, but we chose a local Italian Caffe for lunch which tempted us with its seafood aroma. It served a fabulous brodetto, or fish soup. Then we went to the tourist office in the main piazza and picked up a copy of The James Joyce Trail. In full tourist mode, we followed the little white squares with green lettering that marked the nine addresses where the family had lived while residing in Trieste and the forty-six plaques indicating other addresses of interest. By the end of the day, we were exhausted. That night we decided to rest and eat at the hotel. Bent over our guide, we plotted how we would spend the rest of our time. I wasn't sure how long I would need to accomplish what I wanted to do, but Rufus seemed content with our open-ended itinerary.

"You're a brick," I said.

"I am like a brick," Rufus said, reciting a line. "Sorry, I don't think I'm being original."

I smiled, recognizing how being original was of the utmost importance to my poet.

On our second day in Trieste, we walked to the Piazza Hortis. Facing the square was a large yellow building which housed the public library on the ground floor and the James Joyce Museum on the second floor. Rufus happily visited the library while I explored the museum. Hours later, he climbed the stairs and found me at a table deeply engrossed in my work.

"I thought we could eat lunch outside," Rufus said, brandishing a brown paper bag.

"Aren't you a dear."

"I have to warn you, though, it's hot and humid. I think the temperature has reached thirty degrees Celsius."

"It is the end of July," I said, standing and packing up my computer.

The square was tree-lined with huge conifers and chestnuts. We sat on a bench in the center where it was shady. The city lay sprawled below us. While we ate, we heard the church bells toll from every direction. It was a single sound that echoed the hour.

"I hadn't realized how long I'd been working," I said after swallowing.

"I've never been to this part of Italy. The Istrian peninsula has many different features than other parts of the country. We must take a day off to explore the surrounding hills, the Carso," Rufus said.

"I thought you were being a good influence on my studies and already you're suggesting we play hooky."

"Hooky? As in dodgy?"

I laughed. "No, as in take time off school. Let's, at least, wait until this heat wave passes."

"We have time."

"We do. We have all the time in the world. These are great croissant sandwiches," I said, taking another bite.

"I'm happy writing in the library and walking around the *pedonales*," Rufus said, "so take as long as you need."

Late that night, we took a stroll along the harbour. The atmosphere there was even more lively than during the daytime. Feeling utterly safe, we ventured away from the activity to a corner bounded by the rocky shore and wooden pier. The dark sky was like a planetary curtain with patterns of small sparkles glinting at a distance.

"Look, Isadora," Rufus said, pointing.

My ears absorbed his voice saying my name. It sent a shiver down my spine that was both comforting and cooling. I looked up at the constellation he was identifying for my benefit and smiled in recognition of the Dipper.

"The sky here seems turned upside down," I said. Then I inhaled deeply. "Smell the sea?"

"I do." Rufus nuzzled the top of my head. "And you. I smell you, too."

"What a perfect night."

We returned to the hotel as if walking in a dream.

A few days later we followed the literary trail. When we came across the late author's favourite bookstore, Rufus became very excited. "This place is supposed to be a shrine to the previous owner, the poet Umberto Saba."

We spent over an hour among the shelves. Eventually the current owner asked after our interests. "Then let me show you these," he said, revealing a display of Saba's penciled manuscripts.

Rufus and he lost themselves in the work of the prominent Italian poet. Suddenly, I felt like an outsider, unable to understand anything they were saying as the two were speaking serious Italian, at a language level beyond my comprehension. The experience made me realize how truly generous Rufus had been all week by indulging me in my narrow studies. Humbled, I waited patiently.

"Have you been to the Caffe San Marco?" the bookstore owner asked as we were leaving.

I smiled; grateful he was speaking English. "No."

Rufus grew even more animated and excited. "No, we haven't. We must go there now."

En route Rufus spoke about the literary center that Trieste had been. "It was known as the Austrian Riviera." He hugged me. "I'm so glad we came here."

"Me, too," I said, trying to keep my balance on the irregular pavement of cobblestones while being squeezed around the shoulders.

"The Caffe San Marco has been around since 1914," Rufus said.

We sat outside where the air stirred with a refreshing light breeze. Rufus ordered two espressos. I saw patrons at another table drinking something cool and asked what it was.

"*Frambua*," the waitress said.

"Do you want one?" Rufus asked. "It's like a raspberry smoothie with mint."

"Yes, please. It sounds refreshing."

"*Por favor*," Rufus said.

"You know," I said, leaning into the table. "James Joyce did love Lucia."

"Well, why wouldn't he? She was his daughter."

"When I began my research, I doubted he did. She was devoted to him, but he demanded too much of her and he was partly to blame for her going mad."

"That seems like a modern conceit, blaming the parent."

"That may be," I admitted. "My focus is on dance, but I cannot ignore the domestic situation. When Lucia was born, her father's sisters came to help. They were only too keen to come as they wanted to get away from their father's drinking."

Rufus nodded. "Ah, the Irish."

"First Eva came, but she got homesick, despite the conditions in Ireland which were limited. Then Eileen came, even though the Joyce family lived in rented apartments with little space, and the sisters had to sleep on cots. James was Eileen's favourite brother."

"Yes, well, we saw what those places were like. Mustn't have been too comfortable for a growing family. Of course, nowadays, we're spoiled."

"We are, but James Joyce doted on his baby daughter, even making up songs in Italian for her when they lived here."

"I'm curious. Show me."

I got out my laptop and waited for the waitress to serve our drinks before booting it. Then I brought up the lyrics I'd copied.

Rufus read, "*C'era una volta, una bella bambina / Che is chiamava Lucia / Dormiva durante il giorno / Dormiva durante la notte / Perchè non sapeva comminare*." He sat back and looked into my eyes, translating, "Once upon a time there was a beautiful little girl / who was named Lucia / she slept during the day / she slept during the night / because she didn't know how to walk."

"Thanks," I said, and started to type: Once upon a time…

Chapter Twenty Five

The reward for Trieste was Venice. I could hardly say no to going as it was a fair compromise. While Trieste held Lucia and James Joyce for me, Venice held Elizabeth Barrett and Robert Browning for Rufus. He managed to book a room overlooking the canal. I should have been enthralled by the place but while standing on the Juliet balcony I was transported elsewhere. Trieste was an iconic city for me as it held the visible landmarks of Lucia's childhood. Those memories stirred my imagination. I could picture that city directly across the Gulf of Venice at the top of the Adriatic Sea. Sensing I would have a lifelong preoccupation with Lucia, I became melancholy, feeling as if I was projected into my own future. Looking back at this initial visit, I would surely return.

Trieste was in its heyday when James Joyce lived there. At that time, the bill of lading wherever merchant ships sailed was Via Trieste. Nowadays, it was hardly a remarkable city. While Rufus was happy he had visited, he noted that most Italians hardly knew of its existence, and he was unlikely to return. Maybe, I would have the opportunity to go with my father if and when he was invited to give a talk. However, my father had dropped his own bombshell by telling me I may have to wait to send in my proposal. The Joyce family was getting touchy about their past and ready to sue anyone who revealed anything about their childhood, especially the daughter's.

I heard Rufus stir, get out of bed, and walk barefoot across the floor to me.

"You're sweating," he said, lifting my hair off the nape of my neck and standing so close I felt his bony hips against my fleshy backside.

"Venice in August is hot and humid."

"Are you complaining?"

"No," I said without turning. I kept my gaze on the imagined blue still waters of the sea.

"Had I but plenty of money,
Money enough to spare,
The house for me, no doubt,
were a house in a city square.
Ah, such a life, as one leads
at the window there."
"Let me guess. You are quoting the poet Robert Browning."
"Indeed, I am."
I looked over my shoulder at him. We hugged.
"Let's go back to bed. It's too early to go out."
Rufus's chest was slightly damp against my flimsy nightie. Soon we were slick with sweat. My head felt like sheet lightening. Its brightness gave me a drunken, expansive feeling. Our mutual heat left me tearing at him dramatically. I struggled with the overlap of desire for physical contact and the need for gentle pressure.

Afterward, we took a shower together. The fittings were modern with a high, fixed, wide, rain shower head and an adjustable, flexible hose attached to a smaller shower head. Since the shower cream the hotel provided did not rinse off our skin as easily as gel, we used that as an excuse to vigorously rub each other under the stream of water, playful as toddlers.

The bathroom walls were paneled in cultured marble. The sink and counters were solid marble. The towels the hotel provided were gigantic and plush. Taking turns, we rubbed each other with the soft terry, but no sooner had we soaked up our wetness, then we were damp again with perspiration. We couldn't stop drying the other.

"*Belle tette!*" Rufus said, cupping his hands under my breasts. "*Che bella figura,*" he said, wiping my hips with the towel.

Soon our frisky revelry attracted attention, and someone above stomped on the floor.

Raising his fists, Rufus shouted, "*Pazienza!*"

When we exited the hotel, I realized our room did not face the right direction for imagining the Adriatic Sea in the distance. Since my sense of direction was so topsy-turvy, I grasped Rufus's hand and held on tightly as we made our way through the crowd of pedestrians who were all

listless on this hot day. We had a purpose. We were going to visit the Ca'
Rezzonico on the right bank of the Grand Canal where Robert Browning
died on the mezzanine floor in 1889. At that time, it was the home of his
son, the painter Robert Barrett Browning. Now it was one of Venice's
finest museums. All this was too much information for me. I was in a
conflict of interest as my cognitive brain was preoccupied. My mind was
busy reflecting on my thesis. Most of the time at the museum, I clung
limply to Rufus who expounded enthusiastically on the great poet. I felt
like I was mooning after him, and why not? I was satiated with pleasure.
Yet through the hazy shadow of my thoughts, I did learn that Robert
Browning could not attend either Cambridge or Oxford because his
parents did not belong to the Church of England. They were staunchly
evangelical in faith.

Staring wide-eyed at Rufus, I noted that the cleft in his chin was very
pronounced like the heads of the classical statues on view at the museum.
When I proclaimed my comparative observation, Rufus hinted that he
would not summarily dismiss me, but deal with me later.

Continuing on his quest, Rufus engaged one of the museum guides
in a long conversation while I remained ambivalent. After thanking the
guide, the man said, "Niente." He bowed in a courtly manner from his
waist to the *professore î and îla belle signora.*

Amused by the guide's assumption, I started to speculate. Given that
I was the one working on a doctoral thesis, I was more likely to become a
professor. Pointing to Rufus, I said, "*le bel signor.*" Then I pointed to
myself, indicating that I was the *professore.*

"*Vero?*" the guide asked.

"*Che bella figura,*" I said, eying Rufus and reiterating what he had
said to me that morning.

"*Silenzo!*" Rufus said, grabbing my hand. "*Avanti!*"

Laughing, I followed Rufus outside, tripping over my feet to keep up
with our abrupt departure. "Machismo," I said.

Rufus was not laughing. "What's gotten into you?" he asked.

"Sorry," I said soberly, realizing I was being silly and reminding
myself that Rufus had supported me in Trieste. Indeed, what had gotten
into me?

"Sorry," I repeated, "I'm finding it hard not understanding the language."

Rufus reluctantly agreed. "It is a barrier." Then he shrugged and said reassuringly, "All's right with the world!"

"Who coined that phrase?" I asked, feeling mollified and curious.

"Three guesses."

"I'm in the dark, dear one."

"Hint. Poet."

"Really? R.B.?"

"You win."

We spent another night at the hotel in Venice before travelling north to Asolo. Amid the Venetian Alps, where the landscape was more like buttes than craggy mountain tops, I came to life. The greenery was lush with borders of tall cypress and wispy pines. Best of all, the air was cooler.

Asolo was a walled town. "We must tour the gardens at the Cipriani Hotel," Rufus said when we arrived. "Robert Browning purchased it after losing his beloved Elizabeth. The old villa has been converted into a hotel."

"Sounds wonderful."

It was only a short walk outside town. The unique setting offered views of the rolling valley. The magnificent gardens had a pomegranate tree in the front and a stone walkway around an old medieval well at the back. The air was heavy with the natural perfume of flowers. A solitary woman sat outside. A waiter silently appeared serving refreshment without intruding on the guest's privacy.

"Can we stay here?" I asked, heady with the romanticism of Italy and Robert Browning.

"It's a five-star hotel," Rufus said, not as an enticement, more as a warning. "I'd love to stay here."

"But can we afford it?"

"I don't know. Can we scrounge something up?"

"Yes, let's be brave," I said.

"Aren't I?"

Rising to the challenge, Rufus led me inside to the front desk and boldly asked to see a room. It was spacious. There were dark wooden beams across the ceiling. It was decorated in period furniture. The walls in the bathroom were covered with floral tiles and the floors were covered in terracotta, both local products.

I sighed. It was too rich. "Maybe we could eat here?" I suggested wistfully.

"Maybe we could get married here," Rufus said softly into my ear.

"Is that another one of your mad proposals?"

Rufus twirled me around, laughing with a small tremor of the irrational.

When sober, we returned to town and strolled along the narrow Via Roberto Browning to the main square. There we found a bar with large posters hanging from the ceiling that displayed references to the poet. The owners were twin brothers whom Rufus engaged in noisy conversation.

I looked around the place. It was a mixture of modern and antique. The long bar that divided the serving space from the customers was stainless steel. The bent cane chairs and small round tables could have been a hundred years old. The marble floor and pillars were ageless. It was not a fancy place, but I felt like we had arrived in our natural element. We were comfortable and stayed. People came and went, bringing with them new kinds of desires. Some were locals who depended on the twins to lift their day to the pattern of an acquired Italian life. Many were tourists who seemed to covet the ambiance with infantile dependence. We met a group from Canada being led around by their friend who was Italian by birth. The twins were jovial and full of *bonhomie* for their native son. Cries of *bravaî and imagna* filled the room.

I locked into conversation with the Canadians. They were retired. I filled them in on what I was doing abroad. They too had grown children who studied in Europe. I explained that Rufus was a poet. In fact, he was inspired to write poetry right there and then, so he wandered off to be by himself.

At the end of the afternoon, Rufus left his scribblings with the owners who were delighted to keep the musings of a modern-day Roberto. They asked him to read a verse aloud. Outside, I asked him to translate for me what he had publicly shared.

"It was a poem about the perfume of flowers, the exacting sense of smell so intense at night it attracts the moths who cannot see them, but we can and, because of the moths, we have their beauty during the day."

By evening, we were euphoric, full of the intense reality of underlying feelings we had cultivated toward one another. Hand in hand, we watched the sun set.

"I don't want this to end," Rufus said, his face lighting up with exuberance in the twilight. "I'm challenged to find the words for the thoughts I feel."

"But you're a poet," I said, encouraging him to fill his artistic role and keep the magic of the night between us.

"Where will we go next?" Rufus asked.

"Another town that starts with A," I said, wishing we could hold onto our happiness forever and thinking foolishly we could by staying at the beginning of the alphabet.

"Alba," Rufus said, raising my hand to his lips and kissing my knuckles.

"Perfect," I said, smiling in anticipation, although I was not familiar with the town, but knowing it would be the last place we visited before returning to the villa.

We set off in the morning along the main highway that led to Turin, but rather than turning toward Cuneo, we headed north-east to Alba. Rufus pulled over to the side of the rode. "You drive," he said, jumping out of the car.

"Me?"

He stood outside the passenger door. "Yes, you take the wheel."

"Well, okay," I said, lifting my lower body over the gear box and dragging my legs under the dashboard. Was this a gesture of trust? Was it an acknowledgment of my equality? Or was it simply a need to take a break? Whatever his motive, I found myself in the driver's seat. The secondary road to Alba was quiet that morning which was a relief because I was nervous and rusty like I had been on Antonia's bicycle. Yet, like that earlier experience, after a few false starts, everything went smoothly, and we arrived safely in Alba where we enjoyed a few more days of freedom.

Chapter Twenty Six

My mother had changed. She looked older, mostly because she no longer coloured her hair. It was now natural, somewhere between blonde and grey. She wore it in a tidy bob, kept in order by a black-velvet Alice band which was incongruous with her older appearance. When I introduced Rufus and told her he was a poet she got quite excited and started urging him to read to them.

"Not now," I said, feeling somewhat embarrassed by her outburst.

"You've changed," my father said, kissing my forehead.

When had he ever kissed my forehead? Did he sense other lips had found every part of my body in passionate kisses? Had my mother also sensed the change in me?

Extending his hand, Rufus rose above the occasion. "I'm very pleased to finally meet you, Simon. I've heard so much about you over the years from my parents, and recently from Isadora."

Antonia gave Simon a peck on both cheeks. My father placed his hand on the back of her upper spine while introducing her to my mother. "I'm glad we've finally met," Antonia said.

"Yes," Molly said flitting eyes between her husband and their Italian hostess.

Clive extended his hand to both. "I think it's been a few years since you two met up at a conference."

Antonia and Simon looked at each another. "Let me think," Simon said.

"It was 1990 something."

"Yes, Antonia," Clive said. "You went to Brussels."

"Was that Brussels?" Simon asked.

"I don't remember you ever going to Brussels," Molly said.

"No, no," Simon said, "not Brussels, but somewhere in Europe."

"Antonia's never gone to any conferences outside Europe, have you dear?"

"No, Clive, you're right."

"Well, what does it matter?" Molly asked. "Simon's been to conferences up and down the eastern seaboard."

Clive slapped his knee. "They would like James Joyce there."

I stared at Clive and my parents. I'd never seen Clive behave so gregariously, even when telling his Oxford stories. I'd never seen my parents so suspicious of one another.

Dinah slunk into the hallway and wound her body like a fat skein of wool around Rufus's feet.

"What a lovely cat," Molly said. "What's her name?"

"Dinah," Rufus said, bending to pick her up. Turning to my parents, he said, "I'll show you to your room."

"Let me help," Clive said, picking up Molly's luggage.

"I'll make coffee. Join us in the kitchen when you're settled." Antonia's voice was jaunty.

"Thanks, Antonia," Simon said, flashing her a smile over his shoulder.

Maybe I was reading too much into their exchange, but my father's voice was breezy. Antonia seemed to be flirting. Heaven knows what else she was covertly flaunting.

My mother put her arm around my shoulder. "Come upstairs with me."

I followed.

When the men entered the room together, my mother turned to me. "Are you two in love?"

"Do you have to ask?"

"Has he proposed?"

"Yes. In a manner of speaking."

"What did you say?"

Immediately I felt my Alice in Wonderland life come to an abrupt halt. The family pact changed the contours of my personal landscape. There was nothing for it but to play by the rules, though they smacked of a Harlequin romance novel at worst and a Jane Austen novel at best.

"I haven't given him my answer," I said, recalling Rufus messing around in Verona under Juliet's balcony and at the hotel in Asolo. Here I was presenting his intentions to my mother as serious claims on my affections. "What's your advice?" I asked, hoping to raise my predicament above a Shakespearean drama. After all, our families weren't feuding. Were they?

"Well, I don't know," Molly said clearly astounded. "I must get to know him better."

"Please don't spoil things," I said too late.

"Don't worry. I'll be discreet." Turning a full circle in the upstairs hallway, she asked, "Where's your room?" When I indicated the place, she turned her back on me. "And this must be his room. You have two separate rooms."

"Mom, don't go in."

"I'm just taking a look. What harm is there in that?"

Already, I regretted what I'd said to her.

At that moment the men came into the hallway, hindering Molly's inappropriate snooping. "Let's unpack later," Simon said. "I'd like that cup of coffee."

"I'll join you. Right now, I need a washroom," my mother said making an about turn.

We trundled downstairs leaving Molly on her own. In the kitchen we began with a graceful skittish levity: "After all these years."

"So nice to finally meet your husband and son."

"Your kindness toward Isadora is unparalleled."

Simon was in overload with affluent language and sentiments. I almost felt relief when Molly joined us, until she started lavishing praise on the villa. Since she got no response, she continued headlong, "The drive here was so thrilling, passing lemon and orange trees and olive groves. It's my first time in Italy," she admitted. "How do I say that in Italian?"

"*La mia prima vacanza*," Rufus translated.

"I'm sure it won't be your last," Clive said. "You'll return."

"*Ne vale la pena. Non in attesta della stagione estiva.*"

I thought my mother was going to regret asking for an Italian translation.

"So, you got to Trieste?" my father said, turning his nurturing gaze on me.

"*Stupenda*," Rufus said. "*Lugar maravihoso. Isadora adoro!*"

"We did," I said, "and as you know we stayed at the hotel you recommended."

Simon seemed dumbstruck. He is not a man with a slow brain. He has a doctoral degree. He's been a professor for decades, although not emeritus like our hostess, Antonia. Normally his mouth does not hang open like someone drooling. His aged brain does not have black holes of inactivity from dementia. Yet momentarily, he became a slow-brained, drooling man with suspicious signs of dementia.

Molly rushed in. "So, it seems our children have fallen in love?"

Is this discretion?

"They're young," Antonia said. "But not too young." She looked directly at Simon.

"We were all young once," Clive said.

My father's face turned red.

"Come, Simon. I didn't take you for a protector," Antonia said.

"I already like Rufus," Simon said.

I smiled over at Rufus.

"Where else have you been in Italy?" my mother asked, attempting discretion now that it was too late to save the situation from prying, paternalistic and puritanical parents.

"The Italian Riviera," I said.

"Where they sunbathe topless," Rufus said.

"You went topless?" Simon asked.

"I danced in the sand on the riviera, barefoot," I said, skirting the question. No one went topless while on the beaches at any of the great lakes where we lived, even though they were the size of seas and not crowded.

"You danced?" Molly asked, taking a turn at astonishment.

"While I recited poetry," Rufus said. "Do you want a demonstration?"

"No," Molly said.

"Don't pay any attention to Rufus," Clive said, raising his hand in a papal kind of gesture.

"Rufus likes to tease," Antonia said. "Don't you Rufus?"

My rising feelings deflated like a hot air balloon having an accident. All along, he had been teasing. The truth of our relationship broke into prismatic hues: blue for sadness, red for anger, yellow for embarrassment.

"It's also called the Gulf of Poets. Would you like to visit San Terenzo? San Remo?"

"It sounds romantic," Molly said.

"I was hoping to take you to Trieste someday," Simon said.

"I'd like to go back," I said. "Rufus isn't interested in returning, but maybe we can."

My father laid a heavy hand on my arm. "It is nice to see you. I want to hear all about your research."

"Even though it won't come to fruition as a thesis proposal," I said.

"Someday," Antonia said interjecting. "Isadora told me about your legal concerns. I think there will be a statute of limitations on that front. Just saying, as one of her advisors."

"She's an impressive scholar," Rufus said, dropping his head at a fetching angle.

"Charming," Molly said as if in a reverie. Then she snapped to attention. "What kind of dancing?" she asked, turning to me.

"Modern," I answered. That could mean anything from the last one hundred years. "I took classes from a woman in Oxford."

"Helen," Rufus said.

"Helen," Antonia repeated. "Do you know her, Rufus?"

"No, I understand she's taken by one Michael Joseph," he said, turning to me for confirmation.

"You told him," Antonia said dismissively. "We went to Verona, to the opera."

"Aida," I said, thinking it's always a good tactic to change the topic.

Rufus changed his gaze to my parents. "You'll be so glad to learn that Mummsy didn't plan that for you. Although, if you come back next summer, she might."

"Rufus, do behave yourself."

"I told them you wouldn't mind missing the opera as you never attend at home." Why was I ameliorating for Rufus? After all, he had tried to embarrass me.

"That's right," Simon said, looking soberly at Antonia.

"Verona?" Molly asked. "Isn't that Romeo and Juliet's town?"

"It is," Clive said. "We always attend the opera to see Aida."

"It is a spectacle. Worth seeing once."

"Rufus, are you trying to entice them to return next year?"

"Yes, Mummsy, I am. I have a personal interest at stake." Rufus smiled at me.

"Rufus filled me in on the history of that opera," I said.

"The opera was performed to commemorate the building of the Suez Canal, wasn't it?" Simon asked, seeking approval from either Rufus or Antonia.

"Urban myth," Rufus said, raising his eyebrows at Simon. "See, you have to return to get your history straight. The story behind Aida is as gripping as the opera itself."

"We heard the soprano Amarilli Nizza."

"A blonde bombshell."

"A magnificent voice," Antonia said, taking issue with her son. "We also heard her sing at Covent Garden."

"Ah," Molly sighed. "Pinch me. I must be in Italy. We're talking about opera."

"*Opoglera*," Simon said. "Sorry, I couldn't resist a *portmonteau* in the manner of James Joyce."

"Ogling opera," Rufus said, deciphering Simon's witticism. "What an extraordinary man. I can see why you and so many others study him. We've learned that Mummsy influenced your choice."

"We share birthdays. Hardly influential."

"Well, that is a coincidence," Molly said. "My daughter has probably told you we named her after Isadora Duncan."

"Beware September 14th," Rufus said, imitating a vampire voice.

"Not her birthday, but I'm so glad we're here in time to celebrate it as a family."

"Just don't get her a scarf. I'll write you a poem," Rufus said, tilting his head my way.

"That's so romantic," Molly said.

"I've taken the liberty of inviting my family," Antonia said in her cool voice that was in total contrast to Molly's gushing tone.

"I look forward to meeting them," Simon said.

"More coffee?" Clive asked. "What about something to eat. Biscotti?"

"That would be lovely," Molly said.

"My sister, Augusta, bakes it."

"Homemade," Molly said, continuing to gush. "Isadora, I'm so surprised that you took dance classes. Was this in Oxford?"

"I wanted to experience what Lucia Joyce had experienced, although apparently she was a good dancer. She showed promise."

"You're too modest," Antonia asked.

"Yes, that was her tragedy. She could dance and should have been allowed to dance, but her family and their friends dissuaded her from her true calling. That's my thesis argument." I was as fierce as a tiger in my own defense. I may not have been a good dancer, but I could read, analyze, and put words on paper.

"If Isadora wants an editor, she only needs to ask."

"Please," I said, "you're getting ahead of me."

"I'm confident you'll complete it," Simon said. "We're so proud of you."

"Isadora wants a sister. I have a *cugina*. You'll get to meet her on Isadora's birthday."

"And you have Ed," Clive said, pouring a refill for his son.

"We know you like theatre and ballet," Rufus said. "What about music? Do you like the symphony? I only ask because there is a performance of Respighi's Pines of Rome. It is a 'symphonic poem' that depicts pine trees in four different locations around Rome at different times of the day."

"The pine trees here are majestic. Different from ours," Molly said.

"Isadora wants to go to Genoa, don't you Isadora?"

How did Rufus do it? Since my parent's arrival my emotional landscape ran pell-mell over the fissure and rock of Italy's northern geography. Now I was being offered Genoa. "Yes," I said, smitten by his remembrance.

Chapter Twenty Seven

The photograph taken by Lewis Dodgson was different from my graduation portrait, less conventional but still formal. Molly could not resolve in her mind why I had agreed to sit for this formal portrait. She reminded me that I had always been cranky about having my picture taken.

I was left feeling that by finally doing something right I was still at fault for having done so much wrong in the past.

Rufus fed their unchecked curiosity by drawing attention to the one of me barefoot in the garden that his parents had purchased. Simon and Molly grew more and more curious.

"Barefoot again?" Molly asked.

I felt some empathy for my mother. First, she'd learned that her daughter had danced barefoot and topless on the Italian Riviera. Imagine her surprise to see me barefoot in a proper photograph, although she wasn't quite sure it was proper. I told them about the Charlie Chaplin costume. No point holding back.

"Dressing up?" Molly asked.

This was another surprise. "Like role playing," I said.

"Yes, of course."

"Mother, I didn't expect my full-blown descriptions of the dance lessons I'd taken astonished you."

"Well, you never responded well to the array of dance classes I offered, some taught by me," Molly looked from me to Simon. "And many by various other notable and professionally skilled ladies."

I elaborated on Helen and her studio.

"Yes, yes, I get it. Maybe you were too young."

Antonia was simply skeptical. She doubted such behaviour could be called professional.

"Mummsy never liked Helen."

Antonia turned sharply on her son. "Who told you that?"

Rufus ignored his mother.

Simon took advantage of the lull in the conversation to give us a lecture on the influence of Charlie Chaplin in film. We listened politely. Seeing his audience sag, Simon suddenly became animated and described a scene where a fallen woman emerges from a charity hospital somewhere in the slums of London with a newborn infant in her arms. This scene captivated us. Rufus declared he was thrilled and honoured to be among such brainy people.

Not to be outdone, Antonia followed with a full-blown dissertation on the professional career of Lewis Dodgson as a photographer. Her evidence was no mere subjective analysis of an artist using his imagination, but an examination of his methods in relation to the three theories of truth: correspondence, cohesiveness and pragmatism. She concluded that nowadays a viewer had to recognize the difference between reality and interpretation.

"He was my adviser at the Bodleian," I explained.

"Ah, that's the connection," Simon said.

If I hoped my revelation would put an end to their discourse, I was sadly mistaken. Clive weighed in, willing to tell his guests minute details about Sir Thomas Bodley opening a library early in the 1600s. He seemed used to people paying attention to his chatter like they had on tours around Oxford. The social nature of his mission perked him up, and it impressed Simon who intermittently nodded in recognition of Oxford lore he once knew by heart.

After listening to Clive for nearly an hour, Molly asked, "Who else has these pictures of you?" Clearly, Clive hadn't made an impression on her like he had on me or Simon. Molly wasn't going to be thrown off course by some academic history lesson.

"They're for sale at the gallery," Antonia said.

"They're in a public gallery?" Molly asked. Her gushing surprise was becoming monotonous.

Picking up yet another connecting subject, Clive told us all about Percy, endearingly known to them as Old Winnie, who had bought the gallery when he retired. "He's a dear friend," Clive said. "Maybe you remember him, Simon?"

"I do," Simon said looking at Antonia. "You introduced me to him. You were very close to him as I recall."

Antonia turned red in the face. What was happening, I wondered. First Clive behaved out of character, now Antonia. When had she ever shown embarrassment? My brain felt like a fish swimming in flooded waters. I could only imagine my mother's head space. If we didn't call a halt soon to these proceedings, I could picture her going into overdrive and throwing one of her hysterical fits.

The clock chimed twelve. "Maybe we should all retire," Antonia said. "It's getting late, and these poor people have been travelling for days."

Awake in bed, I wondered about the feelings that were on display earlier. The age gap between Rufus and Lucia was only a few years. She was his substitute sister. He adored her. I was beginning to suspect he'd first found me attractive because I physically resembled her. Surely, since then he had grown to love me for other reasons. I was a match for him intellectually.

Before going to bed, my mother had asked me if I didn't find Rufus too handsome. Her words stung me. Too handsome? The implication was that he was beyond my reach. I was a Plain Jane. I wanted to tell her I was no longer the daughter she knew. Molly had noted the changes in me since living in Europe. Could she not give me any credit?

Unable to sleep, I recalled my conversation with Helen who had older brothers she described as protective of her. I didn't want that kind of male hegemony. Better the devils I knew, but this protective mother was new to me. Did she fear I was experiencing what she had missed? Molly seemed undone by Italy.

My stomach started to feel queasy. Clearly, I found my parents' presence upsetting. I squirmed anxiously on my narrow bed. There would be no nighttime visit. Rufus and I had agreed to be discreet until my parents adjusted to our situation. Now I simply felt resentful. Soon I would have to leave with them. I would be living in Zurich. Rufus would return to Oxford with his parents. We should have eloped in Verona.

I sat up trying to find relief from my troubling thoughts and even more troubling stomach. Why hadn't I taken Rufus seriously? Why hadn't I challenged him? Why hadn't I just said, "Yes," to his outlandish proposals. Maybe they weren't outlandish? Maybe he meant what he'd asked? Maybe he was testing the waters, too shy to appear earnest?

I went to sleep resolved to set things straight between us in the car on the way to Genoa when I would once again have Rufus to myself.

My Father got all excited about the cars. The Fiat owned by Clive and Antonia looked like a small Italian version of a Land Rover, but what really blew his socks off was the sports car. It was an X something. Once again, Simon impressed Rufus.

Dear Clive stood on the driveway filling us in on the details about Fiat. It was founded in 1899 by a group of investors, including Giovanni Agnelli, and was based in Turin. Nowadays, it was the fourth largest European automaker.

Rufus dangled the keys in front of me. "Would you like to drive?" he asked.

Lifting my finger through the ring, I took the keys to the sports car and got into the driver's side. I was confident driving along the Via Cuneo through town. Ahead, my mother kept looking out the back window at us. I told Rufus how my father never let my mother drive.

"Your mother doesn't drive?"

"Yes, she drives her own car, but my father is very nervous having her drive when he's in the car. He says she doesn't know the rules of the road. She does things like driving over the speed limit going down hills and when he tells her to slow down, she says she's driving that way because the car is gaining speed, and he tells her that's what brakes are for. Then she drives over double solid lines onto the bicycle lane to pass a stopped vehicle and, when he reminds her that what she's doing is illegal, she excuses herself saying there was no one in the lane. She doesn't understand that at no time are you allowed to cross a double line. She'd fail her driving test if she had to take it over."

Rufus shook his head in disbelief.

I followed Clive through Cuneo and out of town to the main thoroughfare. Then I panicked. Rufus must have sensed my hesitancy. "Don't worry, Isadora. You'll manage."

His support bolstered my confidence, and I put my foot on the gas pedal after changing gears. On the drive to Genoa, Rufus deliberated on my parents' frame of mind. Did I think their reaction to us was easing? Were they becoming more tolerant of the idea that we were a couple? Although he wasn't sure about Molly's attitude, he thought he was getting on famously with Simon.

Yes, yes, and yes, I said, feeling relieved. My stomach settled. I put a big smile on my face. My prospects were looking up. I could fulfill all my ambitions: finish my thesis, marry Rufus, and live abroad. The wind blew through my hair. What a wonderful life.

Chapter Twenty Eight

On the morning of my birthday, Rufus surprised me before I'd risen. My head was still under the covers when I heard his voice reciting:

"Even in days of thrift
My one birthday gift
A dozen blooms picked by hand
Not cheap, my dear, but grand."

"Rufus, they're lovely," I exclaimed, taking the bouquet and bending my head over the fresh blossoms to inhale their fragrance.

The sound of a flushing toilet greeted our ears when Molly came out of the bathroom. Seeing us together, she came over and stood by my open door. "Happy birthday, Isadora. You're up bright and early, Rufus, and I see you've been out already. Charming," she said and departed.

"Adoro!"

Aware that Rufus was proclaiming his love of the situation, not of me per se, or my mother, I raised an eyebrow.

Rufus growled and leaned closer. "I could eat you up," he said, "but breakfast will have to suffice. *Mi batte il cuore forte ogni volta che vedo amora.*" He handed me an envelope. "For you a love poem as promised."

I took it. "Here I thought you'd already given me my poem."

He took back the bouquet. "I'll put these in water."

Collapsing, I complained, "What time is it?"

"Time to rise. Open the poem later. I don't want you to spoil your appetite." Rufus went into the hallway and made a broadcast that a special birthday breakfast was being served for all and sundry in five minutes. Flashing me a broad smile, he quietly closed my door.

In the kitchen, the aroma of cooking perked up the sleepy adults.

"Maravilhoso," Antonia said, "you've outdone yourself, Rufus." She turned to me, "The only time my son cooks on a special occasion. Take it as an honour."

"I do," I said, sitting at the place set with a single bloom in a narrow silver vase. The bouquet was in a large ceramic vase in the center of the table.

Clive put a CD beside my plate. "We bought this for you in Genoa." Then he rubbed his hands. "Looks scrumptious, Rufus. I didn't hear you get up. I could have helped."

"No need," Rufus said.

Simon and Molly entered with a wrapped gift. "You can open it now, or leave it until this evening," my mother said.

"Maybe, after breakfast." I picked up the CD. "Ah, Pini di Roma. We can listen to this after breakfast too."

Rufus asked me to move the cruet, so he could set a large casserole dish on the table.

"Um, what's this?" Molly asked, leaning forward.

"A crustless quiche with shredded cheese, bits of ham, slices of red and green pepper, as well as some onion. It's spiced with nutmeg and lemon zest." Rufus extended his hand to Molly for her plate to serve her first. "Pass the rolls, please, Papa."

Clive offered the basket to Molly.

"There's orange juice in the pitcher. Anyone for champagne?"

Everyone agreed to save the bubbly for the evening. After breakfast, we retired to the front room where Clive played the Respighi CD.

I lifted the heavy gift from my parents. "What's in this?" I asked, weighing the contents in my arms, but first I opened the card. "I can't believe I'm a quarter of a century old," I said, passing it to Antonia to share around the room.

"Still young," Clive said.

Lifting a pair of ski boots out of the box, I displayed my gift.

"We'll buy you a ski pass this winter," Simon said then turned to Rufus. "Do you ski?"

"Certainly."

"Then you're invited to join us."

I grinned. That cinched it. Everyone grew animated with cross conversations about where to ski, what equipment to wear, and how to assess snow conditions. This talk morphed into anecdotes about skiing holidays and accidents.

Suddenly, breaking the fervour, Molly said, "This is the movement I like best."

Everyone grew still and listened.

"Respighi's fourth," Clive said.

"*Pini di Via Appia*," Rufus said.

"Yes, I like this one, too," Antonia said. "It builds. The haunting wind carries it forward. Then the full orchestra comes in followed by a rhythmic drumbeat. The first movement is all fast and the third all slow. *Pini di Via Appia* is the culmination."

Molly started to sway. "I could dance to this piece."

"Please do," Clive said. "Don't let us inhibit you."

Extending her hand to me, Molly rose. "Isadora?"

"Mother?" I asked, incredulous.

"Go on, Isadora," Rufus said.

I took her hand. Her palm was slippery with sweat but she held my hand with her strong fingers. Her swaying hips encouraged me to find the rhythm. When she lifted her body on the balls of her feet, I rose too. Molly moved beautifully. Her limbs were lithesome and seemed to float in curves as if she had no joints to give her angles. After a few minutes the music ended, and she held me in her arms. "You impress me," she said softly into my ear. "I'm so happy for you." Then curtseying, she held my arm aloft and returned me to my chair beside Rufus.

I blinked back tears, feeling overwhelmed by her gesture of love.

Much later, Octavio and Lucia arrived. We gathered together again coming from various parts of the house and garden.

"*Un'insegnante di danze*," Lucia said when introduced to Molly.

"*Professora*," Rufus said.

Lucia looked confused but smiled hospitably.

"*Un'altra cosa!*" Rufus turned to Simon and Molly. "She doesn't understand." Then he excused himself from the rest of the company and started into an elaborate explanation for Lucia and her family.

Molly said she hadn't known she could cause such a stir.

Immediately, I recognized that my former self would have cynically dismissed my mother's statement as a lie. Now I felt more magnanimous toward her. "Rufus is always very generous with his family," I said.

"*Penso ci dell'apparente errore la vera precisione*," Antonia said, ushering her relatives to the table. "It's time for a champagne toast. We've waited all day for this."

After the toast, we ate and drank until satiated. Then came a birthday cake that Augusta had baked.

"Speech," Rufus said, prodding me to stand.

"*O mio dio*," I said for the native speakers. "What a day it's been: a bouquet of flowers presented very early this morning, thank you, Rufus—more gifts, thank you, Mother and Father and Clive and Antonia—a special breakfast, dinner, and a delicious birthday cake—thank you, Augusta—dancing, a toast,—thank you, everyone—and now a speech." Quelling my jittery stomach, I stood. "Coming to Italy has changed my life," I began.

Rufus translated.

"*Bravissime*," Octavio said.

"*Indimenticabile*," I said, and continued in English, keeping each phrase short and waiting for Rufus to translate. Ending, I said, "*Non sono Italiana.*"

"*Si, Piedmonta.*"

I thanked Lucia. "What I meant to say is, I may not be Italian, but I just want to say how happy I am that I have met all of you and that my parents were able to join us."

"*Stupenda*," Lucia said after Rufus translated.

"We are honoured to be invited and hope to return," Simon said.

"Our home is your home," Clive said, "here and in Oxford."

Weary from a full day, we rose. Everyone helped in cleaning up. Simon and Molly stacked the dirty dishes and cutlery, Octavio carried heavy platters into the kitchen, Lucia lifted the dishes onto the counter, Augusta rinsed everything, Antonia washed, Clive dried, and Rufus and I put things away.

"You know where everything goes," Clive said, handing me a glass.

"She does," Rufus agreed. "She can come back."

I took the wet towel from Clive and whipped it at Rufus.

"You two behave," Clive said. "I need to get a dry one."

When done we all embraced in good Italian style, but Antonia was uncharacteristically restrained. Eventually, I realized this is the kind of observation once made cannot be unmade. I kept looking at her, wondering what was troubling her. Finally, she asked us all to sit down for a serious talk.

Clive played the role of usher. He didn't seem particularly surprised by his wife's request.

She said she had vowed never to tell anybody. However, she felt she needed to be honest with us. "Lucia is not Augusta's daughter." Then she looked directly at Simon.

Havoc ensued.

"*Scempio!*" Augusta raised her arms and said, "*Permissione!*"

What? She'd given permission? Lucia stood and started a spiel in Italian that even the Italians had difficulty following.

"Simon, did you know?" Molly asked.

"No, of course not."

Molly turned to Antonia. "Can you please explain?"

Against a backdrop of raving Italian, Antonia said, "Yes. You know Simon and I were at Oxford together. We were young and when I'd returned home from Oxford I learned I was pregnant." She looked at her sister. "It so happened that Augusta had had a miscarriage, so she pretended to be Lucia's mother. It was easy to fool everyone outside the family. You see where we live. It was even more remote back then. I was able to eventually return to Oxford and enroll in post-doctoral studies."

I sat beside Molly and took her hand. She sat stoically beside me staring down into her lap. Simon stood, then sat back down. Rufus got up and stood beside Lucia trying to calm her. She was quietly hysterical, demonstrative, but not loud. She was concentrating on her cousin's words. Octavio had his arm around Augusta's shoulders.

Clive came around with water for everyone. His presence gave a calming effect on the general hysteria. Then he stood between the two groups and dropped a bigger bombshell. "There's more. You see, I'm infertile."

"But how can you be?" Rufus asked. "I'm your son."

Clive simply turned to Antonia. "You explain, dear, since you're confessing."

Antonia held her son's gaze. "You're Percy Winchester's offspring."

Chapter Twenty Nine

A t night in my garret, I watched the lights go on in the building opposite our apartment. Those lone occupants were my only company as I refused to go downstairs to my parent's flat. I was determined to remain in solitary confinement where I had everything I needed: a single bed, an en suite bathroom, and my laptop. Simon and Molly didn't know it yet, but I was on a hunger strike against the abomination of our family secret.

The drive to Zurich had been hell on wheels. Throughout the entire journey, my mother was hysterical. Her histrionics seemed a manifestation of madness. My father was stoic, mostly because he had to concentrate on navigating the roads. I was demoralized: fragile, fretful, and full of speculation. Just as my life was looking up, my family's circumstances had led me on a downward spiral into a slump of rejection and remorse.

Mostly, I was confused. Was I really related to Lucia? All my life I'd wanted a sister and now that I had a half-one, I felt miserable. Antonia's revelation seemed savagely capricious. What was she seeking? Atonement? Forgiveness? Was she simply unburdening her guilt after years of living a lie? Lucia didn't know the truth about her parentage. That last night before our departure was nightmarish. Of course, Augusta had always known. Augusta, who'd stayed home and miscarried, was a willing accessory to her sister's secret.

What really messed up my mind was realizing Rufus was now a blood relative. I kept returning to that troubling thought. Somehow, Rufus was related. The more I scrutinized our bond the more I was convinced our relationship verged on indecency. We were demeaned by the indiscretions of our parents. I felt as if Lucia's illegitimacy made us illegitimate too. Rationally, I knew I was wrong in thinking that, but I couldn't convince myself otherwise.

Yet Rufus too was in shock. He too was illegitimate. Everything was shocking. Shocking! Shocking! Shocking! Of course, Rufus wasn't related. Since learning that my father was Lucia's father, I immediately speculated that Rufus was also fathered by Simon. But he wasn't. If Antonia was telling the truth. Was she telling the truth? She claimed, after all these years, she was. I saw her as a she-devil: I have gathered you here for the big reveal—your father isn't really your father—your mother isn't really your mother. Antonia was a very small woman to be a fertility goddess. Yet she'd conceived two illegitimate children. So much for being educated.

Lucia was my half-sister. Lucia was also a half-sister to Rufus. We had all got what we wanted. No longer an only child. Raised as an only child, but not.

Shouts. Tears. Anger. Confusion. We fled very early the next morning after a night of insomnia.

Above the fifth storey of the building opposite, I could see the cloudscape of the night sky. There would be no stars tonight, no sparkle to wish upon and make this nightmare go away. There was no consolation in this, and much reproach. Through the squall of emotional upheaval, my father had shown no remorse. I hadn't given him a thought during our long-suffering journey or upon our restrained arrival. My mother had filled our common space, and my own confusion had filled my private world. Now, I felt disapproval toward him. He was a James Joyce scholar who was no better in his personal life than that great literary man, but I knew I was wrong in blaming my father. Irresponsible behaviour was evident nowhere else in his character. His was a naughty deed in an otherwise good life. I told myself not to judge him. All those times he had seen Antonia at conferences, she evidently had never spilled the beans. She had concealed the secret for years. From their brief time together, Antonia and Simon had issued an offspring. Who was the naughty party? Who was nice? Their fairy tale existence mocked.

I closed the curtains, no longer curious about the world outside my garret. Instead, the world inside my head was pressing with the force of a turbine hum, demanding attention. I wanted to make it stop. Too anxious to sleep, I paced the tiny space between the end of my narrow bed and the door to the bathroom. Intermittently, I crossed the threshold and poured myself a glass of water. The world was full of suffering. I was a fool in paradise. My paradise was now tarnished.

Exhaustion didn't claim me. The clock displayed the hour. Precise Swiss time mocked me. No sleep for the weary. No sleep for this pilgrim. I was becoming as hysterical as my mother.

Here was the key. I had to stop thinking of them, those adults who had spoiled everything: Antonia with her child alias her niece, my father with his scholarly companion alias mother of his first child, my mother with her hysterical indignation. She'd been only too willing to travel to Italy to meet the sponsor of my studies and her husband's old college chum. Hah! To visit the ancestral villa. Hah! To take a year off to live in Switzerland. Hah!

And Rufus? Dear Rufus. Poor Rufus. Hadn't I noticed a likeness between him and Percy. What had Lewis said to me, something about we were all young once. Did Lewis know? Maybe I should meet with Lewis, or at least, contact him. I suspected he knew more than he let on.

I was getting angry. Better anger than hurt. I was so riled up that dawn broke and I still hadn't slept. The narrow bed mocked me with its untouched covers. Breathless, I fell on top of the spread where a sudden and debilitating warmth overwhelmed me. Where was the intimacy? That was what I missed. I felt an ambush of tenderness steal over me. I wanted Rufus. He wasn't a blood relative. I had finally fully realized that much. We just shared the same half-sister. How must he feel? He'd always wanted a sibling. He got one right at the same time I got a sister. Lost and found, Lucia was like an urchin. No wonder she was so mischievous and dramatic. Augusta had made the same mistake with her adopted child that she'd made with her own life. Augusta had kept Lucia home, close to her apron strings. No education for Lucia. No independence. No personal fulfillment. No following her muse.

I thought of Helen and our vow. We would follow our muse. We wouldn't let others thwart our ambitions. We wouldn't end up like Lucia Joyce. Rolling over I stared up only to discover I couldn't determine if I was looking at the sloped ceiling or the slanted wall of my room. They were both one and the same. Even my garret was topsy-turvy, much like my life. Conflicted about my future, I lay like that for what must have been hours. Eventually, I heard a soft knock on the door.

"Isadora," Mother called. "Would you like some breakfast?"

"Okay." Soon, she departed. Hearing the muffled sounds of great minds below, I started to laugh. It was an appalling laugh. They would continue with their lives as it was apparent this setback was not going to derail their marriage. They would continue with their careers, Simon gaining more recognition as a Joycean scholar and travelling to Trieste without me, Molly by his side. They would face the world with stoicism, shaking their heads at their one regret, a life marred not by the illegitimate daughter hidden away in a foreign land.

Somewhere in the city a church bell rang. It was a distant clang but pronounced enough to compel me out of my self-indulgent reverie. Rolling onto my side, I placed my right hand under the pillow below my chin and raised myself off the bed. My bare feet touched the cold, wooden floor. I tiptoed over to the bathroom, trying not to make a creaking noise, peed into the bowl, hoping not to make a splashing sound, and poured myself glass after glass of tap water, gulping for air between swallows. Staring at my face in the mirror, I watched my eyes well as warm tears trickled down my cheeks. The drops tasted salty on my lips.

"Can I please just have my life back," I whispered. Of course, you can, dear. Who said that? You're behaving more like Lucia than Isadora, the voice in my head said.

Again, I sat on the toilet. Then determined I needed to get clean, I showered.

When I was freshly dressed, I opened the curtains and let in the daylight. I looked down at the bustling street thinking how the world would go on without me. I could stay for forty days, or I could join the fray. Below the roar of a truck sounded like engines sounded everywhere. My thesis delayed, but not abandoned. My love life delayed, but not abandoned. I must have looked pathetic to anyone who could see me at my garret window. Yet, who was looking? No one. No one was looking in; only me looking out. "Give me strength," I whispered.

Turning to the interior where there was no desk, only a chair beside a dresser, I sat down with my feet propped on the bedside. Opening my laptop, I determined to join the world. My unanswered emails included several from Rufus and one from Helen. Choosing to go gingerly, I answered Helen first, telling her that I was indeed now in Zurich. Obviously, she was online because right away she responded, listing dance classes held in Switzerland that I could attend because I might be interested in investigating a method named after Margaret Morris. I could have responded by spilling out my heart to her, but email messaging seemed too crass for my sensitive subject.

I knew the name, Margaret Morris, having come across her in my research on Lucia. Thanking Helen, I said I would take up her suggestion. Then I bookmarked her email.

I read and deleted all the other emails before opening the ones from Rufus. They made a chronological portrayal of a young man who was clearly tormented by his mother's sudden revelation. While I had been holed up in my garret, he had written. I could track the progress of his thoughts through his emails. His agony paralleled mine. We had been on the same journey, alone. He was sorry. "*Mi dispiace.*"

I emailed back that I too was sorry. I commiserated with him, telling him I had endured similar misery. Then I told him I was going to pick up my work and restore my physical being by taking dance classes in Margaret Morris Method. I said nothing about my longing for his company or missing our aimless days of discovery. With the perspective of memory, I looked back on our time together as unreal. It couldn't last, but I wished for renewal. If our time together meant anything, surely he would desire to reconnect on some level, surely his feelings were mutual, but how could I put my desire in words? Where was the poetry now when we needed it? I sent my feeble reply.

Then I visited the website for Margaret Morris Method. There was a contact that I clicked on and asked for more information about classes held in Switzerland and whether or not I could join. Was I even qualified to attend?

When I returned to my emails, I saw a new one from Rufus. It read: Papa says Margaret Morris was The Dark Flower. Rufus also expressed his gratitude that I had not said, "*Arrivederci.*"

Papa. That was a good sign. Clive was still Papa.

I googled "The Dark Flower". At the bottom of the first page, I saw a site for the book The Dark Flower on Goodreads. There, I read about the main character called Mark Lennan whose Spring, Summer, Autumn, and Winter years and loves are explored with deep sensitivity. I wasn't sure I was on the right subject of reference until I saw the name of the author of the book. John Galsworthy.

I pulled up more information on John Galsworthy. He was an English writer and playwright whose literary career spanned the Victorian, Edwardian, and Georgian eras. He was also a renowned social activist and outspoken advocate for the suffragette movement, prison reform and animal rights. As well, he was the first president of PEN and was awarded the Nobel Prize in Literature in 1932.

There was a black and white photograph. John Galsworthy was a handsome man with a high forehead and defined brow. Rufus had his eyes. Clive had his nose and chin. Yet I knew there wasn't a connection. The similarity was simply a coincidence.

When I googled "Margaret Morris" and clicked on the Wikipedia site, I found she made for very interesting reading. John Galsworthy had encouraged her to open her own school in St. Martin's Lane, London, which she had first called Margaret Morris and her Dancing Children. She was the choreographer and principal dancer for "The Little Dream," a fantasy by John Galsworthy. It was rumoured that as a young woman she'd had an affair with him. I would later learn that it was a platonic relationship, more her wishful thinking. There was also information about her connection to Raymond and Isadora Duncan. He was the original hippie and had taught her the six Classical Greek dance positions which she adapted and used as the basis of her own system of movement.

Remembering I'd come across that connection earlier, I closed my laptop and hunted through my research books until I found a picture of Margaret Morris. She could have been one of his loves. Her beauty was of a dark flower. She wore her hair pulled off her face. She had long limbs and danced barefoot. Clearly, she had followed her muse.

At the back of the book, I sought the references to her connection to Lucia Joyce. At one point Margaret Morris had taught Lucia. So, a student! Immediately, I decided I too would be a student, but unlike Lucia, I would not turn away from dance to be muse to my father.

My resolve was tested. Molly was upbeat, relentlessly so, overcompensating in a way that made me want to call her by her first name. Molly, I wanted to say, struggling to suppress what: mockery, indignation, contempt? Did I want to reveal my feelings to her, my confusion, my disbelief? No! How could she not have known? How could they have not known? Molly had wanted the invitation to the villa. That was Molly's idea. The memory of her asking me over the phone made me want to curl up in weakness. I had done her bidding.

Mother. Molly. Margaret. MMM. I made a connection. Was Margaret Morris a mother-substitute for Lucia Joyce? Maybe, but I could not make such a conjecture without gathering evidence. I could not presume like some ill-trained detective. Just because my relationship with my mother had changed did not mean Lucia had felt the same need. Yet I wondered, do all young women seek substitute role models? It made perfectly good sense if examined through the lens of social psychology. I tucked away that thought to examine later.

Simon sensed I had slipped out of my old skin. His suspicions that I had changed since leaving home were doubly confirmed. Finding true love; discovering a half-sister; substituting my parents with other role models: these were transforming.

Yet I didn't abandon my parents. I had to get on with my work, stick with my resolve, become independent. Until I achieved those goals, I needed some financial assistance. I added applying for a grant to my list of goals. Molly's advice.

Rufus wanted me to tell him what I was feeling. He reassured me that he could help. He told me not to abandon hope. He ended his email, "Do what you have to do."

"What about you?" I replied.

"*Io me so' mmiso scuorno e vergognaria.* I am so angry and embarrassed," he translated.

"Please don't be," I replied. He was upset, and I was too. I could bring sunniness into his world. How could he look at me and not see the resemblance to his half-sister? Was this why he had fallen in love with me? It was a chilling thought, an incestuous idea. Just when I had convinced myself that we were not in an incestuous relationship I was made aware again of that mundane thought. Our lives belonged in a 'True Confession' magazine. Appalling memories of pubescent girls reading those rags purchased from the stacks at the corner convenience store cursed me. I never identified with those girls. They repelled me. They were ignorant bullies always ready to jeer at anyone who showed an interest in learning. They reduced everyone and everything to the lowest common denominator. In this way, they kept themselves down. They wouldn't keep me down.

At breakfast I told my parents of my plans, then slipped away from the apartment and walked the streets of Zurich. Memories of Rufus easily invaded my mind. I became a danger to myself: unfamiliar with the surroundings, I nearly stumbled into oncoming traffic; stunned by the blinding luminosity of my thoughts, I literally bumped into obstacles; burdened by my loss, I carelessly hurtled my body forward. This love was my grief.

After hours of walking, I came to a lake and found a bench where I sat. If only I was more aware, I could appreciate the lovely scenery and my sophisticated surroundings, but I was suffering which seemed silly, but I was too self-absorbed to care how silly I appeared. Hadn't I been happy in love? Wasn't I once seized by love? I came back from the wanderings of my thoughts. Inside, I felt grown up. I could return to calm for a moment. Here was a glimpse of reality. My love for Rufus would never be the same as it was on the mountain top in Italy. Those were our halcyon days. A storm would not rupture our love. Now, I was in the valley looking out over the water, wondering if I was at sea level, certain I had not drowned.

Later I contacted Lewis. "How was Italy?" he asked.

"As you probably guessed Rufus and I fell in love."

"He's right for you."

"Thank you, Lewis," I said, thinking what a sweet man he was. "But Antonia and Clive dropped some family news that came as a shock to everyone. Did you know about Rufus's parentage?"

"Yes, that doesn't affect your relationship."

"No, I just thought you would be privy. You're very loyal."

"A family friend."
I didn't tell him more.

Chapter Thirty

Three weeks later, I took the train to Lausanne. Earlier in my travels I'd put my faith in finding the real Lucia, my hope in revealing her agony, now I expected to discover her happiness. Tracing her route to the one ambition denied her, I followed her footsteps to a dance method she had explored. Whenever my mind wandered off that goal, I reminded myself to stay true to my own aspirations and focus on Lucia Joyce as a student of Margaret Morris. This gifted woman had been her mentor, if only briefly. I could hardly wait to meet those who were carrying on her work. My Swiss contact in Lausanne was Dominique. She invited me to stay with her for two nights, the duration of a special workshop with a guest teacher from England, a woman named Jan Millard.

Earlier in my research, I had read that the young women who were Lucia's friends had admitted to being somewhat afraid of her father. While riding the fast Swiss train, I pondered their attitude. What caused their timidity? What made them anxious? To understand Lucia's happiness, I would also have to understand her underlying anxiety. These friends were all artistic by nature. Was it as simple as cowering under the presence of a great artist? Recognizing that they may have voiced such sentiment, I knew there was more to their fear. They lived in an era that treated artists with suspicion and a time when parents educated their sons. Lucia thought her father knew everything. She was obedient and consequently lived a restricted life. Was it this attitude that made her friends cower?

My musings always brought me back to myself. In some ways I too had lived a restricted life as I had lived at home until the past spring. Yet, unlike Lucia, I was well educated and had experienced a student's life on campus. However, like her, I had no financial independence. Simon was only too willing to fund my weekend trip to Lausanne. He was so full of guilt, he would have continued to fund me as long as I asked, but I had reassured him that it was only a matter of time now before I received a grant which would make me independent of his wallet.

Thankfully, the modern world was freer than Lucia's. Women were enrolled in post-secondary institutions in record numbers. More to the point, I recognized my father did not know everything. Although he was a scholar, his expertise was limited to one author. Yet, he had been my mentor. Both my parents had supported me in my education. I had to give them credit for that much, but I was at a crossroads of expanding my trust. Whether or not my parents fully trusted my decision to pursue the course I was on they still obligingly agreed to assist me in studying MMM. They recognized the amateur dance movement had some bearing on my thesis, so I was at liberty to follow my muse, to further my education, even to contradict them and their work if it came to that end.

Dominique had insisted on meeting me at the train station as she lived outside Lausanne on the mountain side. She had described to me what she would be wearing and reassured me that I could not miss her. True to her word she wore a pink t-shirt with a sparkling figure that celebrated MMM. It was their centenary year and the shirt glittered with the numeral 100. She kissed me on both cheeks in greeting.

Laughing in relief that I was so easily accepted by this gracious woman, I stepped back and complimented her on her top. She told me in a French accent that she had purchased it at Chichester University where MMM held their International Summer School. Then she said we had to wait at the train station for Jan who would be arriving soon, so we found two seats side-by-side where we could watch the arrivals board. Dominique asked me if I had had a good journey.

"My trip was quick and easy, but I must admit I didn't pay any attention to the scenery. It flew by so quickly I got dizzy looking out the window."

Dominique assured me that Swiss trains were always on time. Then she asked if I minded sharing a room with Jan.

"*Pas de probleme*. I can speak French," I said, but Dominique answered that she liked to practice her English with her guests.

"And, of course, Jan speaks English."

"You are being very hospitable. I can check into a hotel or inn if it's more convenient."

"No, no," she insisted. "You will have more fun if you come with us. Jan likes to stay with me because it is for her like a holiday. She works very hard teaching us. With me, she can relax after class. You, too."

"I've never taken classes before in MMM."

"You will learn quickly," Dominique said. Reassuring me, she explained that Jan would be teaching some advanced colours, but not everyone attending was in the higher levels. I was not to worry because Jan would accommodate all the participants, even those, like me, at the Basic level.

"I'm happy just to watch. Sometimes, I'll be taking notes," I said, not admitting I wasn't used to dancing all day, let alone all day for two or three consecutive days.

Dominique laughed and said that everyone takes notes. "We are updating our syllabus."

"Yes, is it okay if I use my laptop in class?"

Dominique shrugged. "That depends on the teacher. We will ask Jan."

"Right," I said, alert to her nuance that I must respect the wishes of a guest teacher. I started to formulate in my mind what I would say to this Jan. Would she intimidate me like James Joyce had intimidated Lucia's friends? There was no predicting an artistic temperament.

Standing, Dominique said, "This is her train."

I remained seated, watching her. Dominique was nervous in anticipation. She was a petite person with sinewy muscles showing along her thin limbs. Suddenly, she ran down the platform to a large woman with cropped, red hennaed hair. They hugged and Dominique took the woman's soft shoulder bag while Jan pulled her hard piece of luggage. I wondered why she carried so much for a weekend event.

Hoisting my weekend bag over my arm, I stood and waited for the two women to approach. They were talking nonstop and laughing constantly. When Dominique introduced me, Jan's eyes bulged in amazement. "Any relation to the Isadora Duncan?"

"None."

"You know Margaret was a contemporary of Isadora's," Jan said.

"Yes. The anniversary of Isadora's death, September 14th, 1927."

"How many years is that? Life must have been so dull for her when she wasn't on stage under the lights with an audience in front of her."

"It was eighty-three years ago."

Jan seemed impressed by my calculation.

"Did you know Margaret Morris?" I asked.

"I met her a few times," Jan said.

"Do you know what Margaret thought of Isadora?" I asked.

"From what I've heard she found her flamboyant."

"Well, her impromptu lightness was her tragic end," I said. I reminded myself not to play the academic role all the time.

"You won't find we're like her. Hardly impromptu," Jan laughed. "Full of discipline."

"Isadora will tell you all about herself in the car. Follow me," Dominique said, disappearing into the crowd, clearly impatient to be on the road.

Out of respect for my elders and my hosts, I sat in the backseat with my luggage. The trunk had limited capacity, only enough room for Jan's two pieces. She and Dominique talked incessantly on the drive. I learned that Jan was a substitute teacher for the workshop, invited after the artistic director became sick.

Anticipating the weekend ahead with the dance group made me feel nervous. Was I really up to the task? Thinking about the past made me depressed and thinking about the future made me anxious. How to overcome depression and anxiety? I needed to be mindful of the present. I was in an unfamiliar place with strangers to learn about an activity I only knew through reading. I told myself to keep my wits about me, to stay alert, and to profit from the opportunity to become familiar with MMM. I would need many such reminders in the days ahead.

Twenty minutes later, we arrived at Dominique's magnificent property. "I'm so glad to be back here," Jan said when she got out of the front seat. Reaching into the trunk to retrieve her bag, she said to me, "We'd better crack on."

I followed Jan to our shared bedroom. Since she had visited before, she knew the routine. While I settled in, she muttered over every item she unpacked. At one point, she scrambled through the piles of papers and notebooks she had arranged on top of the dresser, seemingly unable to put her hands on what she wanted. Then she frantically turned, mumbling under her breath what a ninny she was.

"Can I help?" I asked.

"No," Jan said, not rudely, more in frustration. Abruptly she left the room, calling, "Dominique, I forgot my notes on magenta."

Since I had no idea what she was talking about I minded my own business. Left alone and wanting to touch base with the familiar, I opened my computer and texted Rufus who was still in Italy. He had refused to return to Oxford with his parents. I told him I had arrived safely in Lausanne. Immediately, he replied with an attachment which I opened. It was a love poem:

Before the beginning of Summer
Time was all I had on hand.
The season brought love made warmer
By the company of you, my grand
Passion that blossomed with pleasure.
Your memory is all I have now.
Pain flattens my soul, eager to cure
Your return will lighten my brow.

Breathing nervously under the dread of interruption, I took the time to reread his poem. Hot tears smarted my eyes. His message was clear. My initial response was troubled. Why was I in Switzerland? Why wasn't I in Italy? What would become of us?

Jan reentered. "Oh, dearie, what's the matter?"

Clicking on the red X box, I closed my email account and stared at the blank screen in confusion. Had I accidentally erased his poem? "Just reading an email."

"Did something awful happen?"

Underneath the desire for secrecy was a greater desire to talk about myself. "I got a love poem," I gasped.

"How romantic. I wish someone would send me a love poem." Jan placed some sheets on top of her pile of papers and notebooks.

I gazed at Jan's back. Unable to keep silent, I said, "It's complicated."

"Life is complicated. Love makes life more complicated."

Could I trust this woman? She was a stranger. Why not make Jan my agony aunt? I felt a compunction to describe the labyrinth of my love-life. The protocols of travel had kept me contained. Concealing the secrets of my life made me breathless as if I was starving for air. "He's a real poet."

"Blimey, that's my problem. I've never fallen for a poet. What's he like?" Jan sat beside me on the bed and patted my knee.

Unwilling to reveal the full horror of my predicament, or disturb the approval of her maternal ignorance, I simply told her he was the son of my sponsor at Oxford. She nodded for me to continue, so I told her more bare facts with no embellishments: how I had met him at his family's villa in Italy; how my parents had visited; how I had left with them to travel to Zurich.

"Now you miss him and wish you were there."

"Yes," I admitted, thinking something like that, trying not to imagine how I could return and face him and Lucia without revisiting the awful truth of our relationship.

"Chin up, lovey. It'll all work out in the end. I promise."

I smiled. Jan's way of talking reminded me of Clive. Dear Clive. I started to wonder how he was. In the brouhaha, I had not given him a thought. Now, I felt compassion. Poor Clive. We all deserved some compassion, even my parents, but forgiveness was still unlikely in my mind. Not until I got my life back in order.

Jan jumped up, saying we should get ready to eat. Dominique had the table set. Closing my laptop, I followed her and contemplated how I would later respond to Rufus.

These women were indefatigable. We no sooner finished eating than we had to get ready to go to class. In our room Jan approved of the outfit I wore. I looked down at the bright blue leotards and patterned top with a bra insert, explaining I had purchased some clothes in Oxford for dance classes with Helen.

"Were you there to study dance?"

"No, that was just a sideline. Lucia Joyce is my main focus."

"How, exactly, does Margaret Morris fit in?" Jan asked, turning her back to me. She picked up some notes from her pile and packed her bag.

I could see Jan was losing interest in my academic pursuits, so I decided to leave her question hanging. Her main focus was getting to class. Dominique was waiting for us with the car idling.

When we arrived at the studio, I saw a few others wearing the same top as Dominique. Some were different colours: red, crimson, mauve. One young woman wore a royal blue one. She seemed mentally handicapped in some way, maybe Down's Syndrome, and she was with an older man who appeared to be her father. There was one other man, younger, of Japanese descent. Otherwise, those assembled were females of varying ages. A couple of women introduced themselves to me. They all greeted Jan enthusiastically, but it was another woman, Christine, who led the class in a warm-up. I stood at the back of the class where I could relax in appreciation of the opportunity to move my body and limbs. Those in front of me showed a range of abilities. Some seemed as talented as the professionals in Helen's class, but I was relieved to recognize there were many amateurs, able bodied, but not necessarily stage quality.

Christine formally introduced Jan, although everyone already knew her. Jan assumed her role as guest teacher and thanked everyone for attending, apologizing on behalf of the artistic director who sent his love to all. "I'm going to start with Basic Arm Exercise," Jan said.

Basic sounded all right to me until the music started. It was a classical piece played on the piano. I tried to follow Jan's directions, raising my arms sideways, touching my palms overhead in a diamond shape, moving my arms down to shoulder level in a horizontal line, turning my head to the right and then to the left. I didn't know where to look to keep up with the movement. Everyone but me knew what to do. They were trained. I was the novice.

"Now for White Hurdling Balance." Jan smiled. "I've picked one exercise from each colour. Later, think about what colour exercise you want to review."

This time I knew better than to follow until I had watched the exercise. Again, the music was a set piece. The exercise certainly required balance to perform. On the repeat, I made my attempt and mostly succeeded. When Jan reached the Crimson level, I decided to stop and observe. By then I had already done seven exercises, and my mind was in a minor state of confusion. Sitting in the corner, I watched a choreographed exercise called Side Bend and Balance. The father and daughter joined me. The girl smiled warmly and introduced herself in French.

"Sonja," I repeated and whispered, *"C'est joli."*

The father introduced himself as Jacques and asked where I was from. When I told him Canada, Sonja asked if I knew several people from Toronto, Montreal and Ottawa whom she had met at the centenary workshop. Her father explained that his daughter was very good at remembering names. I explained that I did not know about MMM in Canada and had only discovered it while visiting Europe. We watched the repeat performance of Side Bend and Balance. It was like a small, choreographed dance. Jan did it with effortless grace and classic precision. She was an expert teacher and a wonderful model of technique.

"Do I have any Magenta students here besides Christine and Dominique?" Jan asked after teaching three more exercises at the higher colour levels. She looked around the room. "No."

The others who were not performing Magenta joined us on the floor while Dominique and Christine went to Jan's side. Sonja introduced me to her teacher from home, Marianne. I asked about her classes, explaining that this was my first class. "I had not realized the broad scope of the method until today."

Marianne told me that Margaret Morris had developed movement therapy in response to remediation work she had done with crippled children in the 1920s. I nodded, recognizing the term used then. Marianne also explained that Margaret was asked to study physiotherapy when working in a hospital setting. "Passing that one and only exam she ever sat in her life was significant to the growth of the movement."

I nodded, recognizing that MMM offered more than colour exercises in dance.

At the end of the room, a double door opened to reveal a kitchenette. My eyes took in the whole scene. I found it truly amazing to see nearly two dozen people engaged in a few groups like the one beside me, bent over notebooks discussing the exercises. At the break, Marianne returned with a tray of water bottles, hot tea, and energy bars. I asked her how long she had been doing MMM. Shrugging she looked at Jacques who said they had started together over twenty years ago. *"Et vous?"* I asked Sonja.

"Quinze ans!"

Jacques told me his daughter had been doing MMM since she was three years old. The movement seemed much more appealing to me than ballet. I was terrible at ballet but guessed rightly that Marianne had been trained in ballet. I shared with her that my mother was, too.

With a loud clap to get everyone's attention, Jan resumed teaching. At the end of class Jan said we would begin with improvisation the next morning followed by dance technique. I liked hearing that since I could do improvisation and was familiar with some dance technique. Sonja gave me a hug before departing.

Chapter Thirty One

That night I closed my eyes and immediately fell asleep. Later, I awoke after a dream where I was spinning out of control off a mountain top. In the bed beside me, I heard Jan's quiet breathing which was as rhythmic as her dancing. The dark calmed my anxiety. Turning over on my side, I felt an ache along the length of my thigh muscles and the sides of my ribs. The afternoon of MMM exercises had left their mark. Yet, I was pleased with the physical reminder of a truly enjoyable experience. These memories helped dispel the nightmare from my mind. If I had been in the room by myself, I would have turned on a light and opened my computer. As yet, I had not answered Rufus. I felt such a mixture of elation and sorrow I did not know how to respond. Clearly, he wanted me to return to him. That was why he remained in Italy. Circumstances were so changed from the innocent days of our meeting. His cousin Ed's prejudices were pedestrian by comparison. I thought our circumstances were so challenging they were insurmountable. We needed worldly wisdom and common sense to overcome the force of our inherited attachments. What else would we need? Free will. Hope. Confidence. Where would we find the strength? In love. Only love.

I must have slept soundly after waking from my dream because Jan's bed was empty when I again rolled over on my side. From deep inside the house, I heard an old-fashioned clock chime eight times. I joined Dominique and Jan outside on the patio.

"Good morning sleepy head," Jan said.

"*Guten morgen,*" Dominique said.

Stretching, I breathed deeply. "This mountain air is glorious," I said, looking across Lake Geneva to the distant mountain range. Was I seeing another country? Was I standing on Swiss soil? Was I awake?

"Be a brick and hand me that sheet of paper," Jan said, pointing.

I obliged, then turned to Dominique, "Is your native tongue French or German?"

"Both, mixed parentage," she answered. "Would you like coffee? Croissant? Yogurt? Fruit?"

Sitting, I helped myself to breakfast. "Your garden is beautiful."

"*Merci.*"

"Have you been dreaming about your poet?" Jan asked. Then she turned to Dominique. "Isadora's boyfriend is a poet, and he lives in Italy."

"*Vraiment?*"

"Really," I said. "It's true. He is a poet, and he does live in Italy."

"Is he why you travel here?"

"No, it's a long story."

"Complicated," Jan said.

Dominique shrugged. "But that must be."

"Exactly. They're young."

"Doesn't matter. Young. Old. That is how it is. Complicated. Do I say that right?"

"Yes," Jan answered.

"I don't know what to say to him," I confessed.

"Ah," Jan said, "it's a struggle."

"He makes love to you in a poem. Are you frightened?"

I shook my head in the affirmative to my hostess.

"Is he handsome?"

"Yes," I admitted and was reminded of my mother's comment, too handsome.

"Then, there's no problem," Dominique said. "A handsome Italian. You're lucky in love."

I knew that wasn't entirely true, but what could I say to these older women? They were reliving their youth through me. I had prospects. They were willing to fantasize about my relationship.

"Have you emailed him this morning?" Jan asked.

As if admitting to an act of social defiance, I shook my head.

"Are you feeling vulnerable, Isadora?"

"What's his name?" Dominique asked.

"Rufus Galsworthy."

"So, English and Italian?" Dominique pursed her lips. "Maybe he's conflicted?"

"Conflicted?" Jan repeated. "Your English is improving, Dominique. Galsworthy?" Jan asked, turning to me. "I don't suppose he's related to *the* John Galsworthy?"

"No, I don't think so," I said.

"Hum," Jan pondered. "You do know Margaret was friends with John and Ada Galsworthy?"

"Yes, didn't he name his novel *The Dark Flower* after her?"

"Partly. It's more complicated than that," Jan said.

"Of course, it is."

Jan turned to Dominique. "Do you know the story?"

"I know they helped her open her first school in 1910." Dominique smiled at me, "Margaret and her Dancing Children."

"That was five years after John and Ada were married, but you see, Galsworthy was secretly in love with Ada when she was first married to John's much older cousin. John knew that if his father learned about their love, he would be horrified, and John depended on his father's support for his writing; so, after John's father died, in fact right after his funeral, Ada and John escaped to Monte Carlo so she could get a divorce. Of course, in those days divorce was scandalous. When they met Margaret, she was only nineteen, but she was a very talented young woman, and they thought she showed much promise, so they befriended her. After only a few years, John had to renounce Margaret because Ada was jealous of their intimacy. His farewell letter is full of joy and sorrow. In the end, he asks her to forgive him."

"Poor Margaret," Dominique said.

Jan agreed. "She thought her life was over."

"But her life wasn't over," I said. "She carried on working."

Turning to me, Jan said, "Yes, that is what mattered most to her. John never betrayed his wife. Margaret thought they could remain friends. At the time of their separation, Margaret couldn't accept that she would never again work with him. Galsworthy had introduced her to the theatre, and her life's work became dance, so, in the end, it was all for the best. You should read her account."

"I will," I said.

"Then she married Fergus, *un artiste!*" Dominique said.

"What kind of an artist?" I asked.

"Painter," Jan said, "a colourist. He was known as J.D. Fergusson."

"We must go now," Dominique said, rising.

That morning, I participated in dance class, but after lunch I took a break. Once again, I sat in a corner and opened my laptop. The first thing I did was order Margaret's book online from a U.K. site that specialized in used books. I avoided my emails. I was conflicted. Dominique's choice of word described me. Coming to Switzerland was a revelation to me. Dominique inhabited a world of gracious living made rich by her attachment to the dance movement, her friends, her home, her garden, her view, her languages. I was not unduly impressed, just enchanted. I hated the idea of returning to my conflicted romance. I only wished to return to our earlier enchantment. If only I could exchange my surroundings for these. If only I could recall the joy and excitement of our first meeting. If only I could dispel the weary disillusion that gnawed at my brain and sank my emotions.

Later, I felt the dance draw me in and I rejoined the group. This was restorative, and I found my mind expanding in sympathy and compassion with the others. They had welcomed me, a stranger. At one point, Sonja collapsed, and her father led her to a corner to rest. If only Lucia Joyce had stayed with Margaret Morris and her dancers. Lucia could have come to the aid of the handicapped instead of being someone in need of rehabilitation herself. Why did she spend her life dedicated to her father instead of her art? She could have blossomed instead of having arrested development. I was privileged to be part of this group. I was privileged to live in the times I did. I was privileged to be educated and independent.

Still, I wanted Rufus.

That night, as soon as my head hit the pillow, I fell sound asleep. I did not wake until the middle of the night when another dream disturbed my slumber. In it, I was a grown woman, ripe in years, and gathered around me were little children. Their eyes were bright and eager. I felt all their simple sorrows and took pleasure in their honest joys. When I opened my eyes, I saw Lucia's face looming over me. At first, I thought my pillow was the warm lap of my half-sister. "Wake up! Isadora dear," she said, "you've been dreaming."

"Oh," I said, "how curious." The room was dark and strange. I didn't know where I was. Then I remembered.

Chapter Thirty Two

A t the end of October, I boarded a plane to Italy. Scenes of greeting Rufus at Caselle Airport in Turin filled my mind. I saw him laughing. Then I was in his arms where I wanted to stay for the rest of my life. Yet I was fooling myself if I thought we could avoid the foibles of our parents. Opening my eyes, I resolved not to allow those worries to ruin our relationship. Visualizing them as excess baggage, I parked them on a plane in the bay within my view. Stay put, I commanded, feeling more like an evacuee than someone travelling to meet a lover in pursuit of a shared life.

Once we were in the air, my ears popped. Looking down, I saw the jagged peaks and snow filled crevices of the French Alps. Every detail was stark, making the scene appear so close I thought I could reach out to feel the contours of the earth. Then the plane veered west, and the scene changed. When we flew across the border into Italy, mist hampered the view. In Turin, it was raining. The small mountain range that rimmed the city looked like gigantic mounds of coal. I thought how months earlier when I had first come to Turin, I was feeling gloomy, and the weather was brilliant. Now the weather was gloomy, but not even bad weather could dull my senses. I raced through customs, picked up my luggage, entered Italy, and there he was, standing behind the barricade.

"Rufus!"

"Isadora!" With a strong squeeze, he hugged me, laughing in my arms. We felt a crowd surrounding us.

"We're in the way," I said.

Rufus took my luggage. "*Permesso*," he said, "*mi scusi!*" We passed a group who turned out to be English-speaking.

"They must be going hiking," I said, looking at their backpacks. At his car, we kissed.

"Sorry about the rain."

"Can't be helped."

As we drove out of Turin, I chatted nonstop, filling Rufus in on the details of my latest writings about Lucia Joyce gleaned from meeting the dancers at the Margaret Morris workshop. As I speculated that Lucia had missed her calling as a dancer, Rufus said he thought I had found the kernel of my thesis proposal. "We should all follow our muse," he said.

I agreed but said I would not become a professional dancer like my namesake or develop a modern method of dance like Margaret Morris. "I will write about dance and the negative impact of not following your muse and how that affected Lucia. She knew when her family returned to Paris after their brief stint in Nice that that was what she wanted to do. Listen to this," I said, reaching for my laptop at my feet and scrolling through my research notes. "This is from the book by Carol Loeb Shloss. When Lucia met Margaret Morris, she met a woman who was everything that Nora, her mother, had not been in her life. Dance was as much a modernist movement in Paris then as Joyce's writing." Seeing Rufus nod in agreement, I continued reading from my notes and shared my proposal on that theme.

After half an hour, the flat terrain suddenly changed into mountainous valleys with hairpin turns. "Where are we going?" I asked.

"Piedmont. To begin again where we left off before we were so rudely sidetracked."

I looked out the window and thought, Can we? With each switchback, my mind veered between happiness and hesitancy. We were together again, but in a new reality. His cousin was not his cousin; she was his half-sister, and mine, too. Yet she would remain his cousin. Nothing would change that relationship. Not our awareness, not our knowledge, not our feelings. My father, her father. His mother, her mother. His father was not his father but was still his "Papa," the man who had raised him.

Minutes later, I turned back to Rufus. "Yes, let's. Let's begin again in Alba where we felt joy."

"Actually, I've booked us into a place near Montelupo. It's called Hotel Ca' Del Lupo, family-run, and it has an award-winning restaurant. We'll go to Alba too, later. My mother's treat."

"Does she think we're having a honeymoon?"

"She's making things right."

I smiled and thought, *Maybe*, but said aloud, "Too bad about the rain spoiling the view."

"Yes, too bad. It will clear. Later. Maybe tomorrow."

I laughed and looked outside. As the mist briefly cleared, I saw a villa perched on a hilltop. Beside it a row of poplar trees grew in different sizes, giving the scene an eerily two-dimensional look. "Montelupo," I repeated. "Doesn't *lupo* mean wolf?"

"Yes, but there are none alive now. They only live on in legends."

After two hours of driving, we arrived. Dashing through the rain we entered the lobby of the hotel looking like drowned rats. While Rufus registered, I guarded our luggage and gazed at the beautiful decor of blonde wooden floors and smooth white pillars. Large modern paintings hung on the walls and sleek sculptures rested on stands. Hotel Ca' Del Lupo was an impressive modern structure situated on a hillside. I concluded that Rufus had brought me here as compensation for us not staying at the Cipriani Hotel outside Asolo.

"I hope we're here long enough for the weather to clear," I said. "The view must be spectacular."

"*Si*," Rufus said, continuing his conversation in Italian. Then catching himself, he added, "But not long enough for the truffle festival. They're fully booked at the end of the week."

"A popular place. I can see why. It's beautiful."

"Dinner is any time after eight, in a lower building, the original family home."

Pulling my own luggage, I followed Rufus along a windowed hallway to the lift. "Do they have an underground passageway?"

"I doubt it."

"We'll have to go out again in the rain."

"Are you complaining?"

"No," I said, alarmed that I was sounding ungrateful.

The lift door opened. Rufus pressed the green button. We rode down one floor. The doors on the opposite side of the lift opened and we exited. The hallway was dark, but motion sensors tripped the lights which flickered. Our room was at the end of the hallway. Rufus opened the door with a key attached to a brass fob with a cut-out wolf logo that pictured the animal howling at a full moon.

We walked past a bathroom with no door and a dressing area where we parked our luggage. "Oh, look," I said, finding a pair of room slippers on the bottom shelf of the cupboard. "Their logo is on these terry slippers." Opening the package, I held up one of the slippers that showed a wolf howling at a full moon surrounded by four stars.

"I think that's all you need to wear for now," Rufus said as he began to undress me. I moaned with relief. The big alone together. He took my head in his hands and wiped away my tears. "Why are you crying?"

"Tears of joy."

We lay under the blanket keeping away the chill until our movement caused everything to shift: sheets, hips, torsos.

Later, we found a selection of coloured umbrellas. Arm-in-arm under one umbrella we crossed the cobbled pavement and descended a staircase to a lower level. We followed the lit pathway to the front door where we left our wet umbrella. Our waiter led us past a large room with stone and brick walls that was full of English-speaking guests.

"I think that's the same group we saw at the airport," I said.

Happily, we were seated in a quiet area with glass walls that bordered a reflecting pool on one side and a rose garden on the other. The waiter handed Rufus the wine list. I picked up the food menu.

"We have to sample a Barolo wine," Rufus said. "The Langhe region is known for its great wines and the greatest is Barolo."

The food was great, too: *Insalatina, Risotto al Barolo, Pollo all' arneis.* I quaked at the prospect of another course. Rufus kept tempting me with translations of the dessert menu. "We must try the persimmon pudding," Rufus finally said. "It's local."

"Eating locally grown produce doesn't mean we have to overeat," I said.

"We'll share."

Later, in our room, we sat at the small table and talked. We had missed one another. We had parted in shock. "It will never go away," I said.

"No," Rufus admitted, "but its colour is pale, like the moon tonight. A short time ago, it was bright, like the full moon on a starlit night. *Forse, a poco tempo il passer.*"

"Perhaps," I said, understanding.

The next morning, there was still no view. All we saw was mist. Still, we changed our shoes to walk to Montelupo. Both the hiking guides had warned us not to walk the wolf loop trails as they were very muddy from the heavy rainfall. Outside the air was damp and cool but we felt dry and warm inside our rain jackets. Holding hands, we followed the road downhill, crossed the main road, and walked uphill into the village. At the abandoned post office, we stood in front of a brightly coloured mural depicting The Wolf And The Seven Little Kids.

"Look at that red tongue sticking out of the wolf's mouth," I said. "That's meant to draw your attention to the threat of danger he represents." Then I noticed the repeated flash of red on the woodpecker painted in the tree. No danger there.

Rufus read aloud the caption in Italian while I followed the text in the English translation. The mother goat warns her little ones not to let in the bad wolf who could disguise himself and trick them. She reassures her little kids they'll recognize him immediately by his hoarse voice and black paws. After a few attempts to gain entry, the wolf covers his paws in white flour. In the end the kids are rescued, and the wolf drowns. "Not unlike our story about The Big Bad Wolf," I said.

We strolled along the empty streets. "Does anyone live here?" I asked.

"Not many. Maybe the wolves scared them all away." We stood in front of another mural as Rufus read the title aloud, "*Il Principe Ivan, L'Uccello Di Fuoco E Il Lupo Grigio.*"

"Oh, I like this story," I said, after reading the short caption. "The gray wolf is a helpful animal."

"So, will you read only nice stories to our children?" Rufus asked.

I looked into his eyes. Was he serious? "Are we going to have children?"

"I hope so. Do you want to have children?"

"Together?"

"Is there someone else?"

"No," I said adamantly. "We'll have children together. They'll be our children. We'll know they're our children."

We saw two men drinking coffee. "There is life here."

"*Buon giorno.*"

The men greeted Rufus in return. "Here's another one with a lesson," Rufus said. "Il *Lupo Fifone.*"

"The Wimpy Wolf?" I asked. "We've had the bad wolf, the helpful wolf, and now the wimpy wolf. There once was a wolf," I began and finished with the ending, "Don't be afraid: a crying wolf doesn't look good!"

"And never again will we be alone in the night," Rufus said. "That's a promise."

-End-

Acknowledgments

I am indebted to many sources and people who helped me in writing this novel.

I first came across Carol Loeb Shloss's book *LUCIA JOYCE: To Dance In The Wake* at the centenary celebration of the International Association of MMM (Margaret Morris Method) in 2010 held at the university in Chichester, England. Reading the book affected me profoundly as I immediately recognized Lucia Joyce had missed her calling as a dancer. Also, at that time, I had been trying to start classes in MMM and, not succeeding, was sensitive to the fact that it is still a mad world. I had read *My Life In Movement* by Margaret Morris, and so I reread it. Then I went on to read another of her books, *My Galsworthy Story*. I also read *The Alice Behind Wonderland* by Simon Winchester, *Alice's Adventures Under Ground* by Lewis Carroll, and *Alice I Have Been* by Melanie Benjamin. I found other books most helpful: *TRIESTE and the Meaning of Nowhere* by Jan Morris, *A Place In Italy* by Simon Mawer, *Oxford Memories* by John Mabbott, and *The Dark Flower* by John Galsworthy.

Some of the poetry attributed to the character, Rufus Galsworthy, was written by me, including the haiku, but many pieces were influenced by the poems of some living and some dead poets: Kathleen Winter's shape poem, "Distances," Monk Jakuren's tanka on solitude, Edward Lear's limericks, and Robert Browning's verses.

I wish to credit the following people who most directly helped me with research and editing: Mary Talbot, Victoria Terry, Susan Leswal, Thais Donald, Joe Carlino, Hector Cowan, Patrick Longhurst, and Ian Montagnes. Of course, I would not have conceived of this book without the influence of all my MMM family and to them I am deeply grateful.

Author Bio

Donna Wootton is an author who lives in Cobourg, ON, Canada. She is a retired teacher with a broad range of pedagogical experiences. She is also a graduate of the Humber School for Writers, having studied under the mentorship of Antanas Sileika. She has been an amateur dancer with the Margaret Morris Movement for over four decades.

Donna's most recent novel is called ***What Shirley Missed*** and her earlier novel was ***Leaving Paradise***. Her account of her late father, who was a charter inductee into the Canadian Lacrosse Hall of Fame, ***Moon Remembered***—The Life of Lacrosse Goalie Lloyd "Moon" Wootton, was published by Ginger Press in Owen Sound and is archived in the library at Trent University, Peterborough, Ontario, Canada. Her poetry has been published in various anthologies including ***The Divinity of Blue*** and in all four ***Hill Spirits*** anthologies. She has poems and stories in upcoming anthologies from the Heliconian Club and in a travel publication. She attended a writers' retreat in Bermuda in 2018 and is still an active member of that writers' group. She is also an active member of the Spirit of the Hills Northumberland arts organization. She belongs to The Writers' Union of Canada and to PEN International.

CPSIA information can be obtained
at www.ICGtesting.com
Printed in the USA
LVHW080542180322
713722LV00011B/1188